Plans? Plans for what?

His hand tightened on hers. There was no mockery in his eyes, no trace of humor. His voice level, he said, "I've fallen for you, Deanna. Hard. I need you. I want you with me—forever."

"I—I don't understand," she said huskily, her eyes searching his face. "You refuse to tell me anything about yourself. How can you expect me to accept something like that when you won't even trust me with your name!"

He hesitated, then said slowly, almost unwillingly, "I was testing you, Deanna. I'm sorry, but I had to do it."

"But why, Rick?" she asked, feeling a cold chill creep up her spine.

He said urgently, "Deanna, try to understand! I'm not..."

Dear Reader:

Nora Roberts, Tracy Sinclair, Jeanne Stephens, Carole Halston, Linda Howard. Are these authors familiar to you? We hope so, because they are just a few of our most popular authors who publish with Silhouette Special Edition each and every month. And the Special Edition list is changing to include new writers with fresh stories. It has been said that discovering a new author is like making a new friend. So during these next few months, be sure to look for books by Sandi Shane, Dorothy Glenn and other authors who have just written their first and second Special Editions, stories we hope you enjoy.

Choosing which Special Editions to publish each month is a pleasurable task, but not an easy one. We look for stories that are sophisticated, sensuous, touching, and great love stories, as well. These are the elements that make Silhouette Special Editions more romantic ... and unique.

So we hope you'll find this Silhouette Special Edition just that—*Special*—and that the story finds a special place in your heart.

The Editors at Silhouette

SERL-7/85

ROSLYN MacDONALD
Second Generation

Silhouette Special Edition

Published by Silhouette Books New York

America's Publisher of Contemporary Romance

To Dave, who knew

SILHOUETTE BOOKS
300 E. 42nd St., New York, N.Y. 10017

Copyright © 1985 by Louise Clark

Distributed by Pocket Books

ISBN: 0-373-09261-X

First Silhouette Books printing September 1985

10 9 8 7 6 5 4 3 2 1

America's Publisher of Contemporary Romance

Printed in the U.S.A.

ROSLYN MACDONALD
lives on the Pacific Coast with her husband of ten
years. She is an enthusiastic traveler who enjoys
casual, unstructured holidays in challenging locales.
One memorable vacation in Yellowstone National
Park inspired this story. She can think of no better way
to fix a happy memory in the mind than to set it on
paper to share with others.

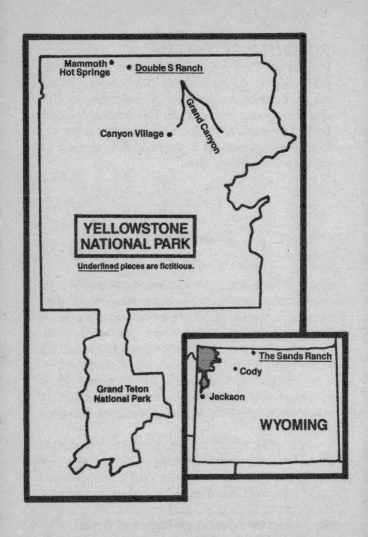

Mammoth Hot Springs ●   ● Double S Ranch

Canyon Village ●   Grand Canyon

YELLOWSTONE NATIONAL PARK

Underlined places are fictitious.

Grand Teton National Park

● The Sands Ranch
● Cody
● Jackson

WYOMING

Chapter One

Jackson, 6 miles, stated the green-and-white road sign. Deanna Monroe suppressed a fatigued sigh as she ran slender fingers through short, golden-blond hair. Large violet eyes, framed by an oval-shaped face, checked the dashboard clock. Five-thirty. Plenty of time to find a motel with a swimming pool. She had started out early and was anxious to make Jackson her stop-over for the evening. Keeping her breaks few and short, she had driven through the heat of the summer afternoon, and now she was gritty, hot and limp.

On the map the route from Los Angeles to Yellowstone National Park, her eventual destination, looked long, but relatively easy. It did not prepare her for the exhaustion she felt after a day of driving through the endless, blazing heat of the deserts of Nevada and Utah, or the twisting, nerve-testing roads of the mountains in Idaho and Wyoming. As she rounded yet another sharp curve, she reflected wearily, for the hundredth time, that she should have flown to Wyoming and rented a car there.

When Deanna had made the reservations for this vacation months earlier she had been designing the costumes for a film due to be completed in June, and an August date had seemed perfect. She'd expected to have lots of time to make the long drive north, stopping whenever something caught her interest. Her ultimate destination was the Double S Ranch, just north of Mammoth Hot Springs in Yellowstone National Park. There she was to join an unknown number of people for a mounted camping trip into the rugged mountains of the famous park. Though the pack trip was only scheduled to last a week, Deanna had planned to be away for three or more as she meandered her way to and from the ranch.

Plans once made just beg to be broken. Nothing went right on the film. First the director was changed, then one of the stars got sick and had to drop out, and after that the producers demanded a key series of scenes to be changed and the costumes redone. The list went on and on. Deanna watched the weeks slip past the June deadline and wondered if her part in the production would ever be completed.

Four days ago it had. That left precious little time to pack her bags, do the endless number of tasks necessary before going on vacation, and drive the hundreds of miles to her destination. She had considered canceling her reservation, but a week in the untamed backcountry with the chance to unwind in a far different setting before her next, and most important assignment, made her cross her fingers and hope she would be able to get there in time.

Ordinarily, she would not go directly from one film to the next. She had a reputation as a competent designer, not a brilliant one, and although she might believe she had plenty of untapped talent, her services were not in high demand.

She made a comfortable living, but the pictures she had been associated with were not lavish productions or big money-makers, and they did little to further her career. That was why this next project was so important. It had a large budget, and a cast studded with famous names. When it was released it would be the focus of public attention, but, even before that, there would be talk throughout the industry. If she did well, her status would shoot up dramatically.

The opposite extreme could also occur. Only, for Deanna, it would not simply leave her stalled in her mediocre niche, it would be a disaster. As the daughter of two Hollywood celebrities, Felicia Grant and Nigel Monroe, there were always accusations that her career was based on who she was, not what she did. Deanna knew it wasn't true, but she still felt the edge of those rumors. This time, though, she was very vulnerable to that particular criticism; her father had written the screenplay for the film and supplied a substantial percentage of the financing. She had been hired because of her potential, not because she was Nigel Monroe's daughter, but if her costumes didn't shine, no one was going to believe it. That wouldn't do her father's reputation any good and it would destroy her career.

Impatiently, she thrust the demoralizing thought aside. The film would be a challenge to her professional capabilities just as this week-long vacation would challenge her physical ones. A whimsical smile curled Deanna's full lips. A pack trip into the wilds of Yellowstone's northern mountains might seem an odd choice of vacation for a girl with Deanna's exclusively urban background. When she had mentioned the idea to family and friends they'd all thought she was crazy. Her father told her flat out she wouldn't enjoy it and suggested she try a week or two at a cottage on a lake somewhere if she wanted to go off on her own. That was a mistake. It roused her stubborn streak and made her more determined than ever to go.

In the beginning she hadn't been searching for a holiday of this kind at all. It was when she noticed a color brochure on the Double S Ranch in a travel agent's office that the adventurous side of her nature was immediately stimulated by the idea of a riding trip into the backcountry. In the spring, when she had made the reservation, it had seemed like an exciting change of pace. Now, with her career about to face the ultimate test, the week stretched as a peaceful haven before the coming turbulence.

Slowing the small Japanese sports car to the posted city limit, Deanna forced tense shoulder muscles to relax. A few more minutes and she would be settled in her room for the night.

A half an hour later she was standing by her car biting her lip in consternation. Jackson, at the southern end of Grand Teton National Park, was the only town of any size in that area of the park and the ever-popular Yellowstone National Park. In midsummer, the height of the tourist season, empty rooms were scarcer than water on the desert. The motel she had chosen after consulting the accommodation guide, was completely booked, as was her second choice, and her third. After several more tries, she had given up looking for pleasing accommodation. Now all she wanted was a place to sleep.

Sighing, she slipped into the driver's seat and started the car. As most of the motels on Jackson's main street sported full signs, she would have to see what she could find on out-of-the-way side streets. A small, unpretentious motel, its exterior in dire need of a coat of paint, caught her eye. Only the bright neon letters spelling vacancy made her pull into the cracked drive. She eased out of the car, drew a deep breath and hoped that the place was at least clean.

The front desk was manned by an obese woman with hard, gimlet eyes that bored into Deanna, assessing the tight designer jeans she wore and the clinging silk blouse, tailored in a trim, masculine style. Deanna was sure that the price of each garment was being added up in the woman's head. As if to confirm this, the round face split into a broad, welcoming smile.

Deanna scanned the room. It didn't reassure her. The walls, like their outside counterparts, needed paint, the furniture was strictly utilitarian, with no attempt at style or atmosphere, and the layer of ground-in dirt on the linoleum floor hid the original color. Drawing a deep breath and lifting her chin a fraction of an inch, she asked if there was a room available.

"Sure is, honey," replied the woman. She named a price well above what the unit should go for.

Deanna gulped, forced down frustration and anger at being taken advantage of, and said in a soft, husky voice, "I'll take it."

"Mighty sensible, honey," said the woman, handing her a registration card. As she watched Deanna fill it in she continued, "By the time folks get to us it means the rest of the places in town are filled up. Which way did you come?"

Deanna looked up, frowning. "From the south. Why?"

"'Cause there's not much north of here. A few places in the parks, but they're usually booked up long in advance. You would have had to backtrack quite a few miles to find a place this late."

"Oh, I see." She handed the form to the clerk along with her money.

Pleased at the cash, rather than a credit card or cheque, the woman hunted up a key as she continued, "This time of year rooms sure are rare anywhere around the parks. Cody, north and west of here, is just as bad. And if you want to stay in Yellowstone—well, I'll tell you, honey, forget it unless you've got a reservation.'' She eyed Deanna interrogatively, clearly doubting that anyone who didn't have the sense to reserve in Jackson would think to do so anywhere else.

"I have a reservation," replied Deanna stiffly, "But thanks for the advice."

"Sure thing, honey," replied the clerk dismissively. The front door had opened to allow a young couple into the lobby. "Hi, folks. Looking for a room?" demanded the woman cheerfully.

Deanna left the lobby, noting with amusement the doubtful, dragged-out expressions on the newcomers' faces. She supposed that was how she must have looked when she first arrived. Maybe she still looked that way.

With a resolute shrug, Deanna retrieved her suitcase from the car, then cautiously entered the small, shabby room. A quick, searching glance told her it was clean, though timeworn, as was the tiny bathroom, with its cracked, garish tiles. Deanna thought once again of the joys of a swimming pool, then wearily resigned herself to a long, cool shower.

Stripping off her silk shirt, she tossed it carelessly on the bed. Her pants followed after she kicked off her Italian leather sandals. Then, clad only in a lacy bra and panties, she padded into the bathroom. As she reached toward the shower stall to turn on the spray, she caught a glimpse of herself in the spotted mirror above the sink. Tiny was the adjective usually used to describe her. Delicately boned, but beautifully curved, with shapely, full breasts, a trim, narrow waist and hips that flared only enough to give her an attractive, feminine shape, she had been alluded to by one appreciative male admirer as a "sexy handful." The observation was double-edged, referring to both her diminutive height of just above five feet and the stubborn, determined, occasionally daring, streak that ran through her sunny temperament.

She tossed her head at the reflection in the mirror and cheekily stuck her tongue out at it. "You're getting vain in your old age, Deanna," she admonished. "Staring smugly at yourself in the mirror. You should be ashamed!" She chuckled and turned on the water, adjusting it to her preference before shedding the last of her garments and stepping in.

The shower only partially refreshed her and, as she stepped out of the cubicle, she was still feeling tired and rather lazy. After patting herself dry, she wrapped a towel around herself and wandered back into the cramped bedroom. Flicking on the television set, she slumped on the bed, leaning against the pillows.

Her small, straight nose crinkled in mild annoyance as the picture brightened into the logo of a well-known program on the entertainment industry, but she didn't have the energy to get up and change the station. She let the voices wash over her without really listening as she tried to persuade herself to dress and find a restaurant for dinner. But her weary body was enjoying its first inactivity of the day and refused to obey her mind. In fact, she moved sensuously to a more comfortable position and was perilously close to dozing off when she heard the host of the program announce that Nigel Monroe was to be the next guest.

Deanna came awake with a start, straightening from her lolling position. She stared at the small black-and-white screen, watching the picture dissolve, then reform into Nigel's familiar features. Why, she demanded silently, did she have to tune into a show featuring an interview with her father when she had come so many miles to escape from all the hype that surrounded her family?

Off camera, the interviewer asked a question about Nigel's new script. Her father answered smoothly and at length. He always did. He knew how to handle the press, how to make them feel each answer was fresh and spontaneous, how to keep the questions flowing in the direction he wanted. Once he had been an actor, a star, now he was a screenwriter of distinction. He knew the business from all angles and he was not a man to be easily caught by a probing reporter.

Slowly, almost tantalizingly, he exposed the bare outlines of the plot, mentioning the actress cast to play the lead and extolling her many talents. Deanna's lips twisted into a faint, mocking smile. Though her father's voice held only sincere enthusiasm about the selection of Colleen Carlisle, she knew he had been furious. His own choice to play the lead had been vetoed by the producers and, after a short, bitter struggle, he had been forced to accept their decision. Now he was putting the best face he could on the selection and, as usual, doing an excellent job of it.

The benefits of being an actor, thought his daughter with sardonic amusement. She only wished she had inherited some of the talent that both her parents could turn on so easily.

But she hadn't. Her expressive face mirrored her moods. If she was happy, it glowed in her violet eyes, it curled her lips, it filled her body with vibrant energy. When she was sad her full lips drooped in a despondent pout, while her eyes darkened to pools of liquid purple. In anger, those eyes hardened to chips of amethyst and her lips thinned to a slash of red in her pale face. But her most telling characteristic was the impossible-to-control color that flooded her delicate features if she was even slightly embarrassed or distressed.

Her father's deep voice was interrupted by the higher one of the interviewer, asking if Nigel had ever considered returning to acting as a career. Deanna slithered from the bed and moved slowly to the low credenza on which her case rested. Opening it, she ruffled through her clothes for a fresh change. Her father, she knew, would never answer this question seriously. His feelings on acting ran too deep.

Much as she expected, she heard him flippantly reply that one actor in the family was enough for any household. This, of course, opened the way for questions about Felicia Grant, Nigel's actress wife of twenty-eight years. The longevity of the marriage between the tempestuous Felicia and the serious, rather stern, Nigel was a constant source of wonder in the industry of which they were both a part. Neither partner discussed their marriage with the press, so rumors were rampant. Deanna, absently stroking mascara on her thick, but too light lashes, reflected that none of the rumors ever came close to reality.

As her father expertly parried the avid questions, Deanna brushed her wavy hair back from her face. Faint, derisive amusement curled her full lips, making the face reflected in the mirror look older than its twenty-five years. She had once, when she was much younger, asked her father why he never defended Felicia, or praised her, or talked about her to the press. His answer was flat and unequivocal. Felicia could take care of herself. To a thirteen-year-old whose head was full of romantic fantasies, the response was a cruel shock. It didn't tally with her view of a lifelong union. Where was all the love, the empathy, the caring that marriage was supposed to stand for?

Now, years later, Deanna knew her parents' marriage was kept alive by Nigel's firm belief that wedding vows were meant to last a lifetime. It was a principle she understood and accepted, but it saddened her to think of her parents tied in a loveless bond, and it reinforced her resolve that her own marriage would only come after a long, slow courtship that allowed both sides to learn every facet of the other.

She grimaced impatiently at these negative thoughts and reached out to flick off the TV. Her father's voice, mentioning her name, froze her hand as it rested on the switch. He was saying enthusiastically how pleased he was to have his daughter working on the new production with him, and then he went on to praise her ability and potential in the field of costume design.

Deanna turned off the set. She wished Nigel hadn't mentioned her involvement in the film. She knew publicity was necessary, but she was already feeling the pressure of this project. It would be much easier to return from her anonymous holiday as simply Deanna, not Nigel Monroe's daughter, to begin work on a project in which she was equally unknown.

Quickly finishing the application of her light makeup, she checked her appearance in the dim mirror one last time, then went out to find a restaurant.

A soft breeze had cut the sticky edge of the early August heat by the time she wandered along the boardwalk of Jackson's quaint main street. Ahead of her she noticed a crowd gathering. Her active mind wondered what was going on, and her step quickened.

She was just in time to see the swing doors of a nearby restaurant fly open. Two extremely scruffy individuals, brandishing revolvers, tumbled out of the building, shouting threats to potential pursuers and orders to each other.

A shoot-out, Deanna realized delightedly, after her initial surprise passed, probably put on by a local theater group. Her designer's eye scrutinized the costumes. The two desperadoes were dressed in loose, faded Levi's, coarse, open-necked cotton shirts, leather vests, and worn, heeled boots. Ten-gallon hats were jammed on their heads and bandannas were tied around their necks. Everything they wore was dirty, and their cheeks were dark with day-old stubble.

A nice touch, thought Deanna, grinning. Bearded men always seemed so much more dangerous than clean-shaven ones.

A shout from the door of the restaurant made her eyes swivel in that direction. A short, plump man, dressed in brown pants and a finely woven white shirt, stood there. An apron was tied around his middle and he was shaking his fist as he demanded the thieves halt immediately. Obviously, decided Deanna, enjoying this more and more, the proprietor and victim of the robbery.

One of the outlaws stopped his headlong rush to escape, turned and aimed. The handgun barked, spitting fire; the plump man fell with a thump.

Several characters gathered anxiously around his limp form, a dancehall girl, wearing crimson satin and black lace, a gambler in an elegant black suit, and a waiter, dressed much like his employer, but in shabbier, less well-fitting clothes.

More shots were fired, and the crowd at the door rushed into hiding. From a side street a short distance away, a tall, husky man appeared. The Sheriff. Deanna grinned and cheered with the rest of the spectators as the two unkempt outlaws got their just desserts, falling to the ground in theatrical death throes.

With the villains successfully defeated, the tableau was over. All the dead magically revived, bowing to the audience's applause. Then, with war whoops, wild rebel yells, and popping six-shooters, the cast energetically retired.

The crowd dispersed with remarkable speed, disappearing into nearby shops or the restaurant from which the outdoor drama had originated. Deanna's stomach grumbled, reminding her that she hadn't eaten since a short break hours before. Noticing the restaurant's menu posted in a window, she stepped closer to take a look.

The fare was standard—steak, chicken, fresh mountain trout, as well as burgers of various sorts. One of these caught her interest. It was made, the menu promised, with Wyoming's choicest buffalo meat. Her eyes flickered as she read the description once again and made her decision. Rather sheepishly, she told herself that one of these days her impulsiveness was going to get her into trouble. She could feel a blush stealing up into her cheeks and cursed herself for being an idiot.

Before she lost her nerve, she marched through the swing doors into the dimly lit interior of the restaurant. It was decorated in imitation of an "old west" saloon, but the twentieth-century clientele were prosperous, well-dressed and dauntingly conventional.

The waitress didn't even blink when Deanna ordered her buffalo burger, which was reassuring. Obviously, it was a popular selection. Still, when the plate was set before her, Deanna bit rather gingerly into the thick sandwich, which could have been mistaken for an ordinary hamburger. She was surprised to find the flavor milder than expected, tasting not much different from beef.

It was dusk when she left the restaurant, her hunger assuaged and a contented weariness sweeping over her. She ambled lazily back to her motel in the soft evening air, planning her schedule for the next day. She would rise early so she could take her time driving the scenic route between Jackson and Mammoth Hot Springs. After her struggle to find a motel here in Jackson she was glad she had had the foresight to book a room in Mammoth when she made her original reservation.

Once back in her room she flicked on the TV set for company, then grunted in disgust.

A movie she knew well was airing—a science fiction thriller set on another planet. Along with a plot that had been done a hundred times before, it boasted terrible dialogue and stars who were picked for their physical attributes, not their acting ability.

It was a cheap copy of a famous box office success, and Deanna had done the costumes for it. The producers had given her very little latitude, but she still felt that the dreadful designs they had insisted upon were more her fault than anyone else's. The heroine's costumes were skimpy, daringly cut to reveal as many sexy inches of her body as the producers thought they could get away with, while the hero wore form-fitting, one-piece suits serving the same purpose. It was not an effort she was proud of.

Her memory of the film was further tainted by the actions of the male lead, who had done his best to coax her into bed. When she had turned him down he had spread a series of rumors about her. Her lips curled in a sneer as she remembered how irresistible he believed himself to be, with his handsome face adorned by a carefully trimmed beard that swept down his jaw to his weak chin. Bearded men, she thought crossly, didn't attract her, especially when they wouldn't take no for an answer.

Deanna switched off the TV, then went into the bathroom to prepare for bed. Being the oldest daughter of a famous show-business couple, it seemed only natural that she enter the same world when her turn came. She had no acting ability and a complete disinterest in writing, but she loved to draw and she loved clothes. The combination had led to costume design, and with her parents' help she had slipped effortlessly into that aspect of film production. Now Deanna wondered if her entry into the business had been too easy. At the time it had seemed natural to let her father recommend her to producers who owed him a favor, or who were personal friends. The opportunities he had created had given her much needed experience, but she suspected that once she started to refuse his help and looked for work on her own merits, the earlier assistance was held against her.

She shed her clothes and slipped a light cotton nightgown over her head. Worrying about her parents and their potential effects on her career was a useless line of thought, she decided, as she switched off the lights and climbed into bed. She was the daughter of Nigel Monroe, film star, television star, acclaimed writer, and Felicia Grant, a superb, passionate actress, whose roles had developed her talent from beautiful starlet through sex goddess to fine, interpretive character actress, and nothing would ever change that. If she wanted to continue in the industry, she would have to demonstrate she was as talented as her parents, to herself, if no one else.

She had decided she would do no more second-rate productions. If she did well on her father's new picture, she would be offered positions on first-class films. And if she didn't do well?

In that case, she was young enough to make a career change to something more suited to her needs and abilities. She had no idea what that might be, but she was sure if she thought deeply on the subject, she would find an acceptable alternative. Options were always available, if only you were willing to search for them.

The shrilling of her alarm brought Deanna out of a deep, relaxing slumber. Yawning, she silenced it, then stretched contentedly before climbing out of the big double bed. This hotel was certainly a vast step above the crummy place she had been forced to take the previous night in Jackson. The furniture was solid and well kept, the room itself bright with the morning sun.

It had been dusk when she finally reached Mammoth Hot Springs after a day spent driving through the adjacent national parks of Grant Teton and Yellowstone. A steady drizzle kept her from enjoying all but a few of the natural wonders, but she did stop at Old Faithful to take in one of the perfectly timed eruptions that made the geyser so justly famous.

The steady beat of the shower and a feeling of subdued excitement brought her fully awake. After washing her hair and soaping her silky skin she let the spray rinse her clean, then stepped out of the shower. Realizing that she had spent longer under the water than she had intended, Deanna hastily toweled herself dry. She combed her hair neatly, not bothering to arrange it in the sleeked back, stylish manner the cut was designed for. Left to dry naturally, it curled around her face, giving her delicate features an appealing feminine softness at variance with the practical jeans she was drawing over her slender hips. A soft green T-shirt completed her outfit for the day, accentuating her ripe breasts and trim waist. The sandals she slipped on her feet were only for the drive to the Double S Ranch. The riding boots she had brought for the pack trip were still in the trunk of her car, along with the small suitcase she'd prepared for the week. In it were only the barest of essentials—a few changes of tops and underwear, soap, a toothbrush, and a small towel. Perfume, make up, dresses, even an extra pair of pants, she left out as superfluous.

It was not until she reached her car that she took note of the time. As she turned the ignition key she casually glanced at the dashboard clock: 9:05. She blinked in amazement, wondering where the time had gone. The letter sent by one Seth Aitken of the Double S to confirm her booking had stipulated that she arrive on the hour, but she doubted a few minutes would cause any problems. She reversed out of the parking spot and headed in the direction of the ranch.

The driveway that led to the Double S Ranch buildings was a rough dirt road, much to Deanna's dismay. She hoped the stones she could hear clanking against the underbelly of her sports car didn't do any more damage than denting the metal. She thought irritably that the road was more suitable to a four-wheel-drive pickup and that the Seth Aitken who had confirmed her reservation might have warned her about its potholed state.

As she neared the buildings, the road widened into a large parking area that had a few cars scattered loosely around it. Deanna drew up beside a late model Chevrolet with California plates and switched off the ignition. Not bothering with her jacket, she slid out of the car. As she slammed the door, she surveyed the tranquil scene.

The ranch house, or what she supposed was the ranch house, was situated back a little distance from the rest of the buildings. It was a long, low bungalow, painted a fresh white with a warm chocolate brown trim. Not far from the barns was a small building she assumed was the bunkhouse. Directly in front of her were the barns, two immense rectangular buildings with fences marking a large corral between them. By these stood a small cluster of people.

Someone from the group waved at her, indicating she was to join them. She raised her hand in response and headed toward the others. Her sandaled feet slapped softly on the bare ground and she was aware that she was being studied by the group she was approaching. An irrepressible smile twitched at her lips. That was okay, because she was studying them as well. After all, these were people she would be sharing a week of rather primitive living with. She was curious to know what sort of individuals they were.

Four of them, two women and two men, were standing more closely together than the remaining three, in a little knot that clearly said they were all well known to one another. This was further confirmed by the physical resemblance between the two men. Obviously they were related, probably father and son. That, she thought critically, was too bad. The younger man was tall, but thickset, with the sloping shoulders and powerful neck of a football player. At the moment he had youth on his side and the bulk in chest, thighs and arms was muscle, not fat. Eventually, though, he would go to seed like the older man, whose tall frame could not disguise the extra flesh around his chest, waist, and hips.

The two women were as different from each other as the men were similar. Wives, identified Deanna quickly. She wondered if the younger one would eventually acquire the tense, annoyed expression of the older. She hoped not. Happiness sparkled in the girl's fine brown eyes, and her expression, as she looked to the young man beside her, was almost worshipful.

A tall, lanky man, leaning casually against the rails watched her advance with a welcoming smile on his long, thin face. His skin was tanned and weathered by the sun and wind, in sharp contrast to his wheat-colored hair. If Deanna guessed correctly, this must be their guide. Between him and the family party stood a slender, medium-tall woman with mousy brown hair and a plain, unremarkable face. Deanna wasn't sure how to place her. Though she was wearing western garb, the fabrics were crisp and obviously new, and her skin was too smooth to have been exposed to the harsh elements as the lanky blond man's had. That meant she wasn't the guide's wife, so she must be another unattached client.

Standing a little away from the group, frowning over a clipboard, was a dark-haired, bearded man of slightly more than average height. Deanna's violet eyes assessed him critically as she drew closer. The thick brown hair, shot with streaks of gold, was a little too long, falling in a heavy lock over his forehead and curling over his shoulder in the back. The lower half of his face was hidden by the thick beard, a shade or two darker than his hair, that covered much of his cheeks as well as his upper lip, jawline, and chin. Despite her preference for clean-shaven men, Deanna thought that on this man, with his broad, muscled shoulders and chest tapering to a taut, flat stomach, lean hips, and powerful thighs straining against snug blue jeans, the rough growth of facial hair suited his tough aura of potent masculinity.

The tall, lanky man shouted, "Hi! You must be Deanna."

"Morning." she responded. "Yes, I am."

As she reached the group the man who had greeted her introduced himself as Jonas Aitken, son of the Seth Aitken who had written to Deanna. He then rapidly presented the other people gathered there, confirming Deanna's suspicion that four of them were members of one family. The older couple were Edith and Hugh Nash from Sacramento. With them were their son and new daughter-in-law, Gavin and Rona. The other single woman was Fay Trent from Atlanta, Georgia.

The bearded man sauntered over as Jonas was finishing. "This is Rick." Jonas added, slapping the other on the shoulder. "He's your guide on this trip. I'm going along as the cook this time, so you'll be well cared for!" he joked.

"Doesn't someone have to look after things here?" asked Fay doubtfully, her voice softened by a southern drawl.

Jonas grinned. "I let Dad do that. We're shorthanded this summer, so I'm filling in where I have to."

Deanna wasn't paying much attention to this exchange. She was staring at the bearded man called Rick, a puzzled frown on her face. There was something about him, about his dark brown, long-lashed eyes that was familiar. Almost as if she had seen him somewhere before, but that was crazy. Where would she have met a Wyoming cowboy?

He must have felt her gaze on him; he turned his head to face her directly and caught her in the middle of her puzzled stare. She flushed at the hard hostility in the almost black eyes and the grim, straight line of his lips. Disconcerted, she turned away, saying brightly, "Well, what happens next?"

It was Rick who answered, his voice harsh, and she was forced, once again, to look into those cold, disapproving eyes. "If you had arrived on time you would know that we were just assigning the horses, mounts each of you can handle. Ever done any riding, Miss Monroe?"

"Yes," she snapped, anger beginning to replace puzzlement.

"You don't expect to ride in those, do you?" he demanded scornfully, pointing to her sandaled feet.

"No, I do not! My boots are in the car. I thought I'd put them on here. They're not particularly comfortable for driving." She kept her voice pleasant, hiding the hot response of her temper, wondering why he would bait her when he had met her only a moment before.

His dark eyebrows rose a trifle, and the brown eyes studied her thoughtfully. Feeling as if his analytical gaze were stripping her bare, Deanna set her feet firmly apart, put her hands on her hips, and thrust up her chin in a challenging way. "Satisfied?" she hissed as his gaze met hers. For a moment there was amusement there, but it quickly vanished.

Behind them came the sound of hooves as ranch hands began to lead out saddled horses. Belatedly, Deanna realized that the selection process had already been made for the rest and wondered what other details she had missed because of her tardiness.

He raised one eyebrow and said mockingly, "I was just trying to decide which of our horses is small enough for you. Sorry, but we don't have any ponies."

Barely scraping over the five-foot level had made her the butt of short jokes for years and, since she had given up hopes of growing any taller at the age of eighteen, she had learned to accept the teasing gracefully. But coming from this man, who had just mentally stripped her naked, the remark was more taunt than tease and it set her blood boiling.

"I don't want a pony! I've been riding since I was four—" a slight exaggeration, but in the circumstances acceptable "—and I can handle anything you've got in your stables." For sheer bravado that topped any boast she had ever made. As soon as the words hurled out of her mouth she regretted them, but she was not about to take them back.

"Is that so?" commented Rick casually, looking down at his clipboard. "Okay, I'll take your word for it." Putting a hand to one side of his mouth he shouted, "Hey, Sam! Saddle up Blackie." One of the cowboys nodded and disappeared into the barn.

"Blackie?" erupted Jonas, who had been watching their confrontation with a slight frown.

Rick ignored him. "Why don't you put on your boots, Miss Monroe, and we'll see how well you handle him."

Chapter Two

Without a word Deanna pivoted on her heel to march angrily back to her car. Behind her she heard Jonas say, "What the hell's gotten into you, Rick?" and one of the campers laugh and ask, "Now what was that all about?"

She pulled the tall black boots out of the trunk, then opened the car door so she could sit on the seat to haul them on. While she struggled she watched Jonas take Rick a little aside and start to argue. It didn't take much to guess that Blackie was the Double S's problem horse, not used on the pack trips.

With one boot on, she picked up the other to shove it ruthlessly on her foot. Arrogant, chauvinistic pig, she thought furiously. She was right, the beard did suit him. Too lazy to shave, he was even too lazy to trim it! Just a smug, conceited, rude man who thought he knew everything. She tossed the sandals he had scorned into the car and stood up. So he thought she was too small and weak to handle a horse, did he? She marched back toward the barns. She would show the obnoxious Rick he had her typed all wrong.

Blackie was not yet in the corral when she reached it, so she shoved her hands into her back pockets and marched over to stand directly in front of Rick. "I'm ready. Where's the horse?"

His lips curled as he looked down at her boots, which were more appropriate teamed with jodpurs than jeans. "English riding boots, Miss Monroe?" he jeered. "Was it your New England daddy who taught you to ride?"

Her cheeks flamed, because in truth her father wasn't much of a rider. Horses scared him. Stuntmen had always done the tricky parts in his movies. "No," she snapped. "He paid for instructors to do it! What do you know about my father anyway?"

"He is Nigel Monroe, isn't he?" queried Rick, the expression in those hard eyes telling her he knew very well he was right.

"Nigel Monroe? Is that a fact?" boomed Hugh Nash who, with the rest of the campers, was watching and listening with deep interest. There was a rustle of excited voices.

Momentarily, Deanna shut her eyes, furious that her anonymity was gone. She opened them to see the hateful, mocking smile once again on Rick's face. Her voice grated as she demanded, "How did you know?"

Rick lifted one hand to let a finger trail down her cheek. "Honey, you must know by now that you're the image of your mother, even if you do lack her inches."

He was right, but that did nothing to tame Deanna's raging temper. She had been told numerous times that she was her mother all over again. The resemblance was especially noticeable with her hair curling around her face in a style roughly similar to the one Felicia Grant had made famous when she had burst into stardom in the 1950s.

Hugh said delightedly, "Of course! Felicia Grant! I knew the face was familiar!"

His daughter-in-law squealed, "Wow! Isn't this exciting? We've got a celebrity in our midst!"

Deanna felt a hot blush creep into her cheeks. "Thanks a lot, mister," she ground out. "Just what a wanted to avoid."

Rick replied jeeringly, "A nice act, Miss Monroe. Trying to soften us all up so we'll be ready when the cameras start to roll?"

"What cameras?" she demanded in honest confusion. She felt as if she had missed part of the conversation.

"Come on!" he mocked coldly. "You're not going to try and make me believe this isn't some cheap publicity stunt."

For a moment she gaped at him; the accusation was so unexpected. "You arrogant..." She bit off the rude epithets hovering on the tip of her tongue. "I doubt you'll believe me, and I don't really care whether you do or not! But for the record, this is *not* a publicity stunt, this is my vacation. The decision to come here was mine and mine alone!" She clamped her jaws shut, determined to explain nothing more to him and furious with herself for letting her rage prod her into explaining at all.

The frown in his penetrating dark eyes as they scrutinized her vivid features made her even more angry. She was glad that Sam chose that moment to reappear, leading Blackie, saving her from another headlong rush into hot, unconsidered speech.

At first glance the horse didn't look like trouble. It ambled slowly behind the ranch hand, its neck stretched lazily, the picture of an old plug. That in itself made Deanna wary. She marched over to the horse without so much as a backward glance at her interested audience.

Thanks to regular swimming and years of battling her sister on the tennis court her muscles were in good shape, but it took nearly everything she had to haul herself into the saddle. Blackie wasn't particularly big, being a quarter horse, but the animal was tall enough to make her mounting an undignified scramble. Blackie didn't help much, beginning to move almost as soon as she put her foot in the stirrup. Jonas hurried over with a shouted offer of help, but her stubborn streak had been aroused and she was determined to mount on her own.

Once safely in the saddle, she felt a mild glow of success. "Okay, Blackie," she muttered as she flicked the reins and urged him forward with her heels, "do your damnedest."

The ears flickered as the animal moved at a decorous walk. Deanna began to wonder if rather than being the wildest horse in the stable, Blackie was the laziest. She thumped its sides again. That was enough. Blackie took off at a canter, rapidly lengthening into a gallop, heading for the fence. Deanna didn't know whether the beast intended to jump the high rails or just crash into them, but she knew she wasn't prepared for either. Desperation, as much as skill, made her pull back on the reins with all her strength, then force the horse sharply to the left.

Nimble-footed, Blackie made a turn worthy of a barrel race at a rodeo and charged for the little group near the other end of the corral. Unintentionally, but quite dramatically, Deanna forced the horse to a skidding, snorting stop right in front of her tormentor. Trembling with anger and reaction, she glared down at him, daring him to make one more jeering remark about her abilities.

"Very nice," he said coldly. "So you can ride a horse around a corral. That doesn't mean you'll be able to manage a week in the backcountry."

Fury gave her the extra strength to vault effortlessly from the horse's back. Sensing her anger, Blackie sidled. She let go of the reins as she moved to stand directly in front of Rick, the horse prancing skittishly away. "What the hell do you mean?" she spat, her lovely eyes cold amethyst gems.

"Just what I said. You haven't the stamina to last the week. Look at you. You're just a little bit of a thing. A strong wind could blow you over," he taunted.

"Okay, mister, you've had your fun with the short jokes," she gritted. "Now, what's the real reason?"

"That's it," he replied, watching her with expressionless eyes.

"That makes it worse!" she hissed. "You've decided that just because I'm not a six-foot, muscle-bound amazon that I can't cope! Well, you're wrong! Dead wrong! I'm as strong as anyone else. I'm not made of glass! And I'll manage very nicely, thank you!" By the time she had finished her voice had risen, her back arched, and her eyes flashed as she spat out her defiance like an angry mountain cat.

Rick reacted to this with a deflating lack of dismay. His cold eyes surveyed her clenched fists and eloquent, stiff posture without even a flicker of response. "Okay," he said flatly. "Suit yourself. Sam will saddle you a gentler horse."

"Thanks, but I'll take Blackie," she replied coldly, wondering if she was crazy. Seven days of trying to control that brute would be sheer misery.

Apparently Rick thought so too. He gave a low chuckle, then said, "Remember, you insisted," before he moved away to arrange the last details of their departure.

"I certainly won't come to you for sympathy," she snarled at his back, determined to get the last word.

Rick turned to look at her. "You wouldn't get any," he replied mockingly, leaving her fuming silently.

Rick and Jonas worked together efficiently, loading three pack horses with food, tents, and cooking equipment, while Deanna and the others transferred clothing and personal belongings into saddlebags that each would carry. Deanna had an amusing vision of a Hollywood cowboy fixing his bedroll of a thin blanket as she fastened her sleeping bag behind the saddle and thought how things changed in some ways, but not in others.

When the sleeping bag looked secure she tugged at it experimentally to be sure it was fitted properly, and felt it slide away in her hand. Feeling a little silly at not being capable of completing this small task, she glanced around covertly, wondering if anyone else was faced with the same problem. It cheered her to see that Fay Trent was standing beside her passive horse looking helplessly at the animal and holding both the saddlebag and the sleeping bag in her arms. The Nash family, however, was coping nicely without apparent problems. Deanna wrinkled her nose as she put the sleeping bag up behind the saddle again, determined to try once more to get it right.

It didn't help when Blackie began to move restlessly, forcing her to reach further and thus making her task more difficult. Not for the first time, Deanna cursed her diminutive size, sure that the Nash family had no problem because of their extra height. When the bag again refused to stay put she muttered a few impolite words under her breath at the same time as she repressed a frustrated desire to kick the offending article out of her sight.

"Swearing won't do any good," said Rick's amused voice behind her. She spun around in surprise, making Blackie snort and sidle. Rick soothed the horse, easing it back to calm. "You do it like this." He quickly and efficiently attached the sleeping bag, making it look simple.

Deanna felt herself flush, embarrassment at her inability to perform the elementary task very close to the surface. "Thank you," she said stiffly.

He raised one eyebrow in an ironic expression. "Can it be possible that Nigel Monroe's daughter doesn't know how to tie a bedroll? Surely your daddy taught you that in the cradle?"

If he meant to taunt her into another outburst of anger, he wouldn't get the satisfaction. Deanna had lived too long with the knowledge that her totally civilized, Boston-born father had acted in the western movies that had made him and his co-star, Max Latimer, famous only to put food on the table and to help further a career in screenwriting. He had no interest in western things; in fact, unlike Max, he despised the tough cowboys and pioneers as barbarians, little better than the Indians they had supplanted.

The stiffness went out of her body as her violet eyes sparkled with amusement. "Sorry to disappoint you, Rick. Were you a fan of my father?"

He replied curtly, "I grew up on a diet of 'The Western Plains.'" That was the name of the early television series her father and Max Latimer had appeared in together so many years ago.

Deanna grinned. "So did I," she admitted. "But I never could associate Gabe Brown with my father. He was not quite as perfect at home."

"I'll bet," Rick said curtly, checking her saddlebags to make sure they were securely fastened. Deanna frowned. His face was shuttered, the expression cool and empty, but the long-lashed eyes were hard, angry, as they surveyed her. He looked away to the activity going on in the other part of the corral.

Deanna thought she knew what had caused that flash of anger. People always reacted badly to the discovery that their idol had feet of clay. Why should Rick be any different, just because he looked tough and competent? Everyone needed foundations to build their life on. Maybe he had used her father's character, Gabe Brown, as a role model. A faint smile tugged at her lips. If he had, he'd certainly chosen a demanding role to follow. Gabe Brown had been the quintessential hero.

Rick's harsh voice interrupted her thoughts. "We're ready to move out. Would you like a leg up?"

She looked into those hauntingly familiar brown eyes and read derision and dislike there. "No, thanks," she said with prim politeness as a flush crept up under her tanned skin. "I'll manage."

He shrugged. "Suit yourself," he said calmly, then walked away. She watched him out of the corner of her eye as she gathered up the reins. He sauntered over to Fay and made her the same offer. To Deanna's chagrin, the other woman had none of her false pride and accepted readily. As she struggled up into the saddle, Deanna had the doubtful pleasure of knowing that she was the only woman who had refused Rick or Jonas's assistance.

They rode out of the corral in single file, Rick leading with the string of packhorses trailing nose to tail behind him. The others fell into a casual, imperfect column with Jonas bringing up the rear.

As she had expected, Deanna discovered Blackie was a definite handful. He had a tendency to want to move at a faster pace than the other horses, and it was all she could do to keep him down to a walk or mild trot. Before very long her arms ached from the unaccustomed exercise.

The even terrain began to climb in an ever steepening slope, giving Blackie an outlet for his abundant energy that didn't require her straining to keep him under control, but Deanna knew that when they topped the ridge the horse would be fighting her again. It made her tired just thinking about it.

Rick set a leisurely pace that everyone else seemed content with. He was riding a big roan with casual grace and outstanding control, even while leading the three pack-horses, and Deanna hated him for it. She wished her stupid pride had allowed her to take his offer of a gentler horse, but by then she had been far too angry to agree to anything he said. And once her haughty refusal had been shouted to everyone standing there, she wasn't able to back down.

They reached the top of the rise and followed a well-marked dirt trail until they came to an open vantage point that gave a panoramic view of the valley below. Rick drew his mount to a halt and they clustered around him.

"We'll stop here for a meal. It will give you all a chance for a look at the Mammoth Valley while we take a break. The horses are trained to be ground-tied, which means if you drop their reins like this," he dismounted in one supple, swinging movement, pulled the reins over his gelding's head, and dropped them on the ground, "they won't stray."

Five people dismounted, emitting various levels of groans and laughter. Deanna stayed in the saddle, not sure how the unpredictable Blackie would take to ground-tying.

"What's the matter, bobcat, afraid to climb off your high horse?" demanded Rick, sauntering over to her. "Here, I'll hold old Blackie's head so he won't run away with you."

She glared at him. Ignoring his last jibe she said, "Why did you call me that?"

"What?" he replied innocently, his expression bland.

Deanna should have been warned and let the subject drop. Instead, she walked right into his trap. "Bobcat."

A grin he didn't try to hide showed her strong white teeth. "Because a bobcat is a lot smaller than a mountain lion, but just as dangerous when it's cornered."

She felt her cheeks flame, especially when the beefy Hugh Nash laughed. "Damn you!" she hissed, jumping down.

"Well, now," he drawled, "you're pretty good at getting off a horse. Too bad you're a little clumsy getting on." He touched two fingers to the broad-brimmed Stetson he wore and turned away, leaving Deanna to ground-tie Blackie and then walk moodily to the edge of the cliff, staring absently at the scene below.

The high mountains of the Gallatin range dominated the Mammoth Valley, making the buildings of the town look like tiny dollhouses, and the hot springs gleamed aquamarine in the warm ivory filigree of the limestone terraces. As she let her gaze linger on the jewel-like pools, she asked herself why she was reacting with such emotion to Rick. She had to admit he intrigued her with his aura of tough masculinity, which she secretly found very attractive. Then, too, there was the faint resemblance she couldn't pinpoint, and the hostility that she sensed had existed before her tardy arrival at the Double S.

None of this explained why she felt such anger in the corral or just now when he'd taunted her. She was sure he was deliberately pushing her to see what kind of person she was. A feeling of amusement began to surface. Rick might never know it, but he had seen a side of her very rarely shown. He had made her lose her usual even temper as if it was a normal occurrence. She never raged at people. She might snap irritably, be cold and aloof or annoyingly amused, but never, never did she expose that passionate, emotional part of herself. It was too vulnerable for the harsh glare of publicity that was always lurking in the background.

Unexpectedly, she laughed aloud, her good humor fully restored as she remembered Rick's recent description of her. To him she was nothing more than a little bit of a thing, a spitting wildcat fighting for its rights. Remarks about her height usually annoyed her, especially when they came from a patronizing male who misjudged her character because of her outward appearance, but somehow she thought being called a bobcat had a definite note of respect to it.

She turned away from the valley panorama and was surprised to find the others watching her. She knew that was another thing she should have expected. Having decided she was a celebrity, they would watch her constantly. She refused to consider that it might be the fireworks that had erupted between her and their guide that had whetted their interest.

Dredging up every ounce of self-possession she owned, she examined each thoughtfully, giving them a taste of the treatment they were subjecting her to. One by one they colored and looked away until she reached the man who had caused the problem in the first place by telling them exactly who she was. She expected him to look away as the others had, but he met her gaze steadily, and in his eyes she read amusement at her tactic. Responding to that, she grinned. It was nice to share a joke with someone who understood.

She pulled herself up short. Though Rick might understand the concept of facing down a hostile group of people, he certainly didn't know what it was like to be gawked at for no other reason than being related to someone famous. If he had, he wouldn't have disclosed her identity to the others.

Jonas, busy with the packhorses, had missed the interchange between Deanna and the rest of the group. He joined them, holding cellophane-wrapped sandwiches. "Lunch," he announced cheerfully. "Ham and cheese or roast beef. Who wants what?"

Deanna chose ham and cheese and when he handed her the thick sandwich she said teasingly, "Some cook. Can we expect this kind of fare for the next seven days?"

Jonas grinned, accepting her ribbing good-naturedly. "Heck no, Deanna. Wait till you taste my steak cooked over an open fire. I believe you'll admit you've never eaten anything better."

Deanna made herself comfortable on the ground, wincing a little as her high boots cut into the backs of her knees as she crouched down. She thrust her legs out before her, resting her weight on one outstretched arm, as she munched the sandwich.

Hugh Nash kept up a steady stream of lunchtime chatter. He talked about everything, from Old Faithful to the weather reports he had heard for the coming week. With a cheerful lack of inhibition, he probed inquisitively into Fay Trent's background and reasons for coming to Wyoming, without discovering any exciting information. Fay, it seemed, loved horses, loved riding, and wanted a holiday that included those ingredients. She worked as a secretary in a large corporation and her life, she admitted cheerfully, contained no secrets. With nothing more to be gotten from Fay, Hugh turned his attention to Jonas and the running of the Double S.

Eventually, he announced the reason for the Nash family's presence. The trip was a wedding present to Rona and Gavin, who had only been married a few months. His pleased smile indicated that he approved of his son's choice of bride, but Edith's rather sour expression didn't change. Deanna guessed that Mrs. Nash, senior, was not quite so happy with her new daughter.

Rona blushed shyly at Hugh's announcement and went even redder when Rick promised, with teasing solemnity, to make sure the tent she and Gavin shared would be located some distance from the rest to give them privacy. Gavin hugged her against his side and stated that suited him just fine. Everyone, except Edith, laughed warmly, but her pinched expression eased a little.

Deanna glanced in Rick's direction, nothing without surprise that when he laughed, with his dark, long-lashed eyes narrowed and crinkling at the corners, Rick was devastatingly sexy. She dragged her gaze away before he noticed she was staring at him. She didn't want him to get the wrong impression. Unfortunately, she met Hugh Nash's eyes, and it was all the opening he needed to demand, quite unabashed by her cool stare, why she had come on this pack trip.

Deanna had no intention of satisfying Hugh's avid curiosity with the truth. Though she was not particularly secretive about her career pressures, she didn't intend to blurt them out to total strangers. She was certain, however, that Hugh would not rest until he had an answer, so she said flippantly, "I came looking for adventure in the 'Wild West.'"

"Adventure in the wild west?" repeated Jonas quizzically.

She smiled mechanically, only now realizing she had obliquely referred to her father's film career. Far from deferring Hugh's interest, she had probably whetted it. But it was too late to back down. She lifted her chin and said lightly, "Sure. Outlaws. Posses. Herds of buffalo shaking the earth..."

Help came from an unexpected source. "A few buffalo we can provide, but that's it," remarked Rick, that devastating smile still on his lips. "Come on, everyone. We've lazed here long enough."

They broke up, each heading back to his or her mount. Deanna shook her head as she came abreast of Blackie. The horse hadn't moved from the spot where she'd left him. In fact, he looked like he was asleep, standing on three legs, his head drooping. "Well," she muttered, patting the sleek neck as she gathered up the reins, "at least you've got good manners about some things."

"Deanna." Rick's voice directly behind her made her jump. That made Blackie snort and jerk his head skittishly. With amazing speed, Rich's hand clamped over the bridle, holding the horse in an iron grip. "We're not that far from home base yet," he said softly, watching her closely. "You can still change your mind about this horse. I'll go back and return with a more appropriate mount, if you want."

"And hold up the others?" she demanded lightly.

He shrugged dismissively. "It doesn't matter. We can always make up the time."

His offer surprised her; it was so out of character with his previous actions. She stared consideringly at him, but his face gave nothing away. He was simply a man waiting politely for an answer. For a moment she was tempted, then the idea sprang into her mind that he was testing her once again, and she said curtly, "No, thanks. I'll stick with this one. I wouldn't want to put you out."

His lips thinned to a narrow slash. "Stubborn idiot!" he snapped.

Deanna's temper flared to match his. "I assure you, Rick, by the end of the day Blackie and I will have come to terms." Haughtily, she turned away from him to mount, but the effect was spoiled by her less than elegant movements, as partially rested muscles protested a return to action.

When she was able to look down the mocking smile had twisted his lips once again. "This beast's name," he said softly, "is Black Devil, which should tell you something. I only hope that when we make camp tonight it's you who has come out the winner!"

Chapter Three

In the soft air of early evening the slanting rays of the setting sun slashed across the small grassy meadow and disappeared into the thick surrounding wall of pine trees. Deanna was walking slowly, carefully, the muscles in her thighs trembling at every step. She carried her sleeping bag and saddlebags in her arms and she had tossed her leather jacket over her shoulders. Behind her the horses were hobbled, unsaddled and rubbed down, settled for the evening. Concentration marked Deanna's face as she headed for the cluster of tents. It was almost too great an effort to keep her legs moving as well as to ignore the ache, but she moved doggedly forward, her mouth pinched and her eyes dark.

As she neared the large canvas tents she counted them—four. That meant she was sharing with someone, probably Fay Trent. Now the problem was, which was theirs? Her mouth relaxed a little with amusement as she noticed a tent well away from the others. Without a doubt it belonged to

Gavin and Rona Nash. That identified one, but what about
the others? To her unskilled eye they all looked exactly the
same.

She paused at the edge of the semi-circle of canvas
dwellings and debated what to do. Toward the center of the
half-formed ring Jonas was building a fire on the scarred
mark of a previous camp fire. Rick crouched beside him,
murmuring something in a low voice. They were the only
ones about; the others were all in the privacy of their tents.
She supposed she could ask which was hers, but she was reluctant to interrupt and to risk another confrontation with
Rick. She was just too tired.

Fortunately, Fay emerged from one of the canvas shel-
ters, giving Deanna the clue she needed, then disappeared
back inside. Deanna groaned inwardly. It would have to be
the one farthest away from where she stood! Pulling herself together for one last effort, she forced tight muscles into
action, despite their cranky protests.

When she reached the tent she dropped to the ground in
an ungraceful flop, letting the bundles and jacket fall where
they would. She pulled off the tall riding boots that con-
strained her calves and bit into the soft skin of the backs of
her legs. With a sigh of weary pleasure, she tossed them casually to one side before she sprawled flat on her back,
staring up at the darkening blue sky. Gradually, the throbbing muscles relaxed in her shoulders, her arms, her thighs,
and she became aware that a lump of earth was digging into
the small of her back, but she was too exhausted to worry
much about that. Her mind noted its presence; her body
dismissed it as unimportant.

Fay reemerged from the tent and sank gracefully down
beside her. Deanna moved her head slightly and smiled
faintly. Talking didn't seem to be worth the enormous effort it would take.

"I guess you figured out we're rooming together," Fay remarked.

"Uh-huh," replied Deanna. The grunt was the best she could manage. Besides, she doubted Fay expected an answer.

"I wasn't sure y'all knew, since Rick mentioned it before you arrived. I've left you the right side of the tent. Is that okay?"

"Sure," Deanna agreed with great effort, wondering how anyone had enough vitality to lay out even a small thing like a sleeping bag.

"We're gonna stay her a couple of days so we might just as well make ourselves comfortable," continued Fay, stretching on her side and propping her head up on one hand. "You look surprised, honey. Didn't you know that?"

"No," Deanna replied, surprised indeed.

Fay grinned. "Talkative, aren't you, sugar?" Deanna grunted agreement again and Fay laughed. "That black horse done you in, did it?"

Deanna groaned. "I have never felt this sore, or this exhausted, in my life. I think that beast took pleasure in making me ache."

Fay laughed again. "I thought when you were grooming that horse you were going to collapse. It looked like every movement was agony."

"It was," Deanna sighed, closing her eyes.

There was silence for a bit. Deanna idly wiggled her toes, enjoying the feeling of freedom after their having been enclosed in the narrow boots. The rest of her body lay supine; she was unable and unwilling to make the effort to move.

"This sure is beautiful country," Fay said softly.

Deanna agreed. They had ridden largely through forests of lodgepole pine, mixed with spruce and aspen, a cool shelter in the heat of the afternoon. Where the sun had broken through the thick stands of trees it had highlighted the dull bronze of fallen needles. Here and there were wild flowers, the scarlet of Indian paintbrush, the yellow of columbine, the deep blue of forget-me-nots, vivid in the wash of dark green. There was little sound, beyond the muffled thump of the horses' hooves, as they traveled through the sweetly scented stands of pine. Despite her battle with Blackie, Deanna had enjoyed the peace and serenity of the backcountry and, tired as she was, she was glad she had not let herself be talked out of this experience.

"Will you look at that," announced Fay, a trace of indignation in her musical voice.

"Do I have to?" moaned Deanna.

"That Hugh Nash," Fay said, faint ruefulness replacing the annoyance. "Where does he get his stamina?"

Deanna moved her head to watch Hugh Nash stride away from his tent, heading toward that of his son and daughter-in-law. "I hope they aren't engaged in—er—marital activities."

Fay laughed. "If they are, they must be blessed with unquenchable energy!"

Deanna chuckled. "Could be a family trait. Besides, they're newlyweds, remember? They're not supposed to be able to get enough of each other."

Hugh called his son's name, then stuck his head into the closed tent. When his body followed a moment later Deanna said with mock disappointment, "Looks like he didn't disrupt anything."

"No," agreed Fay lazily. Her eyes glinted with amusement. "That makes it an even dozen," she added unexpectedly.

"It does?" Deanna had closed her eyes again and was letting her mind drift. "What does?"

"The number of times Rick has glanced—no, stared—at you since I came out here."

Deanna came back to earth in a hurry. She opened her eyes and stared at Fay. "Maybe he's looking at you," she suggested.

"Maybe," Fay agreed, but her tone was amused and disbelieving. "He's a handsome hunk of a man, isn't he?" she observed thoughtfully, watching him from her vantage point.

"If you like men with beards," Deanna replied casually, resisting the urge to sit up and gaze appraisingly at him as Fay was doing.

"I wonder what he looks like without that beard?" murmured the southern woman softly.

"Probably a weak, receding chin and an unsightly scar." Deanna yawned, not believing it for a moment. She had the feeling that a man with the stamp of tough self-control Rick had wouldn't grow a beard just to hide poor features. There had to be reasons beyond that. She closed her eyes contentedly, feeling ready to slip into warm, welcoming sleep. "Why worry about it anyway, Fay? We're never going to see what he's really hiding under that black stubble."

"Deanna," Fay said warningly in the middle of this speech.

"That's all right, Miss Trent," interjected Rick's derisive voice, unpleasantly close. "She's quite correct. I don't intend to shave off my beard this summer. But for your information, Miss Monroe, the reason I grew the beard was convenience. Shaving in the woods is a chore I particularly dislike."

Deanna jerked into a sitting position, surprise and embarrassment coloring her features. "Don't you know it's impolite to sneak up on people?" she snapped, trying to cover her confusion.

His dark eyes gleamed mockingly as he stared down at her. "You are hardly in a position to criticize manners, are you, Deanna Monroe?"

Fay looked from Deanna's flushed face and stormy amethyst eyes to Rick's controlled, sardonic features and stood up. "I think," she drawled carefully, "I'll just join Jonas for a spell." Smiling faintly, she left Deanna and Rick to work out the tension that crackled between them.

His lips curling in a wisp of a smile as he watched her go, Rick said dryly, "Sensible girl." Deanna, still smarting from his cutting words, didn't respond. He crouched down beside her, his dark eyes scanning her strained, weary features and missing nothing. After a moment he asked, "So who won? From the looks of you it must have been the horse."

Deanna wished she had a quick, witty answer to his taunt, but she didn't. She was too tired. "No one won. We called a truce."

"A truce?" he repeated mockingly. "Does that mean old Blackie agreed not to throw you?"

Deanna surprised herself by laughing. "Sort of." That devastating smile, showing his strong white teeth, spread over his face as he laughed with her. She felt her stomach lurch and her amusement fade.

Rick didn't seem to notice her sudden change of mood, but then her temper had been pretty mercurial since they had met, so perhaps he assumed she was prone to wide swings of emotion. Possibly he put it down to nothing more intense than ordinary fatigue. And he might be right at that. She was so weary her body seemed to be weighted with heavy pockets of lead, making each movement a vast effort.

"Come back, Deanna," Rick commanded harshly. She blinked and brought his face into focus. It took her a moment to realize that her mind had wandered. She bit her lip, wondering if she had been staring vacantly at him. "Regretting stubborn pride?" he taunted softly.

She drew in her breath in quick, energizing anger. "No!" Though she hadn't expected the bone-grinding fatigue she was experiencing now, she had known that Black Devil would be a handful. "No!" she snapped again. "Regret is a waste of time."

"And you wouldn't admit it to me anyway," he added perceptively.

She glared at him, not replying. Out of the corner of her eye she noticed Edith Nash leave her tent and glance curiously at her and Rick as she crossed the short distance to the camp fire. Momentarily, Deanna closed her eyes with a weariness that had nothing to do with her physical exhaustion. She had seen that avid, somewhat malicious expression before, usually directed at one of her parents. She could imagine how she and Rick must have looked to Edith—Rick crouched beside her, their eyes at the same level, their lips close enough for a kiss. Edith couldn't see Rick's face, the mocking expression in his eyes, the derisive smile on his mouth. Deanna could only guess at her own expression, or what Edith had thought she'd seen there.

Rick reached out and shook her. "Don't!" she cried angrily, twisting away and groaning a little as her muscles protested. His mouth was grim. She sensed he planned another lecture on her fitness for this trip and said hastily, "Fay mentioned something about staying here a few days. What did she mean?"

The tense lips relaxed. "It's easier to set up a camp for several days and leave the pack horses here. Tomorrow we ride north into the mountains..."

"We're already in the mountains," she blurted out.

He grinned. "We're on a plateau now. The trail takes us up some higher mountains. There's a tremendous view from there."

Deanna, who had thought the view from this ridge was impressive, felt a little stirring of excitement. She cocked her head and smiled naturally, her anger forgotten. "Then we move on?"

"Why are you in a hurry to leave here?" he asked curiously.

"I'm not!" she replied, surprised. "I just expected we would move on to a new campsite every night," she finished lamely.

He sat back, stretching his legs out. "I guess you missed the itinerary. The third day we ride to a trail head and hike the rest of the way to a waterfall at the end of a gorge. It's quite spectacular." He stopped, raising a brow at her dismayed expression. "Problems?" he demanded softly, his compelling eyes searching her face.

After everything else that had happened today she could not bring herself to admit she hadn't expected to be doing anything other than riding, and had no footgear with her apart from the tall boots. He already thought her enough of a fool. She said brightly, "Heavens no! I'm just surprised. I didn't know there were any waterfalls in the area." Of all the stupid things to say, she thought morosely.

Rick, however, didn't seem to mind. He grinned at her and teased lightly, "You assumed all the water in Yellowstone was shot up by the geysers?"

She relaxed a little and nodded. "Why am I the only one who didn't know about this?" she asked curiously.

He said quietly, "Jonas must have outlined the schedule before you arrived." Deanna flushed, reading condemnation in his words because she had been a little late. Before she could retort in her own defense he continued, "On these trips we usually keep the number of campsites down to a minimum to protect the environment. No matter how careful we are, people still affect it. Yellowstone is one of the busiest of the national parks. A couple million people use it a year. Most of them only come to gawk at Old Faithful.'' He paused, his eyes narrowing and amusement creeping into them as she colored. He was too close to describing her usual activities in parks for her comfort. He continued blandly, ''But enough rough it by hiking or riding the back trails for their presence to be felt.''

''I see.'' she said stiffly. ''What else did I miss?''

''Oh that was about it,'' he replied casually. ''Jonas and I take care of setting up the camp and cooking the meals, so you don't have any chores beyond caring for your horse. But you already know that.'' There was a mocking gleam in his dark eyes again. Deanna knew suddenly that he had been watching her inexpert, bone-weary grooming of the black horse. She colored again and he laughed aloud, a low, throaty attractive sound, and reached out to touch her hot cheek, the expression in his eyes amused, but admiring.

The hissing of meat searing over the fire and Jonas' voice calling, ''Anyone hungry? Steaks are on. If you like 'em rare come and get it!'' broke the intimacy of the moment. Rick dropped his hand abruptly, an expression of self-disgust twisting his lips.

He stood up hastily then leaned down, extending his hand to help her up. She grasped it gratefully, knowing she would never have made it up on her own. As it was, he practically had to drag her to her feet by brute force. She stumbled a little as she tried to force overworked muscles to perform and she had to lean against him to keep her balance. His hands automatically slid around her waist, burning through her light T-shirt and making her vitally aware of him. Her head tilted up to let her see his face and for a moment he bent toward her. She could feel her heart hammering in her chest and her throat constricted as she waited tensely for his kiss.

Hugh Nash's booming tones floated over to them, "Come on, you two! After today you both ought to be more interested in food than each other!" He laughed heartily at his own humor.

"Damn!" swore Rick in a savage undertone. Deanna pulled away from his loosened hold, more angry at Hugh for calling attention to them than at Rick for his clear intention to kiss her.

"That won't happen again," he told her harshly, in a low voice that only she could hear. "Can you walk without any help?"

She stared at him a moment, hurt by his sudden coldness, yet hoping she would see another emotion in his face that counteracted his curt words. But his eyes were hooded by long lashes and the bearded face gave nothing away. She took a deep breath, straightened her shoulders, and raised her chin. "I'm fine," she said flatly, wanting nothing more than to lean against him and let herself depend on his strength.

"Good," he said dismissively as he turned away. Deanna clenched her jaw and followed more slowly. As she walked, her tired muscles gained strength and she found the energy to make it to the fire.

Rick had settled beside Jonas, so Deanna made a point of sitting where she was out of direct eye contact with him. Fay was curled comfortably on Jonas's other side and there seemed to be enough room for Deanna to squeeze in between her and Edith Nash. That wasn't a perfect arrangement, but the alternative was to sit between Hugh and Edith or between Hugh and Gavin. Apart from the fact that she wanted to avoid Hugh Nash, it would put her almost opposite Rick, and that she was determined to avoid. Gavin and Rona were cuddled together between Hugh and Rick, completing the circle.

Jonas handed her an aluminum plate with a sizzling hot steak, fried zucchini, and a potato baked in the coals on the side. The beef, a thick New York cut, had been grilled to perfection over the fire. It was juicy, tender, and had the heavenly flavor only cooking in the open can impart to meat. The fresh vegetables were succulent and tasty. The little spurt of energy that had carried Deanna from the tent to the camp fire helped her to wolf down the delicious meal, but as she sipped after-dinner coffee she felt sleep was not far away.

With supper over, Jonas added fuel to the bed of coals he had used for cooking and let the flames shoot up with crackling warmth. The sun had gone down completely and soon darkness would blanket their camp. The night was very still, the only sounds those of the wind and the odd animal moving in the woods. Deanna shivered, suddenly realizing she was cold. While she was eating she hadn't noticed the air temperature lowering, but now she could feel goose bumps on her bare arms. She thought about going back to the tent for her jacket, but decided that would be too much trouble. Instead she leaned closer to the fire.

"That was a lovely meal, Jonas," remarked Edith Nash, with sated contentment. "You have a magic touch with a steak."

Jonas grinned. "Thank you, ma'am, but that's the only fresh meat we brought from the ranch. It doesn't keep, you see, and the wildlife in the park is protected, so we can't do any hunting."

"I'm glad of that!" muttered Deanna into her cup. Beside her Fay suppressed a giggle.

"What do we eat, then?" asked Rona, her high-pitched voice puzzled.

"Canned or dried meat, but fresh vegetables," replied Jonas cheerfully. He laughed at the disgruntled expressions on their faces. "It's not as bad as it sounds. Besides, we've got a fishing permit and I'm almost as good at grilling a trout as I am a steak."

"It's amazing," rumbled Hugh Nash, "how much better a meal tastes when it's cooked out in the open." He looked around the small circle of faces as if seeking agreement.

"I think that's got something to do with the feeling of starvation we all had," Fay remarked drowsily.

"It's the fresh air," Hugh continued blithely. "It builds up the appetite."

Deanna shivered. The evening dusk had given way to darkness and it seemed to be getting colder by the minute. Her coffee cup was empty now and she flexed one leg, before attempting to drag herself to her feet.

The movement caught Hugh's attention and his eyes kindled with interest. "You know, Deanna," he began seriously, "I've seen all your father's pictures and I was a great fan of 'The Western Plains,' that series he and Max Latimer starred in years back."

There was a rustle of sound as Rick moved slightly, to a more comfortable position. Deanna slumped wearily back to the ground, forcing herself to relax. She already knew Hugh well enough to be sure he would keep bringing the conversation around to her famous father until she had satisfied his curiosity. And the others would be happy to let him do it. They were just as interested in the celebrity in their midst as Hugh was. They simply lacked the gall Hugh Nash possessed in such abundance. It was better to get the interrogation over with now, on the first night, as much as she wanted to avoid it.

Apparently unaware of her reluctance, Hugh muttered reflectively, "They don't make decent westerns anymore," before demanding abruptly, "What's he like, your father?"

Deanna sighed. "As a father or as a person?"

"Both," replied Hugh, inevitably.

A wry smile touched Deanna's lips. "You don't ask for much, do you?" she said dryly.

Edith Nash took a hand before her husband could blunder further. "Don't pay any attention to him, Deanna. If you don't want to talk about your family, then don't. But that won't stop Hugh from badgering you, I'm afraid. He's obsessed with old movies, especially westerns. We've got a room full of posters and signed pictures, and goodness knows how many other mementos." She shook her head with rueful affection. "I can't count the number of times I've been dragged to retrospectives of old films. When Max Latimer was killed in that automobile crash and the networks ran all his movies Hugh was in seventh heaven. I couldn't entice him away from the television for any reason."

"I don't suppose you knew Max Latimer?" asked Hugh wistfully, completely ignoring his wife.

"No," Deanna replied coolly. "My parents don't discuss their friends with my sister and I."

"That's too bad," said Hugh regretfully. "I've always wondered what was really behind the quarrel that broke up their friendship and ended the series. It must have been something that went very deep—for both of them."

Rick leaned forward to throw a thick branch, blown from one of the big lodgepole pines, on the fire. In the glowing light his face looked stern, his eyes cold and hard. Deanna wondered if her own distaste was as clearly evident in the flickering fire. She knew the reason for the famous breakup of the fifteen-year friendship between her father and the late Max Latimer, but she had no intention of gossiping about it with someone she had only just met.

Her father and Max Latimer had once been the best of friends, working as a team in a series of hit westerns during the day, then partying and carousing in the evening. They became stereotyped by the roles they played, which in some ways mirrored their real characters and backgrounds.

Max was the rugged, but charming cowboy, born in the rough, wide-open west and knowing no other life besides it. Though he had actually grown up in Houston and had never ridden a horse until his first movie role, Max enjoyed the illusion and did his best to promote it. Eventually, according to her father, Max hadn't been able to separate the real man from the fictitious one.

New England-born Nigel, with his clipped, nearly English accent, inevitably played the refined Easterner, affectionately smoothing some of the rough edges from his western friend and partner, as he instilled a dash of culture into the brash plains. Much more than Max's role, it was based on reality. Nigel, a year or two older than Max, did see himself as mentor to his friend, a sort of older brother who could dare to speak his mind no matter how critical the thoughts might be.

About the time they were signed to do the TV series, "The Western Plains," Max met and married Leah Dewart, a beautiful girl five years younger than he. Marriage did nothing to hinder Max's reckless partying and, until the birth of their son Roderick, Leah did her best to keep up with him, though she made it clear she didn't truly enjoy the artificial social scene. The child gave her an excuse to avoid the constant partying, but it meant she saw less of her husband, who by this time had an image to uphold.

Nigel disapproved of his friend's apparent disinterest in his wife and child and had no hesitation in saying so. Nigel believed marriage was an irrevocable bond and he could see Leah and Max drifting toward eventual divorce. He felt it was his duty to try and bring them back together.

Max saw his intervention as interference and resented it. He also began to resent Nigel's well-meaning strictures on other subjects until eventually he began to brood on past criticisms and Nigel's entire attitude to him.

"The Western Plains" had been on the air for five successful, but exhausting seasons when Nigel finally took the plunge and married the strong-willed, stormy Felicia Grant. Felicia had already achieved stardom, and she was as much noted for her sharp tongue and caustic determination to get her own way as she was for her considerable acting abilities. The press was delighted. They called it a marriage made in heaven, and pursued the young couple unmercifully.

Felicia and Max didn't get along, but she and Leah did. She took exception, on Leah's behalf, to the casual, infrequent interest Max seemed to have in his family. Her dislike and Nigel's continued criticisms eventually drove a wedge between the two old friends. In the middle of the seventh season they quarreled bitterly on the set and refused to have anything to do with one another beyond what was absolutely necessary. The series folded at the end of the season. Max went on to more diversified roles as a leading man and, as Nigel had feared, divorced Leah not long after. Nigel turned to screenwriting and settled down to an apparently happy married life.

Hugh's voice dragged Deanna back to the cool evening, the flickering fire, the sharp scent of pine and wood smoke, the circle of avid faces. "It's a shame, I say, whatever the reasons were for the quarrel. It broke up a great partnership. They made such good movies together. Some classics."

"Yes, they did," she agreed tonelessly, feeling more drained than she had before dinner.

Realizing his present line of questioning was going nowhere, but determined to milk what information he could from Deanna, he reminded her jocularly, "But you must tell us about your father. I haven't seen him in any new movies for a long time. Has he retired?"

"You might say that," Deanna said lightly. "He hasn't acted since the television series ended." By that time, she thought wryly, he had enough money and enough prestige that he didn't have to. "He's been writing screenplays since then."

"He's a writer?" echoed Hugh, disappointment in his voice. "But Max Latimer kept acting, even if he didn't make anymore westerns."

Deanna felt indignation well in her. Hugh's tone made his words almost an accusation. "Perhaps Max enjoyed acting. My father didn't," she said curtly, shivering once more.

"He didn't enjoy acting? Then why did he do it?" demanded Hugh, disapproval and disbelief in his tone.

"Tell me something, Hugh," she said, impatience and anger coloring her normally soft voice, "Where do you work?" She had leaned forward, closer to the fire, in order to see his face, but his features were in shadow. Deanna's face, vividly expressing her feelings, was highlighted by the flickering orange light.

Hugh, though insensitive and thoughtless, was smart enough to know it was time to use caution. He said carefully, "I'm a public servant for the State of California." He added as an afterthought, "In the finance department."

"And do you enjoy your job?" she asked politely.

Hugh, looking somewhat nonplussed by this line of questioning, shrugged. "As much as anyone does."

If Deanna had looked around the circle of silent people she would have seen Hugh's puzzlement mirrored in the others. Except for one. Rick was leaning on one elbow, idly chewing a blade of grass, a quizzical smile curling his lips. It was evident he knew exactly where Deanna's questions were headed and the direction amused him very much. Jonas glanced at him and raised a curious eyebrow. Rick didn't notice, his attention fixed on Deanna's delicate, eloquent features.

Deanna was too intent on forcing Hugh to accept that film stars, particularly her father, had lives and emotions just like anyone else, to notice anything but her quarry. Her fatigue and the cold fell away as she concentrated. "Are there parts of your job you like better than others?" she demanded in the same polite, detached tone.

"Yes, of course! But I don't see what..."

She interrupted, "Are there some aspects of the job that bore you? That you wish you didn't have to do?"

"Now, Deanna," he said with a certain amount of complacency, "we don't want to talk about me! I'm just an ordinary guy..."

"With an okay job that has its good points and its drawbacks," finished Deanna calmly.

"Right!" agreed Hugh, ready to return to the more interesting topic of Nigel Monroe, ex-film star.

"What would you do if you found that the parts of the job you didn't like became more and more essential to it?" she asked with innocent curiosity.

Hugh didn't stop to think where Deanna's question was headed. "I'd quit," he said firmly. "I can take early retirement any time and I've been prudent over the years. Edith and I are well fixed. Life's too short to tie yourself to a job you hate.''

"Exactly," murmured Deanna softly.

Hugh blinked and frowned. His wife let out a short burst of laughter. "She's got you there, Hugh."

He glared irritably at Edith, then said incredulously to Deanna, "You meant it when you said your father hated acting?"

"Yes," she replied, staring into the fire. She hoped that Hugh had gotten the message and would now leave her alone.

Amazement colored Hugh's voice. "How could anyone dislike a glamorous job like that?"

Moodily watching the leaping flames, Deanna said somberly, "If you had ever worked on a movie set you would know that acting is a far from glamorous occupation. Hot lights, long, boring intervals with bursts of exhausting, frenzied activity, fourteen-hour days. Your life becomes public property and you are pestered by reporters, photographers, fans, all complete strangers, for intimate details that should never be revealed. For some people the negative aspects are very minor and the positive parts, the fame, the money, the adulation, far outweigh them. For others, like my father, the flashy side effects eventually become drawbacks. Then there is nothing to sweeten the daily hard work and it becomes a grind that threatens to destroy you. Then you have to quit."

"You sound," said Rick gently, "like you hate the movie business."

She glanced at him, her expression thoughtful and serious. "I don't know. I suppose in some ways I do." She wondered wryly what he would think if he knew that despite her ambivalence, she was part of the industry.

There was a long silence. Deanna noticed that Rona was asleep on Gavin's shoulder, her face relaxed and peaceful, his arm around her waist holding her closely against him. Outside the circle of light shed by the fire the darkness was intense. Above them, in the black velvet sky, stars gleamed and glinted. The flames found a knot in the dry wood, sending up a shower of sparks as the branch snapped and popped. Her eyelids felt heavy and her limbs lethargic. She wished that she, too, had a shoulder to lean on. Rick's shoulder. The name jerked her wide awake. Why on earth had she inserted his name in her mind? Probably, she admitted dryly, because he was an attractive, confident, sexy man, with a latent power that drew her irresistibly. It was a physical attraction, nothing more, and if she had any sense she would make sure she got no more deeply involved with him than she already was.

"You know, it's a strange thing," Hugh injected into the silence.

"What is, Dad?" asked Gavin after a moment, when no one else took up Hugh's opening gambit.

"Max Latimer's son," replied Hugh happily, back on his favorite topic.

Deanna stifled a groan, closing her eyes. Would this impossible man never give up? At least this time he wasn't probing into her private life. She had met Max Latimer only once, at a party with a guest list of five hundred. Max, being a star, was a center of attention. He was surrounded by beautiful, calculating females all under the age of twenty and made up to look ten years older, who hung on his every word, constantly touching him, whispering false compliments. She had shaken his hand and muttered a few polite phrases, feeling uncomfortable as his mocking, thickly lashed brown eyes thoughtfully studied her. She was glad when the chance came to politely escape. She didn't enjoy feeling she had been dissected and found lacking.

Of his son, she knew nothing at all, beyond the fact that he was now in his early thirties and was a very private person, refusing to give interviews to the press.

"Imagine hiding yourself away for six months. Did you know it's been that long since Max Latimer's funeral? It was after that that he disappeared. To his step-father's ranch right here in Wyoming, I believe." Caught up in his obsession, Hugh didn't notice the expression of distaste that flickered across Deanna's face and was gone, or the anger that flashed from Rick's eyes, or the way Jonas stiffened.

But Edith did. She laid one hand gently on her husband's knee and said, "Hugh, that's there's such a gloomy subject! Let's talk about something more cheerful."

Deanna gathered her legs under her and rose, slowly, stiffly, to her feet. "I, for one, am exhausted. If I don't go to my tent now, I'll fall asleep right here. Good night, everyone."

"Do you want a light?" asked Jonas quietly.

She chuckled. "No, thanks. I won't be moving fast enough to stumble into anything. I've got pretty good night vision, as well, so I think I'll be okay." She carefully headed toward the tent and true to her word, walked very slowly, testing every step, though that was more to spare her aching muscles than because she was worried about tripping in the darkness.

Chapter Four

Deanna opened her eyes to bright inviting light that positively begged her not to lie around, but to be up and doing. Fay was still sleeping heavily, so she scrambled quickly into her clothes as quietly as possible. Time enough to disturb her tentmate if the camp was stirring.

After creeping out of the tent she looked around in delight at the scene before her. The meadow was bathed in radiant sunlight that was quickly taking the edge off the coolness of the night. Dew had gathered in droplets on the grass and, as Deanna's bare feet disturbed the shafts, the moisture shimmered and glinted. Bubbling with energy and high spirits, she skirted the blackened shell of the fireplace and followed the lightly trodden path that led to a nearby stream.

Though her muscles were stiff and sent warning spasms of pain if she moved abruptly, she had won out over the exhaustion of the previous night. She refused to let a few aches and pains from stiff muscles stop her from enjoying every part of this trip, and that naturally included exploring the area around the camp.

A wild flower of a soft velvet mauve, sheltering in the shadow of a tree, caught her eye, and she bent down to look at it more closely. She wished she was knowledgeable enough to identify the plant, but her exclusively urban up-bringing had never included an education on the names of wild plant life. She sighed softly as she touched the tiny petals with one gentle finger. There were times when she thought her priorities were all wrong.

She straightened slowly, ignoring creaking muscles, knowing that continued exercise was the best way of easing the stiffening, then continued on her way. The stream sounded close, as it rushed over a rocky bottom, but she didn't hurry. She ambled slowly, enjoying the woodland quiet, her bare feet making little sound over the surface of pine needles.

The stream was bordered on both sides by trees, the point where Deanna emerged being the only small clearing that she could see. The water was flawlessly clear, exposing the dun and gray stones that composed most of the bottom and gave the creek its beckoning gurgle. She crouched down, dipping her finger in the flow to test the temperature of the clear water. It was cold, like most mountain streams, but not so cold as to be unpleasant. A little imp of mischief caught hold of her and she began to roll up her pant legs with a haste that made her shoulder muscles wince.

Near the opposite bank of the stream was a large sand-colored rock, dumped in the middle of the water millennia ago by geological activity. The golden stone was shot through with strains of pink. A shaft of sunlight lay across it, warming the boulder and highlighting the long, oddly shaped surface.

When the legs of her jeans were snuggly rolled up to her knees Deanna stepped gingerly into the stream. The cold water made her gasp, but after a moment her skin adjusted and she found the cool current refreshing. She waded carefully to the golden rock, grimacing a little when the pebbles made for an uncomfortable footing and once nearly falling in when her foot slipped on a rounded, moss-covered stone. Though her heart was pounding when she finished her delicate maneuvering, she felt a sense of accomplishment that she had reached the boulder without mishap. She perched on the edge and looked around her.

It wasn't much of a vista. Downstream the creek bent away sharply and the trees hid anything beyond. In the other direction it flowed straight, then gradually disappeared into the distance. All around were trees, mainly lodgepole pine, with a few broad-leafed varieties scattered through them. She sat quietly, hardly moving when she saw a rabbit crouch at the edge of the water to drink, caution in every line of its brown body. Even though it was only a common rabbit, considered a pest by most, the sight of a completely wild animal so close enthralled her. The little stream might not be an amazing natural wonder or a spectacular mountain view, but it had a peace and serenity that wound its way into the soul and filled Deanna with a deep, soothing contentment. She stretched out on the flat top of the rock, still dangling her feet in the bubbling water, and closed her eyes. The sun caressed her warmly as she lay unmoving, as quiet and tranquil as the scene around her.

Stiff muscles made relaxation impossible after a few minutes, so she reluctantly struggled upright. She decided she should get back to the camp, but first she would splash some of the cool refreshing creek water over her face and arms to help her wake up completely. If it hadn't been for her protesting muscles she knew she would have fallen asleep on the sun-drenched boulder.

She found a relatively level spot in the rocky bed near the camp-side of the stream and crouched down, making sure her jeans were well away from the water. They were her only pair and the idea of spending the day in wet, clammy denim made her shudder. She splashed her arms first then closed her eyes as she cupped her small hands to bathe her face completely. Sputtering a little, she raked her fingers through her golden hair, fluffing the short strands and shaking out droplets that had moistened the tips as she energetically doused her face. Rubbing her eyes with the heels of her palms, she blinked away the last remaining drops of water, then straightened carefully and half turned, arching her body in a luxurious, catlike stretch.

When her gaze rested on the male form leaning casually against a tree she almost fell over in surprise. He moved with lithe speed, grabbing her arm to steady her, then assisting her to stumble onto the bank.

"What are you doing here, Rick?" she gasped, once she was on solid ground again.

"Fetching water for Jonas," he replied evenly, his dark eyes laughing at her. Only then did Deanna notice the gray metal pail. She felt ridiculously stupid. "You're up early," he continued, picking up the bucket and bending down to fill it. "Sleep okay?"

"Yes, thanks. I don't think I moved all night." She watched him lower the container, letting her eyes linger on the play of muscles beneath his shirt. As he turned back toward her she added brightly, "I feel great this morning. A little stiff perhaps, but not enough to matter."

His eyes glinted as if he knew she was being generously optimistic. "That's great. You'll have no trouble keeping up." He set the bucket down well away from the shore, then headed back to the stream, passing her so closely she could smell the tangy scent of him. In a leisurely way, completely ignoring her watching eyes, he stripped off his light cotton shirt before crouching down at the edge of the water to wash.

Deanna felt a blush creep into her cheeks as she admired the broad sweep of his shoulders, the taut, supple flesh that smoothed over well-defined sinew and bone. Despite herself, Deanna felt her own body treacherously respond to the magnetic male promise of his.

He ducked his head close to the stream, then splashed water over his neck and shoulders. Deanna told herself she should way away and leave him to perform his ablutions in privacy, both for her peace of mind and his, but she couldn't force herself to move. She was remembering the electric current that had crackled between them last night and knew she had to stay, if only to discover if Rick really had meant to kiss her before Hugh Nash had interrupted.

With a final splash of the clear water over his face and hair, he stood up. The sun was warm, and in the background Deanna could hear sounds indicating that the camp was stirring. Soon there would be others down at the stream. Deanna kept her fingers crossed that no one would disturb them this time, until whatever was between them had ripened to a conclusion.

Slowly, he turned, picking up the cotton shirt and using it to wipe the excess water from his face and shoulders. The rest he left to dry in the sun. Droplets of water gleamed on his smooth skin, caught in the light covering of dark hair on his muscular chest. Deanna let her gaze roam freely, her throat tightening as she waited for him to move toward her.

Their eyes met and fused, Deanna knowing that hers were mutely begging him to touch her, to caress her, to kiss her lips even though she recognized that there was nothing between them but this intense, fiery physical response. For a moment that stretched into an eternity, she thought he would take what she so willingly offered. His muscles tensed as if to spring into action and his lips firmed into a concentrated, passionate line. Then they relaxed into a resigned smile.

He said softly, "It sounds as if the camp is awake. We'll have the whole troop down here in a minute."

Deanna swallowed and nodded, her eyes staring at the thick flooring of pine needles that effectively deadened the sound of approaching footsteps. He was right. She would be deeply embarrassed to be caught in a passionate kiss with a near stranger by the other members of the group, and it could too easily happen.

She wondered why Rick would be so careful of her reputation. But then, maybe it wasn't her reputation he was worried about. Did Jonas and his father have a rule about fraternizing with the guests? If so, Rick wouldn't want to get caught kissing her. It would probably cost him his job.

She was about to ask him if she had guessed correctly when he said abruptly, "You were upset last night when Nash was asking you about your father. How come?"

She looked at him frowningly, suddenly remembering that it had been his announcement of her identity that had given Hugh the chance to question her. She said curtly, "I wasn't expecting to be known on this trip. I came here for a break and to get away from publicity and prying questions." She sighed, then shrugged. "I can only hope Hugh got the message that I don't want to talk about myself and doesn't bring my family up again."

He slung his shirt over his shoulder and picked up the pail. They began to walk slowly back to the camp. "Let's hope Edith keeps him in line," he said lightly.

Deanna laughed. "I think there's as much chance of that as shaving cream stopping a steamroller."

He chuckled appreciatively, then stopped, suddenly serious. His free hand shot out to grasp her shoulder and hold her still. He said grimly, "Look, I know it's my fault Nash found out who you are, and I'm sorry for that. I had no idea you wanted to be incognito or I would have kept my mouth shut." He paused, his eyes searching her intent features, then added reluctantly, "I misjudged you, Deanna, when I assumed your presence here wasn't on the level. My only excuse is that I couldn't believe a person like you would be ready to brave the backcountry unless you wanted to gain some notoriety. I was sure a horde of reporters would be right behind you."

"You certainly do have a high opinion of people in the film industry, don't you?" she said dryly. With a trace of bitterness she continued, "It seems that people see us in one extreme or the other. Devoted and uncritical like Hugh Nash or contemptuous and cynical like you. You know, Rick, we're people just like everyone else. It's not constant partying and publicity stunts. Most of the time we simply do our jobs and collect our pay checks. Just like the rest of the population."

"I understand," he said gently, his fingers kneading her shoulder caressingly. "That's why I had to apologize. I didn't want you to go on thinking I had some kind of crazy bias against you." He smiled warmly, drawing an answering smile from her. His fingers left her shoulder to trail tantalizingly across the clean line of her jaw. "You'd better hang on to that apology, bobcat. I don't make them often."

Deanna swallowed, but she couldn't force her tongue to shape words of agreement. Rick might be in perfect control of himself, but she was fighting to keep rising desire in check. It was a good thing they were almost back at the camp.

After a breakfast of flapjacks and scrambled eggs they left the packhorses securely tied in the meadow and set out toward a peak several miles away that had an accessible trail. Without the laden packhorses, the group was able to move more quickly and there were times when they passed through an open area that Deanna was able to let her horse stretch into a ground-eating canter. She felt she understood Black Devil now, even if the animal was still resolutely intent on going its own way rather than hers. She could sense when his muscles tightened that he was going to sidle or prance, even occasionally buck, and with this bit of prewarning she was prepared for whatever he planned, and was even able to force the horse to follow her guidance once in a while.

They had been riding over two hours when the trail began to steepen as it wound around the mountain. In another hour the ever present trees began to thin and then, as they approached the summit, disappeared altogether. All that grew near the top of the mountain were scrub bushes and the odd stunted tree.

Rick, who was in the lead, halted the group beside a wide, flat-topped boulder where there was a sparse grass cover and tough-looking bushes. They tied the horses to these, since they planned to remain a while after dismounting, then spread out over the clearing, awed by the panoramic view around them. Mountains stretched away to the north, east, and west without sizable break. To the south, a plateau was just visible in the distance.

Deanna had been near the summit of a mountain before, but she had never been beyond the usual tourist facilities within reach of the average automobile. She was rapidly discovering that without the props of civilization nearby, nature was revealed in all its power, just as the exquisite brush strokes of a master were exposed when dirty, encrusted varnish was carefully cleaned from a painting. It was not as easy to reach the top of a mountain by horse as by car, and it took much more time, but that only heightened the anticipation and made the mind receptive to what was to come.

A cool breeze was blowing, not unpleasant in the midday heat, but it served as a reminder of the potency of nature. It was the wind that stunted the trees on this exposed site and kept the bushes low, hugging the ground. Deanna felt fragile and vulnerable, helpless against the wilderness around her. But, at the same time, the very solidity of the land soothed her, making the problems that dogged everyday life seem pointless and supremely unimportant.

They had sandwiches again for lunch. This time Jonas had made them with tinned meat, corned beef and ham. Deanna chose ham again, eating it slowly as she contemplated the spectacular vista, soaking up the atmosphere of the untamed wilds. After the meal the Nash family and Fay followed Rick to hike another mile to a rocky height that offered a challenge and demanded to be climbed. Deanna decided to remain where she was. The view could hardly be bettered and her boots were not suitable for climbing.

Jonas offered to stay with her and they sat, using the large boulder as a backrest, watching the others scramble up the jagged ridge. They talked idly about Yellowstone and how its varied terrain affected different people, its long history of slow exploration, and its importance as the first National Park.

Eventually the conversation drifted to more personal subjects. Deanna asked idly if Hugh Nash had continued on the topic of her famous father after she had retired.

Jonas shot her a sharp look before replying mildly, "He went on and on about that poor guy, Roderick Latimer, until you made so much noise even he stopped to listen."

Deanna blushed, forgetting for the moment her worry that Hugh would spend the entire week doing nothing but demanding details of her life in L.A. "You heard me?"

Jonas chuckled. "We couldn't help it. What were you doing?"

Deanna bowed her head self-consciously, her forefinger tracing interlocking circles on the hard ground. "I didn't lay out my sleeping bag before we ate. I was so tired I Just dumped everything." She looked up at him, her soft lips curling sheepishly. "I found my sleeping bag okay, but you have no idea how difficult it is to lay one out in the dark. I couldn't remember which side Fay had taken, so I had to feel around on the ground because it was so black in the tent. Then, once I was all settled I remembered my boots and saddlebags were still outside. That was when you must have heard me, because I tripped over something on my way out."

By the end of her recital Jonas was grinning widely. "You don't do anything the easy way, do you?"

"I don't seem to," Deanna agreed ruefully. "But think positively. At least my thumping around like an elephant rescued you from Hugh's obsession with the Latimer family. Or did he start up again after I'd settled down?" she concluded on a mocking note.

"No, we were spared that. Rick and I kept the conversation on other things."

"Sensible," she applauded, her eyes twinkling.

Jonas grinned. "Self-preservation."

There was a companionable silence for a few minutes. The others disappeared, hidden by an outcropping of rock. "I can understand Hugh's interest in Max Latimer and my father. Lots of people are fascinated by the private lives be-hind the figures they see on the screen," she said slowly. Her brow furrowed. "What I can't understand is his interest in Max's son. I don't even think he's an actor."

Jonas looked at her in surprise. "You don't know the story?" When she shook her head negatively, skeptical surprise on her face, he put up both hands and grinned. "We heard it all last night. In detail."

"Okay," she laughed. "Hugh passed it on to you. Why don't you tell me?"

"It all took place down in L.A. You must have heard it and simply forgotten. I mean with your family's involvement..."

"My family?" she protested. "You mean because my father and Max Latimer worked together and were once friends?" She laughed shortly when he nodded agree-ment. "Jonas, by the time I was born Max and Leah Lati-mer were already divorced and Max wasn't a popular person in our house." She added bitterly after a moment of thought, "My father has very definite views about mar-riage. Once the knot is tied that's it. You stay with your partner no matter what problems or emotions surface later. He thought Max used Leah and his young son disgrace-fully." She stared ahead, concentrating on the rugged scen-ery, feeling ill at ease with the revelation she had just made.

Jonas rubbed his chin thoughtfully. "Did your parents ever see Leah after the divorce?"

"Occasionally, I think. Leah married again about fif-teen years ago and moved out of California. I don't know if they still meet." She looked sharply at him. "Why?"

Jonas had the grace to look a little embarrassed. "Just curious, I suppose. The tale Hugh told last night sounded pretty crazy to a country boy like me."

There was a glint of amusement in her eyes at his description of himself, but she didn't take him up on it. "Out with it, Jonas. You have me intrigued now."

"Well," he drawled, "it seems that Max Latimer left all his wordly goods to his son Roderick, with the exception of some property and a sizable trust fund for his first wife, Leah, with nothing to the four ladies who succeeded her."

Deanna moved slightly, easing tightening muscles. "Is that all? I'd heard that much. There was quite a commotion about it at the time, but the will was airtight and there was nothing any of the ex-wives could do about it."

"That's right," agreed Jonas. "The press wanted an interview with the son and heir, but he wouldn't comply. They drove him out of L.A. and here to Wyoming, where his mother and stepfather have a ranch."

"I remember Hugh mentioning that before I went to my tent," she said absently. "You're right. I did hear something about it. Some enterprising reporters invaded the ranch, despite the 'no trespassing' signs and demanded an interview. Roderick told them to leave and when they wouldn't he had them tossed out, then turned the property into an armed camp, with men patrolling constantly." She said thoughtfully, "I suppose it must be the refusal to give an interview that intrigues people like Hugh. He probably thinks Roderick is hiding something."

Jonas laughed. Deanna glanced sharply at him, waiting for him to express what he was thinking, but he didn't. The silence dragged out.

"Poor man," she said after a while.

"Who? Hugh?" demanded Jonas incredulously, "Don't feel sorry for him! He's a deeply contented fellow, believe me."

"Not Hugh, Roderick Latimer." She was staring out at the mountains, her mind far away. She missed the penetrating look Jonas shot at her. "It must be like a prison in-side those walls of his."

Jonas chuckled softly. "Wyoming is a big state," he said lightly. "There's plenty of room for a man to move, even with a gang of reporters barricading the main gate."

Deanna smiled, not really persuaded. Her body was be-ginning to stiffen badly from the prolonged period of in-activity. She stood up and flexed her arms as she walked lazily around the plateau. When she sat down again she noticed that the others were returning from their hike. That brought a topic to mind much more important than Max Latimer's son.

"Jonas," she began, a wheedling note in her voice.

He had been watching her perambulations through half-closed eyes, and now he stared warily at her as he waited for her to continue.

"Has Rick worked for you very long?" she asked, set-tling herself against the rock once again and drawing her legs up before her. With her attention on this, she didn't notice the speculation flickering in his eyes.

"Rick doesn't actually work for us," he said carefully. "We were shorthanded this summer and fully booked through to September. Rick had some time on his hands, so he offered to help us out. We've been lucky. He stayed with us longer than we expected."

She watched the man they were discussing as he agilely picked his way down the rocky path. "Have you known him long?"

"A heap of years," replied Jonas ambiguously.

She nibbled on her lower lip. "Do you have any rules about," she foundered, "well, how to treat the guests?"

Jonas slid her a knowing look. "You mean will he get into trouble for that altercation at the corral?"

"Sort of," she replied in a small voice.

Jonas studied her for a moment, then said guardedly, "Rick is a friend helping us out of a tight spot. I trust him to be sensible."

The climbing party was closer now, allowing Deanna to watch Rick without being obvious. She decided Jonas had very tactfully told her he had noticed the crackling tension between her and Rick and that he wouldn't interfere—only because he wouldn't have to. Rick would be practical and stay away from her.

She let her gaze drift over Rick's well-built frame, the broad shoulders, trim waist, and lean hips, the rippling strength exposed in his thighs by snug-fitting jeans. A formidable man, Rick whoever, and an intriguing one. She wondered idly why he was free to serve as a guide for the Double S Ranch.

"Okay. We leave the horses here. The trail is too rough to take them further." White teeth flashed in Rick's dark beard. "We'll tie the horses to the trees since we'll be gone a few hours."

They were gathered in a small clearing, little more than a widening in the path they had been following. The trail had led them in a north-easterly direction, roughly the same bearing they had traveled the previous day, but instead of climbing up into the mountains it led to a long, twisted valley that had gradually narrowed into a canyon. High rock walls, a few scattered bushes and trees clinging precariously to almost invisible ledges, loomed over them, drawing more closely together with every step the horses took. A stream, which had meandered lazily through the open valley some distance from the trail, was now beside them, swiftly rushing through its more constricted course.

Deanna dismounted with the rest. She looked at her tall boots and suppressed a sigh. Everyone else was changing into more comfortable hiking footwear, but her only option was going barefoot, and somehow she didn't think that would be any advantage over the boots. At least with the clumsy boots on, her feet would be protected.

The trail deteriorated after the point where they left the horses, as Rick had said it would. Rocks and deadfall trees were strewn over the path, forcing them to scramble over or around the obstacles. Although the sky was clear and the day sunny, the rough walls restricted the amount of light that reached the bottom, making the canyon floor cool and dim. It was also moister than the open areas, allowing a greater variety of plant life to flourish. There was little sound beyond the thud of human feet, their occasional low-voiced conversations, and the rustle of the rapidly flowing stream.

As they walked, Deanna felt new muscles begin to ache in her calves and in fresh areas of her thighs and hips. Added to those discomforts, she could feel blisters growing on her heels, an unwelcome reminder of her lack of planning when she chose her clothes and accessories for this trip. She congratulated herself that her arms and shoulders were at least getting a rest, until she had to grab a tree trunk to regain her balance as she lost her footing on a sloping rock. She felt her shoulder muscles wrench as her arms took the weight of her falling body.

She was heartily glad when a new sound heralded their destination, an unnamed waterfall rarely visited due to the difficult terrain, but described proudly by Jonas as all the more beautiful because of its primitive location. Deanna was so exhausted she didn't care what the waterfall looked like; she just wanted a place to sit down and rest.

The walls of the canyon distorted the distance, however, amplifying the noise of the falling water and making it seem closer than it was. Another half hour passed before the canyon widened slightly and brought them out in front of the thundering cascade.

As Jonas had promised, the waterfall had a raw beauty that made it far more impressive than other waterfalls many times its size. Water cascaded over a nearly perpendicular precipice almost a hundred feet high, tumbling into a creamy froth. At the base of the sheer cliff, the rushing water then calmed and formed a clear silver pool.

Deanna found a reasonably flat rock from which she could see the falls, and wearily sank down on it, despite the damp surface. Stretching her legs, she regarded the tips of her black boots moodily. The dirt path had turned to mud because of the constant flying spray from the falling water, and the mud adhered stickily to everything. Now that she was no longer moving, Deanna could feel the fine droplets settling on her, too. Eventually it would make her as wet as the rocks and canyon floor, but she didn't care. Right now she was going to rest her aching feet and body and enjoy this delightful place.

Deanna's physical fatigue had done nothing to dampen her ready sense of humor. Her idle gaze picked out her companions, her eyes crinkling with amusement as Rona Nash incautiously perched on the slick bank of the stream and reached a questing hand to test the water temperature. Her foot slipped, and if her husband hadn't been hovering behind her, moving quickly to drag her back to a safer position, she would have received a dunking. Gavin immediately began to scold, but Rona opened her large brown eyes wide and curled her lips into a pouting smile. Deanna chuckled to herself. Without a doubt Rona had Gavin wrapped tightly around her little finger.

Like their son and daughter-in-law, Edith and Hugh seemed oblivious to the flying spray. Edith had found some unexpected form of plant life and was bending over to view it more closely, engrossed in her inspection. Hugh was eyeing the waterfall disdainfully and wondering audibly if it would discourage fish. Fay had retreated beyond the reach of the spray and was talking to Jonas.

Deanna's heart gave a little lurch then resumed its normal pattern, though at a faster rate, when she noticed Rick striding purposefully toward her, a heavy frown wrinkling his forehead and tightening his lips into a thin line.

"Why the devil are you wearing those boots?" he barked as he came close to her.

She thrust her chin forward aggressively, but replied lightly, "Simple. I didn't have anything to change into."

He said impatiently, "You knew we would be doing some walking today. Why didn't you bring alternate footwear in your saddlebags like the others?"

To Deanna's ears, his tone was saying he thought she had acted purposefully to differentiate herself from the rest. She stared consideringly at him, angry at his assumption and a little saddened by his prejudice. "I told you, Rick," she said wearily, "I don't have any shoes." Deliberately shifting her gaze from his face, she looked toward the waterfall, and her eyes widened. Oblivious to the others, Gavin and Rona were molded together in a passionate kiss. Hugh hadn't noticed them, but Edith had abandoned her inspection of the wild flowers and was staring at them, her hands on her hips, an unreadable expression on her face.

Deanna looked quickly away, feeling as though she were intruding on something private and special. It was crazy, but she wished it was she and Rick who were entwined together at the edge of the waterfall. She felt hot color wash her cheeks and jumped when Rick's hand touched her chin, forcing her to look back into his eyes.

"Are you telling me you don't have any footwear other than those damned boots?" he demanded incredulously.

"Yes," she said curtly, her eyes amethyst-hard.

Unexpectedly he laughed, very softly, deep in his throat. "Deanna Monroe, what am I going to do with you?" he chided tenderly.

Refusing to believe the caressing warmth in his voice, she replied sharply, "Nothing. I can manage quite well on my own."

"Sure you can," he agreed mockingly, laughter thickening his voice. "Tell me, what happened to those pretty sandals you were wearing when you arrived at the Double S? Not that they would have done much good."

"I left them in the car," she snapped, adding, for good measure, "You were so scornful of them I didn't think there was much use bringing them along." That wasn't strictly true. She had dumped the sandals on the floor and forgotten about them because her mind was busy trying to figure out why Rick was so hostile. She glared at him, deciding indignantly that her current physical aches could all be blamed on Rick. She waited for him to say something, wanting nothing more than a flaring quarrel to vent her anger.

Rick didn't oblige. He watched her, his eyes laughing, his lips twitching as he worked to keep a smile from breaking across his face. There was no malice in the expression. He was certainly amused by her predicament, but impressed at the same time by her refusal to complain. Gradually, she felt her anger subside as her sense of humor took over.

"Okay, it was stupid not to bring them along," she admitted with feigned reluctance.

His lips relaxed into the smile that had been teasing them. "I won't disagree with you. Those things must be uncomfortable," he remarked, pointing to her boots.

She grinned, lifting her leg to twirl her leather-clad ankle for their mutual inspection. "I will admit that these are not the best gear for this sort of thing, but I do have an image to keep up, you know."

His eyebrows rose, giving his face a questioning, amused expression. "An image?"

"Sure," she said cheerfully. "Resident tenderfoot."

He laughed mockingly. "You certainly have no illusions about yourself."

For some reason his agreement annoyed her. Rationally, she knew he had every right to think her incompetent, irritating, and a bother, but her body ached and the new blisters on her heels smarted. What she wanted was sympathy and a kind word, not cool agreement. She heard herself sigh wearily, and wondered wretchedly if he would think she was angling for attention.

The expression in his dark eyes became thoughtful, questioning, almost as if he was waiting curiously for her next action. Something about the look in his eyes triggered a memory she could not quite force to the surface of her mind. She had seen that expression before, she was certain of it, but she couldn't recall where or when. It must be fatigue that was making her mind so sluggish.

She put up a hand, rubbing her forehead in a puzzled way. "Rick, have we met before? A couple of times I've had the most extraordinary feeling we have, but I just can't place where. Was it at a party?" She faltered to a stop as his eyes hardened.

He said politely enough, "I doubt it." She nodded, feeling miserably that she had made a terrible blunder. Then he laughed softly, "You are not the sort of girl I would forget, bobcat."

She looked at him sharply, surprised, but pleased by his admission. A rush of emotion made her cheeks color hotly. "Rick, I..."

He extended his hand, helping her to her feet as he had done the first night in the camp. This time he didn't remain close enough to kiss her, but stepped carefully away. "Time to go back, I'm afraid, Deanna. Think you can manage it?"

Though she was chilled by his aloofness, she didn't show it. "Of course," she said proudly, lifting her chin and staring him boldly in the eye. Her coolness matched his as she continued, "As I've said before, I am not made of glass."

The careful, controlled expression lifted for a moment, revealing a warmth and concern that confused her. "I know just how strong you are," he said softly, his hand reaching out to slide lingeringly down her sculpted cheek. "Don't be too proud to ask for help if you need it." He moved abruptly away, as if he couldn't trust himself to remain near her any longer.

It was nearly dark when they reached the camp. Deanna was more exhausted than she had been their first night out. The return hike to the horses had taken more of her energy than it had to reach the waterfall. Rick had left Jonas to lead the way back and there were several times when she was glad of his help over a tree blown across the path or through a slippery spot. That was all she let herself feel, though, as she struggled along. Rick did not confine his assistance to her, but willingly helped the others as well. That made it very clear to Deanna that he did not want to get involved with her. As Jonas had said, Rick could be depended upon to be sensible about this.

With her usual optimism, she had hoped Blackie would continue to be well behaved, as he had the previous day and this morning, but that was too much to ask for. Perhaps the beast sensed her fatigue, or perhaps her hands were not as steady on the reins as they had been, or perhaps it was simply that the horse had been resting, nibbling all the plant life within its range, while Deanna had been expending all her energy. Whatever the reason, the horse was true to his name as they rode back to the camp, using every trick he knew to unseat her and generally acting like a devil. Deanna was as determined to master the animal as he was to get rid of her, and she found from within herself a reserve of strength she didn't know existed.

They caught sight of a herd of about forty elk late in the afternoon. Mainly females with calves, the animals were spread over a grassy meadow protected in front by the meandering stream. To their rear was a thick stand of pines into which they could flee for safety it the need arose. Many were folded up on the ground, their buckskin-colored hides hardly visible in the long, coarse grass. A third of them grazed standing up, taking short bites, then lifting their black muzzles to snuff the wind as their long ears twitched to catch the sound of danger. Slightly apart from the herd grazed a large bull, majestic antlers crowning a proud head.

They were able to watch the peaceful scene as long as they wished. Apparently, the elk sensed there was no danger from the people observing them. The serenity affected them all, even Deanna's bad-mannered horse. Blackie quieted enough to let her gaze wonderingly at the wild creatures grazing calmly not a hundred yards away. But time could not be stopped. It would soon be sunset, and they were still an hour from the camp. At last they moved on, and when they did, Deanna's brief respite was over.

Deanna hadn't thought she would ever see the camp as home, but this night she did. It looked very welcoming to her exhausted eyes because it meant she could give up her unequal struggle with Black Devil. She forced herself to groom the horse, though she didn't think the beast deserved to have his needs seen to before hers, not after the way he had behaved that afternoon. Caring for the horse, however, was fast becoming a habit, and Deanna was working on a subconscious level—functioning, not thinking. She knew that people spoke to her, that she replied; at one point she even heard herself laugh, quite normally, in response to a light tease. The others assumed she was tired, as they were, nothing more. In reality, she was asleep on her feet.

She made it all the way to her tent before she collapsed into a tumbled heap on top of her sleeping bag. She was unaware of Fay entering the tent, chatting happily about the day in her slow drawl, until she realized Deanna was asleep. Nor did she hear Jonas call everyone to the fire to partake of the thick stew he had concocted from dried meats and assorted fresh vegetables that could be carried without refrigeration.

A hand on her shoulder, shaking her roughly, brought her out of her blissful slumber.

"Go away," she muttered, trying to roll away.

"Wake up, Deanna. Supper's ready," said Rick's voice, harshly.

"Not hungry," she mumbled, keeping her eyes firmly closed, as if that would make him disappear.

"You will be by the middle of the night," he responded gruffly, shaking harder. "And there are no facilities here for midnight snacks."

That was true. In order to discourage bears, the supplies were hung from a high tree branch a little distance from the tents. She groaned. "Rick, I'm tired. I'll sleep through the night whether I eat or not. Please go away."

In reply he rolled her onto her back. "Sit up, Deanna," he commanded quietly.

She sighed and opened her eyes to see his face above her, set in grim lines. Even in her sleep-fogged state she realized he would not leave without her. "Okay, okay, I'm coming," she mumbled as she sat up. She rubbed her eyes with the heels of her palms, then let him help her scramble to her feet. As they emerged from the tent she glanced at him obliquely and warned, "I'll get you for this."

Rick just laughed.

Chapter Five

Dressed only in her briefs and a loosely fitting jersey of alternating peach and nutmeg pinstripes, Deanna slumped limply on her sleeping bag, her legs sprawled out in front of her. Gingerly she touched the angry red abrasion on one heel and winced as the light touch shot off a quick shaft of pain. She sighed glumly, reflecting that with a little foresight she might have avoided this latest problem.

She was alone in the tent, Fay having already dressed and joined the others waiting for breakfast. Deanna could smell bacon cooking along with the fragrant scent of burning wood and knew that in a few minutes Jonas would be shouting for the stragglers to hurry up and come out to the fire for breakfast. Right now Deanna didn't feel like eating. She was tired and there wasn't one square inch of her body that didn't hurt in one way or another. She knew, though, that if she didn't show up at the fire Rick would come and get her as he had the night before. She sighed again. She must seem like such a jellyfish to him. It bothered her that he would think her spiritless and it bothered her that she cared what he thought at all.

She inspected her heels again, deciding that what they needed was an adhesive bandage over the blisters to protect the sensitive areas from further chafing. It was possible—no, probable—that there was a first-aid kit amongst the other paraphernalia carried by the patient packhorses, but she was too proud to ask Jonas for it. He would want to know why she needed it, and inevitably, Rick would come to hear of her latest problem. He already thought her helpless enough. She wasn't about to hand him any more proof of her incompetence.

Reaching over to pick up her jeans, she rose slowly to her feet, each careful movement evidence of sore muscles. As she stepped into the pants and hiked them over slender hips, she reflected that her packing job had not been one of her best. But the letter sent from the Double S with instructions on when and how to reach the ranch had added that fancy touches were not necessary in the backcountry and suggested she pack lightly. She was beginning to realize she had been extreme in her interpretation of that suggestion.

Once her jeans were on, she rolled up her sleeping bag and stuffed a few loose odds and ends of clothing into her saddlebags. They were breaking camp and moving more deeply into the wild country, where they would stay for a couple of nights before they began the return trip to the ranch. Deanna wondered how far they would be traveling. She didn't think she had enough energy to face another long, exhausting day. Maybe breakfast would help to cheer her up.

Not bothering with her boots, she strolled across the rough grass to the fireplace. Jonas and Hugh Nash greeted her cheerfully, Fay yawned, and Rona smiled as she leaned drowsily on Gavin's shoulder. Edith hadn't emerged from her tent yet and Rick was busy dismantling the one he and Jonas had shared. Deanna returned their greetings and sprawled on her side, leaning limply on one elbow until Jonas was ready to serve the meal.

Hugh looked up, taking note of the sky, which was cloudy for the first time since they had left the Double S. "Looks like rain," he said wisely.

"Really?" demanded Fay, impressed by his insight. "How do you know?"

"The cloud formations," he replied seriously. "They indicate we're going to get rain in the next few hours."

Fay looked searchingly up at the sky. "You can actually tell that from a little ol' cloud?"

"Sure can," replied Hugh. "Isn't that right, Jonas?"

Deanna, who didn't think Hugh was the most reliable authority on predicting the weather through natural phenomena, watched Jonas instead of the sky. He smiled rather absently, apparently concentrating on his cooking, and agreed. Hugh was delighted and he proceeded to give Fay an outline of the different types of clouds and what kind of weather each promised. Jonas looked up, caught Deanna's eyes on him, and grinned.

"Come on, Dad," said Gavin, as Fay began to look a little swamped. "You're going to put us all to sleep if you keep this up."

"I thought Fay was interested in cloud formations," rejoined Hugh mildly, not in the least put out by his son's interruption.

"I am," Fay interjected, with hasty politeness.

Unfortunately, Deanna picked that moment to yawn. Gavin laughed. "See what I mean, Dad?"

Hugh shook his heavy head in mock resignation, "You win, son. End of lecture."

"That's a relief," said Rona, gently teasing her father-in-law.

He sighed theatrically. "No one appreciates me." His son laughed and cuffed him on the shoulder, forcing Rona to sit up. She straightened, blinking sleepily.

Rick joined them a moment later, settling in beside Jonas, after he made sure the cook was stocked with enough wood. Deanna could feel his steady gaze probing her features and wondered uneasily what he was seeing. Were her eyes shadowed by blue smudges of exhaustion, was her skin pale and drawn? She had no idea how she looked because a mirror was one more thing she hadn't though to bring. She carried one in her cosmetics case, but that was securely locked in the trunk of her car. All she knew was that she felt like a wreck, and from the expression on Rick's face, that was exactly how she looked. Her only consolation was that Rona and Fay were obviously feeling tired too, so she wasn't the only one who found the extended exercise exhausting.

They started out later than usual that morning because breaking camp, though smoothly organized by Rick and Jonas, meant the tents had to be taken down, the pack-horses loaded, and the fire securely doused.

By late morning the clouds that had so interested Hugh, long, wispy mare's tails high in the stratosphere, still remained, but they did little to obscure the sun as it blazed down on the open meadow they were riding through. Deanna looked around her with interest. She was sure she had seen this place before. For a moment she wondered if her memory was playing tricks on her, as it had yesterday when she had seen that fleeting resemblance to someone unknown in Rick. That had bothered her—it still bothered her. Usually her memory for faces and places was excellent, a by-product of her observant, artistic eye.

She felt Blackie lurch under her as the horses scrambled down the slight bank of a stream, splashed through the shallow water, and lunged up on the other side. As she concentrated on managing the horse, she remembered why this clearing seemed so familiar. It was the one where they had stopped to watch the elk feed the previous night. But there were no elk now. The open ground slept, peaceful and serene, under the hot sun.

With the packhorses fully loaded, their speed was necessarily slow, relaxing for the others who could sit on their ambling horses and look around at the birds and wildlife. But for Deanna it was just the opposite. Black Devil was getting irritable at the crawling pace and fidgeting. With the ford behind them, Deanna decided to let the horse stretch its legs while they were in the open, unexacting meadow.

After crossing the creek, the others had spread out over the open space, abandoning the line formation they usually used when riding in the midst of the trees. Gavin and his father were riding beside each other talking, while Rona hovered to one side. Edith rode behind, watching the three of them with blank, expressionless eyes. A little to the rear were Jonas and Fay.

Deanna eased the reins a little and nudged the black horse's sides with her heels. The animal needed no further urging to lengthen his stride. She felt a warm glow of pride as she kept the horse to a tight, controlled canter. Over the past few days she had truly learned how to ride, and it was nothing like an hour or two spent on a well-groomed trail within sight and sound of the city. Riding for the whole day, battling a spirited horse, and winning gave her a powerful sense of accomplishment that transcended aching muscles and bone-weary fatigue at the end of the day.

She guided Blackie in a sweeping arc around Rona's ambling mount, then brought the animal back toward Rick.

She knew she was showing off her newfound skills, but she didn't care. She wanted to be sure Rick saw how capable she was now.

He did. She slowed the horse as she drew near him, deliberately proving it was she who was in control, not Black Devil. There was amusement in his dark eyes as he said dryly, "You've made your point, bobcat. I'm impressed."

She laughed gaily, a lovely rippling sound full of warmth and high spirits. "Another apology, Rick? I never thought I'd hear it!"

Black Devil's pace, though slower than it had been, was rapidly taking her past Rick, who was hampered by the trudging packhorses. She half turned her body, knowing that the meadow was safe and her horse well under control. There was a wicked grin on Rick's face, answering her own teasing expression, and she wondered how he would respond to her banter.

Suddenly, the idyllic scene shattered. Deanna felt the horse jerk sharply to one side and rise on its hind legs. With her body half turned she didn't have a chance to regain control, and she landed on the ground with a thump that drove the breath out of her body.

She heard Rick shout her name, then call for Jonas to go after her frightened horse. A moment later he was on the ground beside her asking—no, demanding—to know if she was hurt.

Unable to talk, she grinned feebly to let him know she was all right as she struggled to draw breath back into her lungs.

"That damned horse," he muttered, as his hands ran quickly over her body to determine if there were any breaks.

"Not his fault," she gasped as soon as she could manage.

Rick paid no attention. "Damn it! I should never have let you ride that beast. He's too much for you."

"Wasn't paying attention," she whispered, not sure what he might do in this angry state. Her eyes, wide and dark, searched the grim lines of his face. He cares, she thought, happiness flooding through her. He was worried she might be injured, that was why he was so angry at the horse—and himself.

"I don't think there's anything broken," he muttered, more to himself than to her. He stroked her short, silky hair away from her face in a gentle movement, almost as if he had to touch her to reassure himself that she was unhurt.

Her breathing was back to normal, but she lay quietly, enjoying the light caress and wishing they were alone so it could deepen into something more. She could hear Rona exclaiming, Hugh announcing he had kept the packhorses from bolting, and Edith's tart tones telling him not to be silly, the horses had been standing still, in no danger of going anywhere.

Unwillingly, her eyes twinkled. She saw the tension ease in Rick's face and a grudging smile curl his lips. "I guess you're okay if your sense of humor is back." He drew his hand away—reluctantly, she thought—and helped her struggle into a sitting position.

"I'm fine. Nothing damaged but my pride," she agreed lightly. "What happened? Did you see?"

He shrugged, his narrowed eyes watching her closely. "Something ran in front of Blackie, or between his legs. I couldn't be sure what it was. It spooked the horse and made him rear up."

Her lips drooped in a rueful expression. "Then I definitely deserved the tumble for my carelessness. How stupid can you get?" she added in disgust.

He smiled at her emphatic self-criticism, but didn't immediately have a chance to reply. Jonas arrived, leading Black Devil and wanting to know if she was hurt and the details of what had happened. Rick gave him a short, terse rundown, concluding with, "I'll take Blackie from now on, Jonas. Deanna can ride my roan."

"No!" she shouted, scrambling to her feet, her eyes sparkling like jewels, her chin determined.

Jonas looked a little taken aback by her furious reaction, but Rick was prepared for it. "Yes!" he snapped, rising to tower over her. "I'm not going to discuss this with you, Deanna. I'm doing now what I should have done before we left the ranch. This horse is too spirited for you, too strong, and too damned dangerous! You'll ride the roan."

She looked at his horse, placidly cropping grass. She knew why Rick wanted her to ride the roan. It had the temperament of a stuffed teddy bear. "Everyone falls off a horse sooner or later," she tried desperately. "Just because I took a tumble doesn't mean you have to make a federal case out of it!"

"It isn't only the fall. That horse drains so much energy out of you that you're limp by the end of the day. Can you honestly say you've been enjoying yourself?" he demanded furiously, his hands moving to hold her by the shoulders.

"Yes!" she cried agonizingly. "I didn't think I was capable of riding Blackie, but I proved I could! That's important to me, Rick." She put her hands on his chest pleadingly.

His expression softened. "I know that, bobcat," he said gently, tightening his grip on her shoulders. "But there isn't anything left for you to prove. Ride my horse and enjoy yourself for the rest of the trip."

She looked at him bitterly, knowing that nothing she could say would change his mind. Her emotions heightened by shock, she lashed out at him in frustration. "Your conscience bothering you, Rick? Because it was you who put me up on Blackie in the first place? And were so sure I'd fall off and make a fool of myself. And you wanted that, didn't you, Rick?"

His hands fell from her shoulders and he stepped away from her. "The matter is decided," he said curtly. "You'll ride the roan from now on."

Her mouth opened, more scathing words trembling on her lips. Jonas interrupted hastily, saying, "Rick is right, Deanna. We're pretty far from civilization out her and if you were injured it might be a while before we could get you to a doctor." His lips twitched into a smile. He looked from one angry face to the other, then added softly, so only they could hear, "Come on you two, be friends. You know it's what you both want."

Rick shot him a furious look, which was met with a bland expression, and abruptly snatched Black Devil's reins from Jonas's hands. Deanna, shaken both by her fall and Jonas's perception, watched him swing up into the saddle without protest. Not for a minute would she admit that Rick was right, but secretly she was relieved she wouldn't have to battle the horse any longer. Still, it galled her to see Rick's effortless control of the animal. It seemed to highlight all her deficiencies.

Jonas touched her lightly on the arm. "Come on, Deanna. I'll give you a leg up."

They camped that evening on the edge of a small, peaceful lake, its bottom visible through translucent water. It was fed by streams originating in the high mountains to the north, which kept the temperature cool all year-round. Jonas promised trout for their dinner the next day, caught fresh from the lake.

There were no beaches and the ever present pine trees grew thickly almost to the water. A thin, level strip, hacked out of the surrounding forest by countless campers, made a perfect, secluded, tranquil spot to pitch the tents. These were placed close to the trees for shelter, but circling the camp fire and facing out toward the unspoiled lake.

After a dinner of thick chicken stew, a simple salad, and rolls Jonas had baked over the fire in a heavy cast-iron dutch oven, Deanna was glad to let the conversation eddy around her as she sipped her cup of after-dinner coffee. Her body ached with more than its usual share of sore muscles, and one hip had begun to stiffen badly, having taken the brunt of her fall.

During the afternoon she had finally admitted to herself that Rick had been right to force her to change horses. The roan's placid temperament had given her the first truly relaxing afternoon of the expedition and had allowed her to focus on her surroundings rather than her fractious mount. After covertly watching Rick's handling of the black horse she reluctantly accepted that Black Devil needed a larger, stronger rider to keep him under control. She didn't have the strength, not on a prolonged basis. That she had survived as long as she had without a tumble was more a credit to her determination than anything else.

Her mind wandered as she slowly consumed the hot coffee, but her thoughts were all on Rick. She regretted now the sharp, cruel words, meant to hurt, that she had hurled at him and wished they could be unsaid. She had caught his watchful gaze on her a couple of times during the afternoon, but he hadn't spoken to her since her fall, and she couldn't guess how deeply her words had affected him.

She sipped coffee and thought how little she knew about him. There were so many questions about this man, from small ones, like his reasons for refusing to divulge his surname, to large ones, like where he had acquired the aura of command that he couldn't hide, and why he was here in

Yellowstone working as a backwoods guide. He and Jonas were friends, not employer and employee, but it was clear Rick was not a man used to being constantly outdoors, as Jonas was. She was willing to bet that under his heavy beard Rick's skin was several shades lighter than the bronze of his hands and forearms, whereas Jonas's tan had become almost permanent weathering.

Her reaction to Rick provided almost as many puzzles to her as the man himself. Whenever she was near him she felt an undeniable jolt of attraction. As yet he had done nothing more than imply he was going to kiss her, but when he touched her, when he smiled at her and let his eyes rove freely over her body she felt desire kindle and knew a frustrated longing for deeper satisfaction. This intense reaction confused her. She had dated men the same age as herself, as well as older, more mature, ones and none of them had inspired this flame of response to a word or a look. Her senses told her that meant something, but she wasn't sure what.

Unconsciously, a wistful expression crept over her delicate features. Once she left Yellowstone she would never see Rick again. She knew it was crazy, but she would miss the way his teeth flashed white in the dark beard when he was genuinely amused, his quick competence in every situation, the relaxed attitude that signified his cool self-confidence. She would even miss those occasional, arrogant assumptions he made about her abilities and attitudes. She felt ridiculously close to tears.

Across from her, Rick's eyes narrowed intently as he scrutinized her features. He had been watching her closely all day, to be certain she had suffered no ill effects from her fall and he could see the weariness marring the lovely contours of her face. Deanna blinked, suddenly aware of his steady regard. She felt a sharp rush of heady excitement that made her wish they were alone here in the Yellowstone wilderness. For a delicious moment, she let herself fantasize making love with him in the peace of these woods before she ruthlessly brought her inflamed imagination under control. They were not alone, nor would they be. Resolutely, she wrenched her eyes away from Rick and, after asking Jonas to refill her cup, forced herself to pay attention to the conversation around her.

She woke early the next morning, though she wasn't quite sure why when she needed all the sleep she could manage. Perhaps it was the morning sun changing the color of the tent walls, or the birds chattering and singing in the surrounding trees, or even the quiet sounds of activity around the hearth. All she knew was that when her eyes opened to the new day she was wide awake and it was pointless to try to sleep any longer.

It dismayed her to discover she was favoring her left hip as she moved around the tent, pulling on jeans and a fresh T-shirt. Before she left the privacy of her tent, she forced herself to forget about her aching side. She was going to walk normally and not let anyone, especially Rick and Jonas, know of the result of her fall.

She was surprised to find only Jonas sitting by the camp fire, his legs crossed in front of him, the picture of indolent ease as he sipped from a chipped coffee mug. He didn't notice her approach as he poked the smoldering hardwood fire with an immature deadwood branch.

"Good morning," she said softly, as soon as she was sure he would hear her lowered tones. "Are we the only ones up?"

He jerked in surprise, sloshing a little coffee over the rim of the cup. "Good grief, Deanna! I thought you would sleep for hours yet!"

She grinned and sat down beside him, facing the lake. "Once I'm awake, that's it, although I'm not promising I won't be ready for a nap after lunch." She pointed at the pot. "Enough coffee for another cup?"

Jonas nodded and hastily poured her one. She added sugar and powdered milk as he said with some amusement, "Of everyone here, I expected Hugh Nash to be up first."

"Hugh? Why?" Deanna raised thin, beautifully arched eyebrows. That made Jonas grin even more, amused by the incongruity of her tousled hair and casual clothes with the delicate features and occasionally haughty expressions.

"He said something about starting early, while the fish are biting. Although with Rick splashing around out there he would have been disappointed."

Since Deanna had never done any angling, the comments about the subject meant little to her. She ignored them, seizing instead on the information that did interest her. "Do you mean Rick's swimming in that lake?" She peered at the water, a frown forming on her fine features. "Are you sure, Jonas? I don't see anyone."

Jonas glanced casually at the placid, mirrored surface. "He's probably close to the other side by now."

"He's swimming across the lake—in that freezing water?"

Jonas laughed at her remark. "It's not that far, less than a mile across, and the water's not so bad, once you're used to it."

She tried not to look skeptical as she sipped her coffee. She liked Jonas and didn't want to insult him, but it stretched her imagination to believe anyone would enjoy water that cold. Last night, after they had set up camp, she had gone down to the edge of the lake and dipped her bare feet in it. Her toes turned to frigid blocks of ice and the skin whitened as the blood was driven to warmer areas of her body.

The others began to straggle out of their tents, Hugh Nash first. He moved with pointed quiet to where Jonas and Deanna lounged beside the fire. When he spoke it was in a hoarse stage whisper. Deanna sipped her coffee, listening with silent amusement as he explained that his wife was still sleeping and he didn't want to wake her. He then accepted a cup of coffee and demanded to know where Rick was and why Jonas wasn't making breakfast.

He got the same answer Deanna had and looked just as appalled, but apparently he was more disconcerted by the idea of swimming that distance than by the coldness of the water.

As she listened to the two men, Deanna kept her gaze fixed on the lake as she searched for Rick's location. When she pinpointed him, she saw he was swimming away from the far shore in a smooth, energetic crawl that sent ripples out around him. He was still some distance away from the camp, but his stroke remained steady, as though he was on the first leg of his swim, not the last.

She heard Jonas telling Hugh that today was a holiday. Dragging her thoughts away from Rick, she said curiously, "A holiday, Jonas? What on earth do you mean?"

He slid a glance at her from the corner of his eye that she found impossible to interpret, then shrugged. "Today is a free day. This morning we laze around the camp and do a little fishing. This afternoon, if anyone is interested, we take the horses and go in search of wildlife. There is usually a herd of buffalo in this area, but there's no guarantee we'll find it."

"Buffalo?" she breathed, delighted. "Honest to goodness wild buffalo?"

Jonas nodded, but didn't smile at her enthusiasm. He shot her another veiled look and seemed relieved when Fay joined them, rubbing her eyes and yawning.

"You didn't have to get up so early," Deanna teased lightly, as Jonas handed Fay a mug of coffee. "Jonas tells me we have a free day today. You could have slept for hours yet."

Fay yawned and stretched, oblivious to Jonas's interested observation of her. "With you guys making so much noise out here?" she drawled casually, her half-closed eyelids masking the twinkle in her eyes.

Hugh immediately rose to her bait. "I was very quiet! I deliberately spoke in undertones!"

Fay smiled lazily. "I know. I could hear whispering and muffled movement, so I was sure something exciting was going on. When I discovered Deanna was already up, I was positive I was the only one not awake yet." She paused and yawned again. "I wasn't going to be left behind. I figured if Deanna could rise and shine, so could I!" she concluded, with a broad grin directed at her tentmate.

Responding to her sally, Deanna pouted playfully. "Why do all of you have such a jaundiced view of me?" she demanded mournfully. Jonas laughed and Hugh looked as though he intended to explain, in detail, the answer to her question. She shot him an indignant look.

Fay giggled, rescuing her hastily. "Why don't we wake everyone else up so we can eat? I'm starved."

"We don't have to do that," Jonas said lazily. "I'm just waiting for Rick to get back, then I'll start. He'll be hungry."

"Get back?" repeated Fay. "Where is he?"

"There," Deanna muttered hoarsely, pointing to the shoreline. He was hauling himself out of the lake, the muscles in his shoulders and upper arms flexing fluidly to lever him safely to dry ground. Picking up a towel that had been hidden in the long grass, he roughly scrubbed the water from his thick, sun-kissed dark hair, leaving it attractively ruffled as he applied the cloth to his torso and long, muscular legs. Then, after a quick wipe of his arms, he sauntered toward the tents, smiling pleasantly, but clearly intending to dress before he joined them. Deanna watched the sensual, almost pantherlike way he walked, her eyes drawn to his flat belly and lean, muscular hips, covered only by the triangle of black cloth that was his immodestly brief bathing suit. That first morning, when she watched him by the river, she had thought him an attractive, fit, virile man. Now, seeing him virtually naked, his well-knit body covered by a light mat of dark hair, she felt a flush of primitive excitement rise in her and again wished they were alone in the secluded clearing at the edge of the stream.

When he reappeared he was dressed in a checked shirt and faded, well-worn jeans that hugged his thighs and hips, sending Deanna's fevered imagination rushing into channels not wise to dwell upon. By then, breakfast was well on its way, and the scent of Jonas's cooking had drawn Edith, then a sleepy, and rather rueful, Gavin and Rona, out of their tents.

Once the meal was over, the dishes washed and the remains cleared away, the real business of the morning began, as everyone but Deanna and Fay went fishing. The fishermen spread out along the shoreline, settling themselves comfortably, apparently prepared to make a day of it. Deanna and Fay talked in a desultory way about their respective cities of Los Angeles and Atlanta and some of the misconceptions they shared about Wyoming and Yellowstone. Eventually Fay wandered off to the tent, leaving Deanna to stretch out beneath the increasingly warm sun. She felt an almost drugged indolence wash over her in slow,

seductive waves as the mellow heat caressed her and eased her bodily aches from the forefront of her mind.

From somewhere nearby she heard the low rumble of voices, but in that confused state between full waking and deep sleep she couldn't be sure who was speaking, and she felt too lethargic to bother finding out. Eventually there was silence again. She must have dozed until a new combination of voices, much closer this time, brought her slowly to full attention. She was able to identify the voices easily. Rick and Fay were talking placidly about Atlanta, Georgia, and the south in general.

As she listened, Deanna realized that Rick was skillfully drawing Fay out, giving her no opportunity to question him about his background. It made her wonder who the real Rick was, what he usually did for a living. It was impossible to tell, because he never talked about himself. Was he a doctor, a lawyer, a businessman? And why would he hide himself away in the fastness of Yellowstone? Maybe there was a simple reason for his presence here. She considered the idea. Perhaps he was a teacher, or a university professor, who had the summer free of regular commitments. This might be his holiday, too. If so, why the mystery about his name and background? No, the answer to the puzzle of Rick's identity wasn't a simple one. It was as complex as the man himself.

She heard Rick say something that ended with her name, but she hadn't been listening carefully enough to discern the words. She felt a mild irritation that grew into annoyance when Fay replied with a gentle laugh, "You needn't worry about Deanna. She's done nothing strenuous the whole morning. Right now she's sound asleep."

"I am not." Deanna snapped querulously, sitting up quickly. The other two were relaxing not far from her, Fay sitting cross-legged, plucking at the long grass, while Rick lay stretched on his side, his head propped on one hand. His eyes caressed Deanna gently, but she refused to look at him, clinging to the resentment she felt at his discussing her with Fay.

The southern girl didn't seem at all put out that Deanna might have overheard her conversation with Rick. She said mildly, "Then why didn't you say anything? You were so quiet I was positive you were sleeping."

"I was thinking," replied Deanna curtly.

"Oh? What about?" Rick asked mockingly, dark eyes narrowed intently as he stared at her sleep-softened face and angry eyes.

Deanna flushed. She could hardly tell him she had been thinking of him. "The sun," she said hastily, "and how warm it is."

From the raised eyebrows and humorous twist to his mouth, it was clear Rick didn't believe her. She sent him a piercing, irritated look that made his white teeth flash in his bearded face.

"It is hot," Fay agreed, oblivious to the currents exploding around her. "It would be nice to go for a swim. What's the water like, Rick?"

He smiled lazily. "Cold."

Fay laughed softly, "That leaves me out. I'm used to warm southern seas. I hate cold water!"

Deanna ran her fingers through the grass in front of her sprawled legs. "Can you dive in anywhere?" she asked innocently, looking at the shoreline, not at Rick.

"Not if you want our enthusiastic fishermen after your blood for spoiling their sport," he said, teasing her gently. Pointing to a low peninsula that jutted out into the lake, he continued, "That would be a good spot. Far enough away not to disturb the fish, and the shore's not too high for safe diving. Why? Are you planning to go in?"

Deanna looked at him, then shook her head. "No, I didn't bring a suit." One more thing she hadn't thought to include when she packed.

"You could always strip down and swim in the buff. I'm sure if you asked nicely no one would look," he suggested softly, with the faintest of leers in his voice.

"What is it with you? Would it give you a thrill?" she spat angrily. When Fay gasped and she realized how her words must have sounded she blushed hotly. Rick's throaty chuckle only intensified her feelings. With an abrupt, angry gesture, she jumped up and hurried away.

At the edge of the low cape Rick had pointed out, she stopped and stood looking out over the water. The surrounding mountains were reflected on the still surface as perfectly as in a mirror, but her mind was not on the peaceful scene. Instead, her thoughts revolved around her childish response to a bit of harmless teasing. She had been embarrassed to have to concede yet another example of her unpreparedness to a man she wanted badly to impress. That, on top of her silly refusal to acknowledge that she had been asleep, like an overtired child too stubborn to admit her own exhaustion, made her feel like a complete fool. For once she wished she could get the better of Rick. Just once.

Hearing footsteps behind her, she turned slowly. She knew it was Rick and she knew her emotions were still too close to the surface for her to talk calmly to him. "Go away," she said clearly.

"Still sulking?" he demanded derisively.

"I am not sulking," she countered stiffly.

"No? What do you call it then?" he asked mockingly, advancing to within inches of her.

A wild light of irrepressible mischief flashed in Deanna's eyes as they burned into his, making him lose his air of lazy assurance and carving a frown between his brows. Her rampaging thoughts told her that here was a chance never to be repeated; she could either take it or turn on her heel and walk away. Deanna was not the kind of girl to chose prudence over action. She lifted her chin, a challenging smile on her lips.

Rick began urgently, "Deanna, don't..." as she put her small hands on his broad chest and, exerting all her strength, pushed.

Chapter Six

He landed in the water with a resounding splash. Fay shrieked and ran over to where Deanna was standing, watching the water complacently, waiting for Rick to bob to the surface. She felt no regret or guilt over what she had done and, in fact, was having great difficulty stifling her bubbling laughter. She knew Rick would be furious and didn't think it would be wise to be giggling helplessly when he came up for air.

"What have you done?" cried Fay, peering into the blue depths of the lake.

Deanna was saved a reply as Rick surfaced a little distance from the shore, spitting water and shaking the shaggy, water-darkened hair from his eyes.

"Thank God you're all right!" shouted Fay. "You must be freezing! Do come in!"

Rick remained where he was, treading water with practiced ease. Across the short, blue distance, Deanna felt the pull of his eyes and raised hers to meet his gaze. There was anger burning hotly there and a kind of devilish, wicked amusement. Deanna felt a tingle of excitement slide down her spine as he swam expertly to shore, despite the encumbrances of his heavy, wet clothes and boots.

At the shore he grasped the edge of the turf for balance. When he tested it the earth fell away in his hands. He looked up at Deanna, his eyes glinting. Lifting his other hand, he said to her, "Looks like you're going to have to give me some help. The shore won't take my weight."

Deanna laughed and jumped backward. "Oh, no! You're not going to catch me in that trap! Pull yourself out!"

"Deanna," he said in a bored voice, "give me your hand. The water's cold. I'd like to get out before I freeze."

"I'll help you," offered Fay obligingly, coming over to the side.

Deanna thought she detected a flash of irritation in his eyes and congratulated herself on having the good sense to keep away from the edge.

"Thanks, Fay," he said calmly, "but I think Deanna should do it. Besides, I'm really too heavy for you. I don't want you to strain yourself."

Deanna felt a piqued stab of annoyance. "What about me?" she flashed, knowing she lacked a good three inches on Fay, "I'm a lot smaller than she is!"

"I thought you were the one who didn't want any concessions because of your size," he retorted coldly.

The truth of that touched a vulnerable spot. She studied him as he bobbed gently in the water, looking for signs of deception. The irritation she had noted before wasn't because Fay had interfered in any planned retribution, but because he worried about her ability to cope with the effort.

Drawing a deep breath, she snapped, "I don't." Two tentative steps and she was at the edge, holding out her hand, keeping her eyes fixed warily on his face, intending to flee if she noticed any telltale change of expression. His dark eyes, framed by thick, spiky lashes, remained hard and fathomless. She let him grasp her warm fingers with his cold, wet ones, then strained backward to haul him up. The shark jerk on her arm caught her off balance. Just before she hit the water, she noted his eyes were blazing with a wild, roguish light, then her body was being jolted by icy cold that made her open her mouth to gasp. She took in a mouthful of water and began to choke, fighting her way to the surface instinctively, coughing as soon as she reached air.

She felt Rick's arms go around her waist, holding her head well above the water level while she concentrated on drawing in great, shuddering breaths. "You little idiot," he growled in her ear, "Why didn't you hold your breath?"

Deanna shook her head, unable to speak.

Rick made a disgusted sound in his throat and began to tow her back to shore. His moment of relaxed vigilance gave Deanna the opening she needed. Putting both hands on his thick, wet hair, she pushed his head under water. But Rick's hold on her waist tightened, and in a lithe movement that proved he was just as much at home in the water as on land, he dragged her under with him.

A shaft of sunlight penetrated the clear water, bathing them in unearthly, diffused light. Deanna saw his eyes gleam and felt one hand leave her waist to slide gently over her cold skin to caress her breast. Feeling powerless to stop him, and not really wanting to, she let him cup the soft mound, his fingers splaying over it to find the tip, hardened by the freezing water, as his mouth came down in a harsh, punishing kiss that meant to teach her dominance, not passion. The cold kept her from feeling pain as her lips were ground against her teeth, but she knew in a few hours she would remember, as clearly as if he had put his brand on her, that he was not one to take challenges lightly.

They surfaced for a few short seconds, his body shielding Deanna from those on shore, one hand still possessively on her breast. She gasped in a few quick breaths, enough to refill her lungs, but not for her to give voice to an indignant demand for him to release her, when he dove once more, this time into darker water. Deanna writhed and struggled, but his hands were like iron and, afraid she would run out of air, she gave up. He kissed her again, this time gently, almost coaxingly, seeking a response she was reluctant to give. His mouth was warm and throbbing in the cold that surrounded her, promising a fire that would drive all knowledge of the icy chill from her shivering body. Instinctively, her lips parted beneath his, to allow his probing tongue access, as one hand remained tantalizingly on her tender breast and the other circled her waist to hold her cradled against his hard body.

Slowly they rose to the surface, too absorbed in their own reactions to notice, but as their heads broke from the clear water Deanna suddenly remembered they were not alone. They were far enough from the shore for Rick's more intimate caresses not to have been observed, but Fay must have witnessed their close embrace. It was difficult to know how much the others could see, scattered as they were along the shoreline, or if they would even be interested.

That, she thought, was a futile hope. Of course they would be interested. Hugh Nash would be intrigued, his wife amused or faintly disapproving; even Jonas would be curious. She twisted agilely out of Rick's grasp, swimming a short distance away. Far enough to be out of his reach, but close enough so they could talk in normal tones.

Her thumping heart was sending her blood pounding through her veins as his compelling dark eyes lingered on her face. She felt the almost physical caress of them and searched her mind for something—anything—to say to break their potent spell.

"Why did you do that?" she demanded huskily, feeling betrayed by the desire that thickened her voice.

His brows rose in incredulous surprise and amusement tugged at his lips. "You have to ask?"

She bit her lip, feeling the hot color in her face exposing the sudden shyness she felt. He was right; it was a stupid question. Breathing deeply, she demanded, "Why here, now, in front of an audience?"

"No one could see anything," he replied curtly.

"They could see us surface together. They all have imaginations. They could guess!" Her voice rose, betraying a fear she rarely expressed.

"What's eating you, bobcat? Afraid the press will come to hear of it?"

"Yes!" she hissed. He frowned, taken aback by her vehemence. "But that's not something I'd expect you to understand!" she added angrily.

He responded with the cool, mocking amusement that had infuriated her on the first day. "Oh no? Try me."

A short distance away there was a whoop of glee. "I've got one. I've finally got one!" shouted Gavin. "Look, everyone! A fine, fat trout! Hey, Rick, come on over and take a look!"

"Damn!" he muttered, his tone no less explosive for its quiet.

"You'd better go," she said harshly. "We've already called enough attention to ourselves."

After a moment of indecision, he swam quickly to the shore and heaved himself easily on to the grass. Treading water, Deanna watched him saunter over to Gavin, apparently oblivious to the sodden state of his clothing. She wrenched her eyes away from him when Fay called, "Deanna, you'll catch your death, honey. Come on out!"

She laughed. "I'm wet now, so I may as well enjoy the swim. Don't worry about me, Fay." She didn't wait for an answer, diving into the clear water, trying to ignore the goose bumps that had erupted all over her skin.

For another fifteen minutes she swam, dove, and played happily. For a few of them Fay watched her worriedly, apparently certain that the cold water would produce a seizure of some sort, but eventually she wandered away, seeking more convivial companions. Deanna enjoyed her solitude, feeling alone in a vast wilderness, soothed by her unspoiled surroundings. She was idly treading water and telling herself she wasn't ice cold, when she noticed Rick standing at the edge of the peninsula.

He had replaced the saturated jeans with dry ones, but hadn't bothered with a shirt, leaving his muscled chest bare. The sight tantalized Deanna. She stared appreciatively, her eyes hungrily noting the sinewy shoulders and upper arms, then lowering to the lean hips and muscular thighs. She had a sudden memory of his nearly naked body as he crossed from the lake to his tent only a few hours before and felt a shaft of desire that made her shiver.

He squatted down and held out his hand. "You've been in long enough, Deanna. Come out. Now."

"Aren't you afraid I'll pull you in?" she taunted, unwilling to do what he ordered, even though she knew he was right.

He smiled faintly. "No. These are my only dry pair of jeans. I don't think you would deliberately soak them."

Deanna wrinkled her nose, knowing he was right, and swam forward to let him help her out. Sitting panting on the grass, she closed her eyes, raising her face to feel the warm kiss of the sun. It was nearly noon and the sun was hot, the air still.

Slowly, she opened her eyes when she heard Rick say, "You must be cold." He stood above her, his hands on his hips, his eyes drawn irresistibly to her gently curved shape. The T-shirt was clinging to her body, outlining her high, rounded breasts, the nipples still hard from the cold and her own barely controlled desires. She saw his jaw clench as he strove to master his own response. Not waiting for her answer, he stretched out a hand to bring her to her feet. She grasped it firmly and rose, deliberately moving with exaggerated slowness, letting him feast his eyes on her sensual, barely covered form.

She knew that she was teasing him unmercifully, but the opportunity was too good to miss, just as it had been when she'd pushed him in the lake. His hot gaze caressed her and went a long way to warming her chilled body.

"You'd better get changed out of those wet things," he said huskily when she was standing upright. He dropped her hand and stepped backward.

She bit her lip, mumbling grudgingly, "I don't have anything to change into."

His forehead creased in a frown as he wrenched his eyes from her curves to gaze penetratingly into her face. She met his look levelly, although she knew he must be annoyed. "You're serious, aren't you?" he said slowly, after a moment's intense inspection.

She nodded solemnly, suddenly feeling extremely foolish as exasperation flashed in his eyes.

He drew in a deep, steadying breath. "What exactly did you think this trip was going to be? A jaunt in a city park?"

"Well, no," she said, looking down at her bare toes.

He waited for a moment to give her time for a further explanation, but when she was silent he continued inexorably, "You insist on riding a completely unsuitable horse..."

"That's not *my* fault!" she flashed, her head coming up swiftly and the abashed look fleeing from her eyes.

He continued, ignoring her outburst. "You compound that by wearing boots useless for anything but sitting on a horse and don't even bother to bring walking shoes or hiking boots with you...."

"Seth Aitken's letter said to pack light!" she shouted, wishing she could make him stop.

"Now I discover you didn't even have the sense to bring an extra pair of jeans! What would you have done if you'd torn these on a tree branch or a bush?"

"Sewn up the tear!" she snapped promptly.

His eyebrows rose in polite inquiry. "With all the other things you omitted from your packing list, you thought to include a needle and thread?"

Color splashed up her neck and into her cheeks with a betraying rush. She bent her head, knowing it was useless to try and deceive him. "No," she mumbled. Then, with a resurgence of spirit, she looked back up at him, lifting her chin proudly, "But I would have managed somehow."

His eyes were enigmatic. "That I do not doubt. You are like a cat, Deanna Monroe. You always land on your feet." He studied her for a moment, a faintly indulgent smile on his lips. "How are you going to do it this time?"

"I don't know, but I will!" she spat angrily, annoyed by his superior air.

"Like I said," he mocked, "I don't doubt that in the least."

The afternoon was sunny, hot, and silent. Deanna yawned lazily, tucked her feet beneath her and rose, wincing a little as her bruised hip twinged at her sudden movement. Near the fireplace her jeans were laid out, drying in the sun. She ambled over and picked them up, grimacing slightly as she realized how damp they still were. It would be best, she thought, if she could drape them on a bush or hang them on a tree branch, but the forest was in shadow, out of the direct path of the sun, and she couldn't take the chance. Denim took so long to dry, and she would need the pants tonight. She moved stiffly over to a dry patch and spread them flat again, damper side up, then limped back to the spot where her sleeping bag lay open on the grass, doing service as a beach towel. With a little sigh she settled on her stomach, exposing her back to the sun, and let her thoughts drift.

As she had promised Rick, she had solved her problem, in a way. Fay had come to her rescue, offering Deanna her bathing suit until the jeans were dry. She confided to Deanna that she, too, had been guilty of poor packing and had brought no spare pair of slacks; otherwise she would have been glad to lend them to Deanna instead of the bikini. Deanna accepted the offer of the bathing suit gratefully, not realizing until she stripped down and slid on the moss-green bikini how little there was of it. Fay was longer in the body than Deanna, but of an equally slim build, so the bottoms fit perfectly. The bra top was a different matter. Fay's breasts were smaller, less rounded, and when Deanna fastened the top of her full breasts spilled over the edge of the skimpy pieces of cloth in a most enticing way. Deanna bit her lip, realizing she could not wear the bathing suit outside of the tent without something to cover it. That wasn't a problem though. She just pulled a T-shirt over it, leaving her beautiful, slender legs bare.

After lunch the rest of the group had opted to go with Jonas, searching for wild buffalo. Deanna would have liked to have joined them, but with her jeans wet and no alternate clothes, she was stuck. She consoled herself with the thought that she was better off being completely lazy all day.

Once the commotion of departure was over, and stillness returned to the clearing, she had collected her sleeping bag from the tent and settled down for an afternoon nap, discarding the T-shirt to let the sun play on her creamy, California-tanned skin.

Remembering that she had been sleeping on her stomach for more than an hour, she rolled over. She didn't think she would get a sunburn, but there was no sense taking chances. The tiny bathing suit did little to hide her charms, but she wasn't worried. She was alone, except for the birds and other wildlife, and they wouldn't care if she was naked! She let sleep claim her once more.

She dreamed, and in her dream it was not the warm caress of the sun her skin felt, but of a man's hands moving slowly down her rib cage to trail feather light across the sensitive skin of her stomach, then up toward her breasts. She moaned in her sleep, a husky sound of pleasure, hoping the tantalizing caress would continue to the aching crests of her breasts, but it did not. Instead, the hands left her body to stroke sedutively along her jawline, then to touch and outline her full pink lips.

By now she was awake enough to know that the hands stroking her body were not a dream. Peeping out from beneath her lashes, she saw what she already knew. It was Rick who seductively caressed her, and he was watching her intently, waiting for her to respond. He probably already knew she was awake, she thought, but she kept her eyes closed and her body relaxed, deciding to play out the game a little longer to see how far he proposed to go.

It was difficult, pretending not to be aware of his caresses. Despite herself, she felt her breasts tauten as one gentle finger blazed a path of fire down her slender neck, past her collarbone, to outline their perfect shape beneath the bikini top. Deanna swallowed an obstruction in her throat and opened her eyes abruptly to see Rick's serious, smoldering features. Her hands lifted to touch the warm, slightly damp skin of his naked chest and felt his heart pounding with powerful, urgent strokes.

His arms slid around her to encircle her back and cradle her against him as his lips moved to cover hers in a tender, teasing kiss, his teeth nipping gently at her full lower lip, making her groan again and press more closely against him. She could feel his hands working at the strings of the bikini top, but she didn't protest. Already she was acting more on instinct than conscious thought.

With the strings untied and her back bare, the kiss deepened. His tongue persuaded her lips to part and admit it within. His hands stroked gently down her spine as his tongue plunged and probed. She let her own hands slide up his chest to his shoulders, clinging to the powerful muscles there, as if to draw strength from his strength. The tip of her tongue teased and tantalized his, setting off an explosion within him that made his hold tighten and his kiss grow more demanding. Her fingers dug into his shoulders as he lowered her back to the ground, using his slackened grip to toss away the useless bikini top.

His lips left hers to fasten on the susceptible pleasure point at the base of her neck. She drew in a deep shuddering breath, aware of nothing but her own sensations and the man who was creating them. Her hands eased their clinging grasp on his shoulders to cup his neck, then travel down the hard lean muscles of his back. She didn't move them consciously; she was so caught up in the heat that had grown in her loins and spread like wildfire under she felt it might consume her.

The thick, dark beard that hid his jaw and cheeks was no impediment to her pleasure, as she might have thought, if she was capable of composed reasoning. The bristles were not hard and scratchy, but soft. They tickled enough to tease her delicate skin to new heights of sensation. When his lips left her shoulder to fasten on her breast, his tongue lapping and caressing the nipple while the beard teased and tantalized the rounded mound beneath, she felt her body ache with the need for fulfillment. She heard herself whisper hoarsely, "Rick! Please! I need you! Don't wait! Please!"

He responded to the urgency in her voice by lifting his head, leaving her abandoned while he stared at her intently. "Are you sure, Deanna?" he demanded harshly.

"Yes!" she cried, her hands moving up to tangle in his thick hair. "Please Rick, don't stop! You're driving me crazy!"

He smiled slightly at the longing in her voice, then lowered his head to drop butterfly kisses at the corners of her mouth, lower to her throat, in the hollow between her breasts. She watched him, her hands fluttering around his shoulders and neck, part of her wanting this delicious temptation never to end, more of her demanding fulfillment. She groaned out his name, desperate for him to quench the blazing fire inside her.

He looked up, his eyes tenderly amused. "You're overdressed, sweetheart," he teased, one hand following the line of the bikini bottoms across her flat abdomen to her hip, then down to her desire-tautened thigh. Deanna moved her hips convulsively to aid him in ridding her of the unwanted garment. A shaft of pain lanced through her from her bruised limb, and unthinkingly she gasped, a very different sound from the desire-filled moans of a minute before.

Immediately, his stroking hands stilled. "What is it, Deanna?" he demanded soberly. "Am I hurting you?"

She bit her lip. If she told him about her hip she was afraid he wouldn't continue, but she couldn't let him believe his actions brought anything but pleasure to her. She let one hand trail down to his face, running her fingertips through the thick beard on his jaw. If she could just persuade him it was no more than her normal quota of aches and pains.

"It's nothing," she said huskily, "I'm just a little stiff, that's all. I moved the wrong way I guess."

His eyes bored into her, testing the truth of her reply, and she felt herself color. His expression softened. "Liar," he said gently, rolling away to rise to his feet in one fluid motion.

Deanna sighed. She had to be the worst actress in the world, a pretty sorry commentary, considering who her parents were. Feeling let down and lethargic, she slowly re-tied the bikini top and prudently decided to pull the white T-shirt over it. Rick was standing with his back to her, staring out toward the lake, his stance rigid as he fought to control his rampaging desire.

"Are you decent?" he demanded curtly.

"If you mean, do I have my top on again, the answer is yes," she said irritably.

He turned around, smiling faintly when he noticed that she had donned the T-shirt as well as the bikini top. She glared mutinously at him as he sat down beside her, notic-ing sourly that he kept enough distance between them to make touching difficult. Prudent, but provoking. "Why did you cry out?" he demanded bluntly.

Deanna ignored the expression of concern in his eyes as she snapped, "I told you. It's nothing more than stiffness."

"We both know better than that," he replied evenly. "Stop being difficult, Deanna, and tell me what the problem is."

"Difficult?" she repeated softly, feeling temper replace the flaring heat of desire. "I am not being difficult!"

His warm eyes scanned her belligerent features and kindled in amusement. He reached out to touch her face, almost as if he couldn't resist being so near without feeling her silky skin against his fingers. Deanna held herself tensely, knowing it would take very little for her body to catch fire again. She nursed her anger, using it as a guard against his potent attraction, but when he cupped her head and brought her close to him for a kiss, her ire melted away as if it had never been.

His lips moved over hers in a tender, pliant caress that was more sweet concern than passionate desire, but Deanna wasn't thinking—she was responding. She placed her hands on his chest, not to hold him off, but to enjoy the tactile pleasure of his skin beneath her fingertips. His lips left hers to tease the lobe of her ear, and she heard him whisper, "Tell me."

For a moment she stiffened, but his hands had wrapped around her slender body and his lips on her shoulder were making thought difficult, if not impossible. "Don't stop," she murmured hesitantly.

"Tell me, sweetheart. Let me help you," he commanded persuasively.

"I... My hip...when I fell off Blackie I bruised it. That's all. Ummm, that's nice," she added as one hand stroked the length of her thigh, pushing the T-shirt up to give him better access to her damaged limb.

He laid her back down on the sleeping bag and concentrated on his inspection of her hip in a purely clinical manner. Deanna sighed and propped herself up on one elbow to watch him. His long fingers probed the area, where the shadow of a major bruise was just becoming visible, with such precise competence that she said, half humorously, "You wouldn't, by any chance, be a doctor, would you?"

"No," he replied absently, "an architect." He must have felt her tense in surprise, for he abandoned his inspection, looking at her with frowning concern. "That shouldn't have hurt...."

"What do you mean, you're an architect?" she demanded, sitting up so that they were at an equal eye level. The expression on his face became guarded, which told her without words that he had admitted something he didn't want known. Why? Architecture was a perfectly respectable profession. And what was he doing here, guiding pack trains in the wilderness of Yellowstone National Park?

"We were talking about your hip," he said coolly.

"You were, I wasn't. What are you hiding, Rick?" she demanded, her curiosity strong. "I think I deserve an explanation after what almost happened today."

He eyed her consideringly. "You don't want to know about my past, bobcat. It's not very exciting."

"I'm easily entertained," she replied casually, hiding her interest.

Rick wasn't taken in by her act. He grinned at her, his teeth very white in the dark beard. Deanna felt herself melt inside and wished he would trust her. After a moment of reflection he said with a shrug, "I was bored with my life."

Something in his guarded tones told Deanna there was much more to it than he was admitting, so she remarked cautiously, "You seem very much at home with," her hand fluttered to indicate the terrain, "all this."

"Just because I design buildings doesn't mean I don't respect the environment, or that I can't cope outside the parameters of concrete and glass," he said, his voice soft, his eyes mocking.

She realized with a swelling of indignation that he saw right through her attempt to gather information on his past. So much for subtlety. Maybe the direct route was the answer. "Okay, so I'm curious. Who are you, Rick? I don't even know your last name!"

There was a long period of silence that seemed to stretch and lengthen with each passing moment. Finally, Rick broke it, his voice low and husky. "Tell me something, Deanna, when you came her did you expect anyone to pry into your past?"

She flushed. His arrow had hit home. "No, but they did. I understand what you're saying, Rick. You don't want me, or anyone else, probing into your background." She felt incredibly hurt. He had been using her. He didn't trust her, he probably didn't even like her, yet he had been prepared to make love to her a few heart-stopping minutes ago. "What's the real story?" she queried, her voice harsh with self-loathing. "Did you rob a bank? Break out of jail?"

He began to laugh, a deep velvet chuckle of very real amusement, as if she had said something hilariously funny. The dark, rich sound rasped against her bones like chalk squeaking against a blackboard. She shivered, standing up abruptly and limping over to inspect her blue jeans.

There was an angry explosion from the man behind her. "What the hell have you done to your ankles?"

For a moment she couldn't understand what he was talking about. She stopped and looked frowningly down at her feet, then realized that he must mean the blisters she had acquired on the trek to the waterfall. "Oh, that!" she said casually, proceeding on her way to the jeans. Crouching down, she fussed with the moist cloth, using it as an excuse to ignore Rick.

"Yes, that!" he growled, coming up behind her. "How long have you had those damned blisters?"

"A couple of days," she said calmly, not daring to look at him because she knew the expression in his eyes would be one of angry condemnation.

His hand on her chin forced her head around. She lowered her thick, light lashes to hide the vulnerability in her eyes, but that leveled her gaze to the dark, curling hairs on his chest and brought back hot memories of a few minutes before. Quickly, she raised her eyes to his face. Seeing his anger was better than suffering from unquenchable desire.

"Why the devil didn't you tell me about it?" he demanded harshly. She opened her mouth to answer, but he continued in an exasperated voice, "Do you never listen? I told you to ask for help if you had any problems. Did it even occur to you to come to me?"

"No," she muttered.

He made a disgusted sound in his throat and dropped his hand as if her words had scalded him. "I'll get the first-aid kit," he told her grimly. "Go on back to your sleeping bag and get comfortable."

Deanna didn't move. She realized, quite suddenly, that she had hurt him by not trusting him. He stood up and stepped carefully around her, heading for his tent. She said clearly, "After the way you criticized my boots at the falls I thought you would only be mad." He stopped and slowly turned to face her. She swallowed. "You have to admit you've been pretty scathing about my ability to cope on this trip."

"That wasn't contempt, Deanna, it was concern," he responded levelly, a frown between his eyes as he watched her rise clumsily to her feet. "You didn't talk to anyone about what to expect before you came on this expedition, did you?"

She shook her head. "There was no one to ask."

"Especially not your proper New England father," he said grimly, his mouth set in a straight, wrathful line. Abruptly, he turned away toward the tent, leaving Deanna to limp slowly back to her sleeping bag and settle on it once more.

When she returned with the first-aid kit she let him bandage her heels without any protest. They both knew that she could have managed on her own and they both knew that he would insist on being the one to do the job. She watched him apply the adhesive bandage to one heel, then extended the other.

"How come you're here?" she asked idly, "I thought you went off with the others."

He smiled tightly. "One of us had to stay behind. Since it was my idea, I was the lucky one to remain."

"Do you mean you planned all this?" she demanded indignantly.

He paused as he was about to place a second bandage and looked up. "Yes. I thought you needed a day to rest."

"I didn't," she snapped, moving restlessly, as if she intended to jump up and flounce away.

His long, powerful fingers closed over her slender ankle, imprisoning it and her, in an iron grasp. "Stay still," he commanded. "I'm not finished yet."

It wasn't easy to sit passively while she burned with hot animosity, but she swallowed the rush of adrenaline that made her want to pace the length of the small clearing and let him complete his task. "How were you planning to keep me from joining the buffalo hunt?" she demanded rhetorically, then answered her own question. "Dunk me in the lake? You must have been delighted when I was obliging enough to do it for you!"

"Nothing quite so complicated," he said calmly, attaching the bandage to her red heel and grabbing her wrist before she could move away. "I would have simply forbidden you to go."

"And you think I would have complied?" she cried hotly.

"Yes," he replied quietly.

"Well, I wouldn't!" she spat indignantly, glaring into his dark eyes.

He shrugged. "Then Jonas and I would have led the party through easy terrain, or you and I would have become separated from the rest and be forced to return...."

"You conniving skunk!" she shouted wrathfully.

That only made him laugh. Idly, he lifted her chin with one lazy finger. "I can see my plan worked. The circles are gone from beneath those beautiful violet eyes, and the marks of strain have disappeared from around your delightfully kissable mouth." His lips descended to meet hers with a fleeting, promising touch.

Furious, she wrenched her head away. "I asked for no concessions," she said tightly. "And I wanted none!"

"Brave words," he replied softly, watching the quick interplay of emotions on her expressive features. "But how long would it have been before you collapsed completely?"

Deanna felt the turbulent anger drain from her as quickly as air escaping from a pricked balloon. His words were concerned, compassionate, revealing emotions she hadn't expected to find in a man, especially one she had known only a few days. "I'm stronger than I look," she said halfheartedly.

Surprising her, he acknowledged softly, "I know that." She watched the hint of a smile playing at his lips and found herself smiling back. "Or you would have given up the first day." She blushed under the compliment, and he laughed.

"That's the last thing I ever expected to hear you say," she remarked lightly, to cover her confusion.

He chuckled. "Bobcat, you may be willing to tackle anything, but a woodsman you're not. You need someone to take care of you."

The truth of that statement made her say provocatively, "Like you did?"

His brows rose. "Are you protesting?" he demanded softly.

She allowed her lips to tremble into a smile as her eyes gazed deeply into his. "Oh, no," she said huskily, "not at all."

He stared at her for a moment, then took the kiss she was so plainly offering. His lips moved over hers, teasing, enticing, skillfully stoking the fire. She knew that Rick was rapidly losing his thin layer of control and that this time there would be no drawing back for either of them. His fingers moved, impatiently tugging at her white T-shirt.

She could have cried when the sound of high, excited laughter heralded the return of Jonas and his troop of buffalo hunters. Rick drew back, looking equally disgusted.

He slanted her a glance from hooded brown eyes and said wryly, "Talk about rotten timing."

Deanna couldn't help herself; she began to giggle. "I can think of worse moments."

He stared at her, then saw the humor of the situation. "Minx," he said softly, running a careless finger down her cheek.

She stood up, knowing it was safer to put some ground between them if they didn't intend being caught in a compromising situation. Striving for normalcy she said, "Where were you this afternoon? I mean before you," she choked, "woke me."

Fishing," he replied briefly, watching her.

"Where?"

Pointing to the trees he explained, "There's a path leading to one of the streams that feed the lake. It's about a quarter of a mile away, maybe a bit more. It's an excellent spot for fishing." He added mischievously, "In the afternoon it's shaded. Not all of us are sun worshipers."

She grinned, then limped slowly over to her jeans. "Catch anything?" she asked over her shoulder.

"A three-pound rainbow trout," he told her absently, his eyes following her halting pace. "You're limp is less pronounced, bobcat. Feeling better?"

Somewhat surprised, she realized he was right; her hip wasn't as tender as it had been. She paused to grin cheekily at him. "I told you it was just stiffness."

"A little more than that," he murmured. She wrinkled her nose at him with mock disdain and crossed the remaining distance to her pants. He watched her with narrowed, assessing eyes until he was satisfied her injury was nothing more serious than bruised and stiffened muscles, then he bent to fold her sleeping bag.

Chapter Seven .

That was how the others found them, Deanna inspecting her jeans with worried absorption while Rick, across the clearing from her, quickly carried a sleeping bag toward the tents. In the confusion of their arrival, no one noticed that he dropped the down-filled bag in Deanna's tent, nor did they question that Rick had spent the afternoon fishing while Deanna dozed in the sun. They were too busy regaling both with descriptions of the animals they had seen and meticulously detailing all that Deanna and Rick had missed by remaining at the camp. Neither paid much attention. They had far more potent memories of the day than the others would ever imagine.

Deanna slept restlessly that night, her dreams a confused distortion of the incident in the clearing that afternoon. When the gray light of early dawn crept through the canvas walls of her tent it easily dissolved the misty haze in her mind, bringing her to sharp awareness. For a while she lay on her back in the cozy warmth of the sleeping bag, trying to sort out the welter of emotions that were the aftermath of yesterday's lovemaking. Instead of relaxing, her muscles tensed, until she knew she had to leave the tent or scream with pure frustration.

She scrambled out of the bag, pulled on her jeans, cool, but blessedly dry, added a gaily colored T-shirt of blue and red diagonal strips, and picked up her leather jacket. As she stepped from the tent the ground was cool and damp under her bare feet. She pushed her arms into the buff jacket, but left it open. As with most summer days on the Yellowstone plateau, it would be hot by noon, and even now it wasn't unpleasantly cold.

She paused by the scarred, blackened fire pit, staring out at the tranquil lake. The scene was beautiful, but Deanna felt an overwhelming compulsion to move, to slip away from the clearing, where any minute another member of their small expedition might wake and decide to do exactly as she was doing.

Still, she hesitated, unsure of herself in these wild conditions. If only there was a path she could follow as she had that other morning when they were camped by the stream. She smiled faintly, remembering how startled she had been when Rick had appeared at the water's edge.

To her right a movement caught her eye and she padded silently toward it. It was a bird, a large one, blending into the undergrowth with uncanny accuracsy. What was it? A pheasant? A grouse? Did either of these two species live in the Yellowstone area? Her eyes searched the timber for another glimpse of the small creature, but without success. She did notice a gap in the trees, though, which suddenly brought back another memory from yesterday; Rick telling her he had been fishing in a spot where a creek entered the lake. This must be the path that led to his clearing.

Cautiously, she entered the woods, carefully watching her footing. The path was little more than a widening in the trees, but it was well-defined enough to follow without getting lost. The surface, however, was littered with roots and fallen branches, making it clear the path was rarely used.

That suited Deanna perfectly. She wanted a place where she would be undisturbed and she was sure no one would follow her here. Now that she was on the move, she began to relax and the tautness of her muscles eased. She was pleased to notice that her hip wasn't giving her any trouble this morning, and for the first time she was free of the nagging ache of stiff, overworked muscles. She felt a wonderful sense of physical well-being, despite her emotional confusion.

The path broadened into a natural clearing where a wide, but shallow creek opened into the lake. Rick's fishing spot. She moved to sit on the edge of the bank, then imagined him in that very place, holding his rod, a moody, thoughtful expression on his face as he waited for a fish to take his bait. The rod curved and tautened as he fought to bring the fish in. Her heart lurched and she felt a warm flush of longing. This was not the place to do any cool, objective thinking about her relationship with Rick—what there was of it.

Beyond the open area the creek curled lazily into the trees. Deanna looked at it thoughtfully. What harm was there in walking a short distance beside the water? It would be a simple matter to find her way back to the clearing with the creek as a guide.

Her feet making little sound on the soft floor of pine needles, she picked her way along the bank until she came to a spot where a fallen log, beside a still standing lodgepole pine, provided a comfortable seat. She sank down on it, leaning her back against the tree, and stared up at the canopy of branches so far above. As she sat motionless the sounds of the forest wove gently around her as birds and small animals, alerted by her presence, returned to their normal activities. The scent of pine was heavy on the air, and the whole setting had a tranquil beauty that opened the mind, letting thoughts flood in.

Yesterday she had almost made love with a man she hardly knew, something she had never done before. A man, moreover, who obviously didn't trust her, or he would be willing to tell her his name and his reasons for being in the wilderness. He knew everything about her, but she knew nothing of him. How could she surrender so easily to a man like that, especially when it violated all of her deeply en-grained moral standards?

Her physical response wasn't surprising under the cir-cumstances, she decided grudgingly. He was an attractive, virile man and in this rather unusual situation, which had thrown them so closely together, a chemical response be-tween two healthy people was natural. What amazed her was the way she had quickly come to desire his good opin-ion as well. That suggested she was more deeply involved with him than she would ever have expected in a few short days.

Her forhead puckered in a frown as she wondered if part of her interest in Rick stemmed from the mystery that sur-rounded him. His refusal to discuss his background made disclosures like yesterday's casually dropped information all the more intriguing. She tried to think of Rick in a city, designing and erecting buildings, but found she couldn't imagine it. He seemed so much a part of the vast Wyoming wilderness that it was impossible to picture him cooped up in an office.

If Rick was not a city person, she certainly was. Here in the woods she was completely hopeless, always doing the wrong thing and making trouble for everyone else, especially Rick.

She shivered suddenly, feeling cold for reasons that had nothing to do with the weather. She wanted to make love with Rick, but she also wanted to get to know the man behind the good-looking exterior. That took time and it would need commitment from both of them. She and Rick had neither one—tomorrow they would be back at the Double S, where he would stay while she left. Even if they did want to make things more permanent, the barriers in their way seemed enormous.

She smiled, rather ironically, into the sunlit grove. She had come to Yellowstone for a breather before she began work on the most important, and taxing, assignment of her career. Her plan for an anonymous, carefree vacation had been shattered from the beginning by the very man who had come to dominate her thoughts.

Rick had walked into her mind and, she was afraid, into her heart, until he absorbed all her emotions. The importance of her coming assignment dwindled in the face of her overwhelming need for him.

The thought depressed her and she sighed, her expression grim. It was stupid to think she cared for Rick in an emotional way. That would imply she had fallen in love with him, which simply wasn't possible. Love, real love, only existed after a slow, meaningful uncovering of ideas, beliefs, and feelings. It was not a quick, electric charge that emptied the mind of everything but the need to be one with your partner, to touch, to feel, to help. That was infatuation. It had to be.

Her wayward thoughts forced her to remember the conversation that had followed their interrupted passion. When Rick had shown her that he cared about her, her heart had leapt with pleasure and excitement. For the first time in her life she wanted to depend on a man, to accept him and have him accept her. When he had been hurt by her stubborn refusal to trust him, she knew instantly how he felt, and had responded by trying to soothe the injury she had caused.

Was that love? By her definition it couldn't be, but in her heart she knew what she felt was the very core of any successful, loving relationship.

She sighed again, the slight quiver of sound lost in the cheerful gurgle of the nearby stream. Her parents' stormy, quarrelsome marriage had begun in just this way. A short, passionate infatuation, demanding fulfillment, had led to years of empty separations and violent shouting matches that reverberated off the walls of their elegant home and terrified their eldest daughter.

Long ago Deanna had promised herself she would never be caught in the bitter bondage that held her parents. Yet in less than a week, she had abandoned all her principles over a man whose last name she didn't know, who refused to trust her, who teased her unmercifully about her size and her ability to cope.

She shifted uneasily on the log, seeking a fresh, somewhat less knarled spot to sit. It was unfair to blame all her present problems on her parents and her upbringing. It was true that the image of their battle-scarred marriage haunted her, making her ultracautious in her romantic relationships, but they had always been supportive of her interests and ambitions, especially her father. Though they never consciously directed her into the movie industry, she knew they were both delighted when she chose costume design as a means of putting her talents to work.

Like any proud parents, they assumed she was extremely gifted, capable of unlimited success. Inevitably, because of her parents' status in the industry, that view was shared by everyone she came in contact with. A swift, meteoric ascent to prominence was predicted by her parents and her business associates alike.

That rise had never occurred. Over the past few years she had failed to meet those early expectations. Deanna knew she had talent, but she worked badly under pressure, and in the movie industry pressure was ever present.

Idly, she scuffed her bare toes in the floor of pine needles. The picture she would be working on when she returned to L.A. would be more highly pressured than most, since it was her father's script and one of the year's major productions. She wanted desperately to do well, to design costumes that enhanced Nigel's vividly drawn characters. If she succeeded, she would finally establish herself. If she failed, she would have difficulty finding anyone willing to risk hiring her.

She grimaced at a woodpecker that settled on her log and began its staccato search for grubs in the rotting wood. The real problem was not whether she would be employed again. She could always find work doing something. Perhaps she could teach costume design at a college specializing in theater arts.

No, what she feared was letting her father down. He had encouraged her, helped her, supported her these last few years, and she hated the idea that she could not meet his exacting standards. That was why she wanted to do well, to prove to him she was as capable as he expected her to be.

She shook her head moodily and the woodpecker took fright, winging away into the trees in a blur of speed. She flexed her leg muscles, thinking that it was time to shelve her gloomy thoughts and head back to camp. She hadn't solved any problems this morning—her career was still in limbo, her feelings for Rick, irrational as they were, still existed, and they still didn't fit into her pattern for love. A despondent hopelessness settled over her as she rose to her feet.

And froze, delight chasing away the grim anguish. Wrapped up in her thoughts, she had moved quietly, not disturbing the forest peace as she stood up. Now, just beyond a low thicket that obscured her vision while she was seated, she could see a deer drinking at the creek. Never in her life had Deanna been so close to a wild creature at home in its own habitat. If she walked forward a few steps, she would be able to touch the elegant creature with its big, melting brown eyes and sleek, well-fed body.

She watched it, entranced. The deer was a female, a graceful adult doe whose wariness never left her, even as she drank at the stream. Her muzzle would lower to the water for short seconds, then jerk up quickly, the large ears twitching expressively, while her soft brown eyes scanned the forest for danger.

The intense caution of the wild creature fascinated Deanna, making her wonder if there was a pressing reason for it. Perhaps this lovely doe had a fawn hidden away in a thicket somewhere, sleeping while its mother went out to stretch her legs and take a short break.

Deanna grinned mockingly at her mental pairing of the deer and a human mother. Of course there was no comparison. But when the doe took her last drink before moving silently away, Deanna followed, careful to make as little sound as possible. The opportunity to see a wild fawn was too intriguing to be missed. She told herself she would only follow the doe if it remained close to the stream. As long as she stayed by the water, or within range of its rippling gurgle, she couldn't get lost. She was as safe as she would be in her own neighborhood in L.A.

The doe moved with a silent, swift delicacy that amazed Deanna as she trotted along behind, her mind concentrating on keeping the animal in sight at the same time as she kept her footfalls as quiet as possible. The forest creature must have come a long way from her fawns, Deanna thought at one point, for the doe had shown no sign of stopping.

She continued to follow it until she accidentally stepped on a brittle piece of deadwood that cracked like a rifle shot in the surrounding quiet. The doe melted into the forest, leaving Deanna on her own. She sighed, then told herself sternly she was a complete idiot for chasing the beast, but she didn't really believe it. Seeing the animal so free, so natural, meant more to her than the extra few minutes it would take to cover her tracks as she returned to the camp. With calm assurance she turned to head back the way she had come.

Slowly her gaze raked the bush around her, seeking the right direction. Though she made a complete circle, no part of the forest looked familiar. Even the gurgle of the creek, as it rushed over its stony bottom, had faded into nothing. While she had followed the deer, blithely telling herself there was no danger, she had done exactly what she should not. She had walked away from her markers and paid no attention to where she was headed.

She was lost. The words and the frightening significance of them hammered in her mind. She fought for control before panic set in and she ran screaming even deeper into the green maze. Forcing herself to look around once again, she thought she detected a pair of trees that looked different, more familiar, than the rest. Keeping her fingers crossed, she stepped purposefully in that direction.

It didn't take her long to conclude that she had made the wrong move. There was no path, nothing familiar about the encircling trees, except that each one seemed a mirror image of the other, with no defining marks to help her identify her location. Panic caught at her, knotted her stomach with fear, drove her on through the trees, despite her confusion about direction. It was not until she ran right into a solid pine trunk, the broken, scarred bark biting into the soft skin of her cheek, that she snapped out of her unreasoning terror.

Lost, she thought desperately. Her fingers clasped the tree for support, digging into the bark until all the blood was forced from the tips, leaving them white from the blind force of her grasp. She drew a long shuddering breath and tried to reason with herself.

By now the camp would be awake. They would be having breakfast. Someone would ask where she was. Fay would say she hadn't been in the tent this morning and they would begin to search.

"Hang on," she muttered aloud, wanting the comfort of a human voice in the heavy silence of the forest. "Help's coming. Stay where you are."

Panic began to rise in her again, despite her brave assurance of imminent rescue. What if she hadn't been gone as long as she imagined? What if the camp was still asleep? How long could she stand it? The forest seemed to be closing in on her.

"Oh, Rick," she breathed. "I need you! Help me!" But there was no sound in the quiet, except her own ragged tones.

Panic welled in her once again, urging her to run, anywhere, just to escape the overpowering forest around her. The sane part of her knew that would be foolish. She could blunder around for days, stumbling in a circle, never moving any closer to the campsite. The sensible move was to stay where she was, to let Rick find her, not run about frantically looking for him.

Rick. Her mind grasped his name, using it to anchor her composure and keep her legs from moving unbidden into the surrounding trees. He would find her—she knew he would. When he did he would snap at her and tell her what a bother she was, that she had once more made a complete fool of herself, that she wasn't fit to be left on her own. This time, she promised herself, she would listen meekly to every word, because each would be true. She had been stupid, she was a terrible encumbrance, she didn't have the sense to stay away from situations she didn't know how to deal with.

"Rick! Rick, come for me. Soon. Now! Don't you know I need you?" she mumbled into the tree. "Please come! Oh, please!"

But there was only silence. No sound of rescuing footsteps, no loved voice shouting her name, nothing but the empty silence of the hostile forest. Weariness overcame her and she sank to her knees, uncaring that her fingernails were broken and torn as her hands, still gripping the tree trunk with desperate strength, trailed down the uneven bark.

She bit her lip, telling herself she must remain calm, but that was an almost impossible task. Fighting down constant urges to run, to scream was draining the strength from her and making the panic that much more difficult to fight. She knew she would soon give in to those urges, but refused to do so any earlier than necessary. She closed her eyes and clutched at the tree, focusing all her concentration away from her predicament to happy moments and positive thoughts.

The voice she desperately needed to hear came when she had nearly succumbed to the panic. She was shaking all over, her muscles taut and trembling with the exertion of the battle within her.

"Deanna! Dammit, where are you? Deanna!"

Rick's voice. Sounding blessedly annoyed and so very, very normal and sane in this terrifying world. She was on her feet in a moment, poised for flight into his welcoming arms.

"Rick?" she screamed. "Rick, I'm here! I can't see you. I don't know where you are." Her voice rose shrilly, panic edging in.

"Deanna!" he roared. Then, a little more softly, he added, "Thank God! Do you have any idea how long I've been searching for you? Stay where you are, but keep calling. I'll come to you."

But she had huddled against the tree trunk for too long. Blindly, she ran toward the comforting sound of his cool, composed voice. Vaguely, she was aware that she was calling his name as she crashed noisily through the undergrowth, but her senses were all trained on the sound of his voice. In her concentration, she didn't notice a large root growing above ground level. Before she knew it, she was flat on her face in the spongy loam with the breath knocked out of her and her bare toes throbbing from the impact with the root.

The heavy silence that followed stretched for endless moments as she tried to catch her breath, then she heard Rick bellowing her name, asking if she was hurt, demanding that she answer. Drawing a great shuddering breath, she tried to call, but the words came out only as a shaken wheeze. She heard Rick shout her name once more, his tone short, curt, angry. Then there was silence.

Renewed panic made her heart thump crazily. I've done it again, she thought irrationally. *I've provoked him so much that he's leaving without me. He doesn't care if he finds me.* Impelled by this new fear, she scrambled to her feet, ignoring the grazes on her tender toes.

"Rick!" she screamed. "Don't go! Please!" A sob tore at her throat and she whispered again, "Please, don't leave me." Her body began to tremble and she grabbed a tree for support. The forest was so quiet she began to wonder if she had ever heard the sound of Rick's voice, or if her terrified imagination had conjured it up like a mirage in the desert.

She moaned his name softly, her tone one of hopeless defeat.

"It's okay, honey," said his soothing voice. "I'm only a few yards away. Turn around and you'll see me."

Very slowly, Deanna did as the disembodied voice commanded, half afraid this was all part of her hallucination. Her eyes scanned the trees, at first seeing nothing, then a movement caught her attention and Rick's hard, masculine form materialized before her. With a surge of relief she flung herself at him, wrapping her arms around his neck and sobbing his name as her shaking body pressed against his solid length.

He swept her up in his arms, cradling her against him and telling her she was safe over and over again. In the recesses of her mind, Deanna realized he was saying it as much for his own benefit as her own, but she didn't care. The sound of his voice was taking the edge off the uncontrollable shudders that wracked her body and helping her pull herself back to calm.

Though the worst of her fear had abated, she was still shaken when his hands found her shoulders and thrust her roughly away from him.

"I want an explanation, Deanna, but it can wait until we're back on the path," he growled, his fingers biting painfully into her soft flesh as he clamped them around her lower arm to drag her forcibly back the way he had come.

Deanna winced a little, knowing she would be bruised there the next day, but she didn't complain. She was still terribly frightened of becoming separated from him, of being left alone in the woods, and his firm grip reassured more than it hurt.

When they reached the familiar clearing by the creek where Rick had fished the day before, he halted. Grasping her shoulders with angry force, his dark eyes blazed fiercely into hers.

"Now, what the hell did you think you were doing going off on your own like that?" he raged, his voice rasping in his throat.

"Please, Rick, you're hurting me!" she cried.

He eased his punishing grip, but his hands didn't leave her shoulders. "Well?" he snapped, his mouth a tight, angry line.

"I—I—I—" she choked, finding that she could not explain while staring into his furious dark eyes. She lowered her lashes and moistened her lips nervously.

"I'm waiting," he said coldly.

That didn't help her composure any. She drew a deep breath and said in a rush, "I needed to think."

"Think?" he repeated incredulously. "What, in the name of heaven, is so important you have to go out and get yourself lost in the woods in order to think about it?"

"I didn't get lost!" she blurted out. "At least, not at first. Not until I followed the deer...."

His eyes widened at this information, then narrowed to cold, angry slits. "What deer?"

She swallowed uneasily, then explained reluctantly, "I came down to the creek to think, but I saw a doe drinking just before I planned to return to the camp. She looked so beautiful standing there that when she moved away it seemed natural to follow her. So I—I did."

That made him furious. He drew his breath in a sizzling hiss. "So. Because you've decided you can't think in your tent, or down by the lake, you blithely go off into the woods without telling anyone, then compound it by chasing after a wild animal and paying no attention to your direction. Is that it?''

''Yes!'' she cried, as if the admission were being wrenched from her. The expression on his face frightened her. Set and grim, his strong jaw clenched, he was snarling out the choleric words through barely moving lips. His hands slid from her shoulders to wrap around her upper arms in a painful iron clasp.

''Did it not occur to you that the rest of us might worry when you didn't turn up for breakfast?''

She swallowed uncomfortably, knowing he had every right to be furious. ''Yes. But—''

''But?'' he prompted when she stopped.

''I didn't notice the time.... I was sure if I stayed near the creek I could find my way back, but when I looked...when I tried to return, I was lost! All the trees looked the same and they seemed to stretch for miles in every direction. I couldn't hear the stream and it was so quiet!'' She put her hands on his chest and gazed up into his eyes as she admitted softly, ''I didn't plan on getting lost, Rick. I didn't want to frighten anyone! It just happened!''

''I'm going to make damn certain it doesn't happen again,'' he said thickly, dragging her against him and covering her lips with his own in a hardy, angry kiss.

Deanna strained away from him, her hands pressing on her chest in a futile effort to break his hold, and twisted her head to escape an embrace that was bittersweet. Nothing would have pleased her more than to have Rick kiss her, but in passion, not anger.

Her resistance only served to inflame him further. She heard him mutter, ''Little wildcat,'' as one sinewy arm wrapped around her waist to pull her against him, while his free hand slid up from her arm to catch the nape of her neck and hold her head still for his kiss.

Imprisoned, she gave up the uneven struggle. Now, perhaps because he knew she was powerless to escape, this kiss lacked the brutal force of the other. It was no coaxing kiss, though. His lips fiercely demanded a response as his probing tongue plunged inside her mouth, exploring the moist depths to tantalize and delight. She slid her hands up his chest, feeling the rough cotton of his shirt give way to the smooth warmth of his skin. For a moment her fingers caressed his neck, then sank beneath the shirt to stroke the taut muscles of his powerful shoulders. He pressed her against him convulsively, his tongue touching the tip of hers lightly before plunging within. Her hands clutched at his head and tangled in his thick hair, her only thought to prolong the caress indefinitely.

Her avid response ignited a flame within him. The arm that had been holding her in an iron band moved to creep beneath her clothes and stroke her naked back. His lips softened, as if once sure of her passionate response they desired a more sensual one. The probing tongue retreated to stroke her tender, sensitive lips as the hand that had held her prisoner to his first, heated demand found the silken mound of her breast and caressed the tip into taut awareness. Lost in a sensual excitement that made her oblivious to everything but Rick, Deanna moaned deep in her throat, craving fulfillment.

It was Rick who drew away at last, having a better idea of how close they were to the camp and the likelihood that they might be interrupted at any time. She murmured his name, her eyes deep, soft violet pools of longing. He smiled and nibbled her full lower lip tantalizingly. "Not here, sweetheart," he whispered thickly. "It's too public."

His words brought a glimmer of sense into her passion-drenched mind. Slowly she became aware of things other than the man who held her. The gurgle of water, the raucous scream of a jay. The pungent scent of the pines. She realized too that Rick was holding her only lightly now, but that his expression was tender as he smiled down into her bemused face.

"I'm not going to apologize for that," he said, a faint undercurrent of laughter in his voice. "I enjoyed it too much!" Suddenly serious, his eyes scanned her face. "You scared the hell out of me, Deanna, thundering through the bush, shouting and crying, then nothing! I wasn't sure what had happened to you."

"I tripped," she muttered ruefully, staring fixedly at his chest. "When I caught my breath I couldn't hear you. I thought you'd given up. I was terrified! You must think me a useless burden," she added wretchedly. "You'll be glad to get rid of me tomorrow."

He tilted her chin up, forcing her to gaze into his grave, questioning eyes. "What makes you think that?"

She swallowed. "I'm a city girl, Rick. I can cope just fine on Mulholland Drive and I'm a whiz on the L.A. freeways, but put me out here, where there are no stop lights or directional signs, and I'm lost. Literally! I've done nothing this week but blunder from one scrape to another and this morning...." She stopped, her lips twisting contemptuously. "This morning I didn't have the sense to realize my limitations. I wanted to follow that deer so I did, as casually as I would walk around the block at home!" She shook her head, obviously disgusted by her own actions.

There was a mocking gleam in his eyes. "So you think you don't measure up."

She sighed. "I know I don't!"

He looked down at her, the mocking gleam warming to tenderness. "That's what makes you so special," he said huskily, pushing her jacket away to nuzzle the hollow at the base of her neck.

Deanna wasn't sure she had heard him correctly. "What do you mean?" she stammered, her body reacting electrically to his lightly nibbling lips.

He raised his head to smile down at her. "Exactly what I said. I've been watching you, Deanna, the way you lift your chin when you're facing something unpleasant; then you clench your jaw and simply do what you have to, no matter how little you like it. The way your beautiful eyes sparkle when you laugh. The damned sexy way you walk!" he finished on a low growl, his arms tightening around her.

Deanna let her body melt against his, feeling warm satisfaction at his words, which told her that Rick, too, wanted something more than quick, physical affair, over almost as soon as it had begun. Reaching up, she trailed one slender finger down his beard-roughened jawline to his lips as she smiled tremulously into his eyes. His tongue darted out to lap at her finger and she felt her flesh quiver with an unexpected response. His dark eyes smoldered wickedly as he felt her body's reaction, and she knew if he hadn't been holding her steady she would have sagged to her knees. As desire coursed through her already heated veins, she closed her eyes and arched against him, the tip of her pink tongue darting out to moisten suddenly dry lips.

His breathing was ragged as he lifted one arm to take her hand and place it firmly on his chest, his own larger one covering hers. She felt him inhale deeply to calm himself and gradually the mist of passion that held her faded away. She opened her eyes and looked into his, thinking tenderly how wonderfully expressive their dark depths could be.

"Tomorrow," he said thickly, "When we're back at the ranch, stay behind when the others leave. We can talk then, and make our plans."

Putting her head to one side she smiled mischievously, "Plans? Plans for what?"

His hand tightened on hers. There was no mockery in his eyes, no trace of humor. His voice level, he said, "I've fallen for you, Deanna. Hard. I need you. I want you with me—forever."

"I—I don't understand," she said huskily, her eyes searching his face. "You refuse to tell me anything about yourself. How can you expect me to accept something like that when you won't even trust me with your name!"

He hesitated, then said slowly, almost unwillingly, "I was testing you, Deanna. I'm sorry, but I had to do it."

"But why, Rick?" she asked, feeling a cold chill creep up her spine.

He said urgently, "Deanna, try to understand! I'm not…"

"There you are! I thought I heard voices. Dammit, Rick, you might have let us know Deanna was all right! We've all been sitting in the camp biting our nails with worry." Jonas strode angrily into the clearing as he spoke, coming to a sudden halt when he noticed their closeness. His eyes narrowed in considering thought as Rick moved to stand in front of Deanna in a leisurely way, to give her time to tuck in her shirt, straighten her jacket, and bring a little order to her tumbled hair. Then he grinned and said mockingly to Rick, "I'm glad to see you and Deanna are—friends—again. Work out all your problems yesterday?" He added teasingly, "I must admit, I thought you would make the perfect couple."

Apart from a wary glance, Rick ignored this jibe. Deanna had the feeling he was afraid Jonas might blurt out something Rick would rather keep secret. She felt a shiver of cold apprehension run down her spine, but ignored it. The confused, but intense feelings she had for Rick were obviously reciprocated, and they both needed to bring them out into the open to talk about them. She wasn't ready for the kind of commitment Rick had hinted at, but he deserved an explanation for her reasons. Marriage to her was a serious, lifelong affair, to be entered into only after considerable thought by both parties. It was not something based on the sudden flaring attraction she felt for a mysterious stranger.

Rick ignored Jonas's teasing, replying instead to his initial accusation. "I was giving Deanna a moment to compose herself." She moved to stand beside him. He looked down at her, smiling with mocking affection as he slipped his arm around her shoulders to hug her against his hard length. "My Deanna is not the greatest woodsman, you see. Having wandered off to be alone, she then proceeded to chase a deer until she was thoroughly lost."

Jonas frowned at her. "That's not a good idea, Deanna. Deer are usually timid creatures, but occasionally, if you corner them, they'll charge you, especially a stag."

Deanna smiled thinly. "This was a female, but thanks for the tip. Next time I'll stay well away from the animals I'm stalking."

"There won't be a next time," snapped Rick. "From now on you stay close to camp, where Jonas and I can keep an eye on you."

Deanna gasped indignantly, her face flushing as she glared at him. Hot words sizzled on the tip of her tongue, until she remembered she deserved every mocking jibe Rick cared to dish out. She had been incredibly stupid, taking a needless risk that might have ended in disaster.

Jonas broke the tense little silence that followed, complaining blandly, "I'm confused. Why was Deanna chasing a deer anyway?"

Between them she and Rick described what had occurred as they sauntered slowly back to the camp, in deference to Deanna's tender feet. She also described her feelings while lost in the woods, shivering with remembered fear. As Rick's arm tightened around her shoulders in silent comfort, she burrowed as close to him as she was able, enjoying the solid strength of his hard male body against her. She closed her mind to the future, content, for the moment, to remain firmly in the present.

Chapter Eight

We'll be back at the ranch in another hour," remarked Jonas casually, as they sipped a final cup of his coffee.

"I hope the rain holds off," said Hugh, looking doubtfully at the sky.

"Dad doesn't want another soaking," laughed Gavin.

"I should think not!" Edith snapped tartly. "He was wet clear through to the skin. If he doesn't get one of his congestive colds from it, he'll be very lucky."

"Now, Edith...." soothed Hugh.

Deanna stifled a sigh. Hugh wasn't the only one who had been drenched by the storm that had dumped a hugh amount of water on them late the previous afternoon. They had to pitch camp early, because it was impossible to go on in the rain and twilight gloom. Jonas and Rick had rigged an awning over the fire so they could eat, but the ground was wet, the fire smoky, and no one felt much like sitting around the billowing blaze once the necessity of eating had been taken care of.

"I hope you all enjoyed yourselves," Jonas was saying, and his words were met by a chorus of murmured agreement. "You know, the weather we had was exceptional, even though yesterday's rain was unexpected and today is rather miserable."

Jonas had the gift of understatement, Deanna thought wryly. It hadn't rained yet today, but the sky was leaden, the temperature cool. Tendrils of mist hung near the ground and clung to the sides of the surrounding mountains.

Hugh stood and, after clearing his throat, made a short, formal speech expressing thanks to Jonas and Rick for their professionalism and knowledge. Jonas smilingly acknowledged this apparently impromptu speech for both of them, while Rick looked sardonically amused. Then it was time to douse the fire and mount their horses for the last time.

Their return route was different from the one they had followed when leaving the Double S the week before. Instead of a steep, direct trail into the mountains, the path meandered down the slopes at a gentle angle, bringing them out behind the ranch buildings, so that the barns and house obscured the parking area and road.

At the corral there was a confusion of voices, as Fay and Deanna said good-bye to the Nashes and each other. Deanna's attention was on Rick, more than the other campers. She noticed he and Jonas were discussing something intensely, but they were far enough away that she couldn't hear what they were saying. It was clear from the way Jonas ran his fingers repeatedly through his sandy hair that something was troubling him. The conversation ended with Rick clapping him on the shoulder in a friendly gesture. Jonas nodded, then grinned ruefully, before hurrying over to wish his clients as safe journey home. Rick gathered up the reins of two of the horses and disappeared with them into the barn.

Deanna fiddled about, trying not to make it obvious she was staying behind while Jonas shepherded the others toward the parking lot. When they were safely out of sight, Deanna grabbed the roan's bridle and followed Rick into the dim light of the barn.

"Rick?" she called when she couldn't see him in the gloomy interior of the cavernous structure.

"Over here, Deanna," he shouted in reply.

"You would be in Blackie's stall," she remarked dryly, as she paused at the opening. "Mind he doesn't kick you."

He grinned. "Black Devil's got some bad habits, but biting and kicking aren't among them. Thank God!"

She laughed and indicated the roan she was leading. "Where does this fella go?"

"Two stalls down," he informed her casually. "Don't bother with the saddle, but please replace the bridle with the rope halter. I'll groom him later."

"Sure," she said, cheerfully ignoring his directive after she had substituted the halter for the bridle. By now she was able to remove the saddle with practiced ease, but lugging it around the gloomy stable as she searched for the tack room was more than she was capable of, so she balanced it on the half door of the small stall.

"Where is everyone?" she called, picking up a wisp of straw to give the horse a sketchy rubdown. "I thought the Aitkens had a number of hands who stayed here on the ranch?"

There was a slight pause, then she heard Rick slap the horse's hide and mutter irritably, "Move over, Blackie." Speaking in a louder voice, directed at her, he answered, "They do. Usually when a pack trip is due back, there are two or three men ready and waiting to look after the horses. I'm not sure what happened today. Maybe they got an unexpectedly large number of day trips."

"I didn't know the Double S did trail rides as well," she remarked, watching the roan horse stick its nose in the water trough. She grinned to herself, thinking that to an outsider the conversation must sound completely innocuous, two casual acquaintances talking, but saying nothing at all. Yet the tension was there between them, crackling below the surface, held in check until the necessary tasks were done. "Where's Jonas now?" she asked, wondering how long she would be alone with Rick before Jonas reappeared.

"He went over to the house to see if he could find out where everyone is," replied Rick, coming up to the stall.

"Have you finished with Black Devil?" she asked softly, feeling his eyes rake her up and down, knowing hers were doing the same to him.

He nodded, saying huskily, "You didn't have to bother with the roan."

She shrugged awkwardly, feeling a little bashful. "I wanted to."

"Thanks." He held out his hand, commanding softly, "Come here."

She moved slowly, mesmerized by the warm glow in his dark eyes wordlessly telling her that he had nothing more on his mind than the need to hold and kiss her in the intimate gloom of the barn. Her hand touched his and was clasped strongly as he pulled her hard against him, using his free arm to encircle and tighten around her trim waist. Wondering, with a flash of humor that curled her lips in a bewitching smile, if they would ever get around to talking about the future, she lifted her face to receive his kiss and knew that she didn't care. She could feel the desire raging in him and her own soaring to meet it. Her flesh molded itself to his as she let coherent thought slip away and raw, delightful sensation rule her body and her mind.

A sudden flash of light broke the smooth rhythm of their pounding pulses and alerted Rick that they were not alone. As a second explosion occurred, Deanna, still dazed by the unwelcome interruption, realized the dazzling light came from the flashgun of an experienced photographer. Her mind cleared and her body chilled at this offensive intrusion into her privacy. It shouldn't have surprised her though, for there had been enough people around when Rick had announced her identity a week ago. Plenty of time for someone to tip off the press.

The flash exploded again, capturing her curled against Rick with his arms wrapped protectively around her. A voice from behind the camera chortled, "Well, well, well. Isn't this cozy! My editor is going to love this!"

I'll bet, thought Deanna. She could imagine the malicious caption, just short of libelous. Glancing up at Rick's face, she saw it was a carved mask of rage and she was terrified that he might do something violent.

The hateful, sneering voice continued, "Yes, indeed. Miss Deanna Monroe and..."

"Keep your damned mouth shut!" Rick snarled, letting Deanna go and advancing menacingly on the photographer.

The man laughed, apparently not in the least disconcerted. Deanna's vision had cleared and she could see the smug triumph reflected on a round, pasty face as malignant pleasure burned from tiny raisin eyes. He continued as if Rick hadn't spoken, "And Mr. Roderick Latimer, caught by yours truly in as tight a clinch as anyone could imagine."

Deanna froze. Roderick Latimer, the man had called Rick. Roderick. Yes, the name fit. Rick could be a nickname for Roderick.

The light streaming in through the doorway was momentarily obscured by the figure of a tall, lanky man. "Rick?" called Jonas, anxious concern in his voice. "Are you in there?" He advanced into the barn. As his eyes adjusted to the dimmer light he noticed Rick, but Deanna and the photographer were obscured by shadows. "There are a bunch of reporters up at the house."

"And one right here, taking pictures where he had no business being," interrupted Rick savagely.

Jonas heard the violence in Rick's voice as clearly as Deanna had. He said quickly to the photographer, "Give us the film, then get off my property and we won't have any trouble."

"Are you kidding?" gasped the man, the beginnings of fear in his voice. "This is dynamite! Roderick Latimer and Deanna Monroe smooching in a barn. The second generation healing old wounds, so to speak. The public will eat this up!"

Rick didn't give him a chance to say anything more. He was on the photographer before the man had a chance to prepare, driving his fist into the protruding belly and doubling him over. The camera crashed to the concrete floor of the barn. Deanna didn't wait for any more. She stumbled from the building as Jonas joined the melee, more to keep Rick from killing the man than because his friend needed any help. She felt confused and numb. Paramount in her mind was the desire to get away before the other reporters Jonas had mentioned descended on the barn. More than anything else she needed time to sort out the tumultuous emotions that her discovery of Rick's identity had roused.

Deanna drove without being conscious of her direction or where exactly she was going. She knew she was still in the park because traffic was slow and heavy. People were constantly stopping their cars abruptly so they could gaze at yet another natural wonder. The irregularity of the pace, forced Deanna to concentrate on keeping herself, and her vehicle, from becoming involved in an accident and she stored her problems away in the back of her mind.

The road twisted up the side of Mount Washburn, through Dunraven Pass at nearly nine thousand feet, then down again to the village of Canyon. There Deanna stopped to get her bearings, have a coffee and a snack, and change from her jeans into something more comfortable.

Canyon, she discovered as she sat in a large, echoing restaurant sipping coffee, her emotions held rigorously in check, was the site of Yellowstone Falls and the most spectacular viewpoints of the Grand Canyon of the Yellowstone. It was also a junction point for roads leading to the western and southern parts of the huge park. Unfortunately, there was no direct route out of the park from the village; she would have to take one of the other roads.

She asked herself, as she absently nibbled on a slice of apple pie, if she did actually want to leave the park, but her mind refused to answer. When she'd fled from the barn to her car it had been a purely instinctive action. The photographer's maliciously given information had shaken her badly, and she hadn't wanted to cope with the news of Rick's identity in front of the probing, observant eyes of a mob of reporters. She was too poor an actress to hide her feelings for the man she knew only as Rick and her shock at his true name.

Sitting here in the restaurant in Canyon, it was easy to rationalize her action. If the reporters ever discovered Rick had kept his identity from her it could cause even more speculation than the bald information that they had spent a week together in Yellowstone's backcountry. So she had done Rick a favor by running before the press was upon them.

Miserably, she toyed with the coffee cup. The truth was that she'd panicked, just as she had yesterday in the woods, and left Rick to face the avid curiosity of the press alone.

Now that she was a safe distance from the flash bulbs and the angry male bodies, she could think more clearly. It would have been best if she had stayed on the Double S, faced the press with Rick, and carried whatever personal questions were asked. With things still undecided between them, however, that might not have been possible. She knew she couldn't have kept up a facade that they were just friends, and she wasn't sure if they were more than lovers. They really needed that long discussion they were due to have before they met the press. That meant that what she should have done was returned to the Mammoth hotel where she had a reservation for the night and locked herself in until Rick could get to her. But would he have wanted to? Should she turn around now and return to Mammoth Hot Springs and take the chance that Rick would still want to see her?

She thrust the pie away then rubbed her temples, feeling confused and indecisive. Abruptly, she pushed her chair out from the table, knowing she could not bear to sit still a moment longer. She hurried out to her car, rummaged through the suitcase until she found a light wraparound skirt that went well with the T-shirt she wore, then, after picking up her sandals, returned to the restaurant where she slipped into the ladies' room, using one of the spotlessly clean stalls to change. When she emerged, holding boots and blue jeans, she felt better, but still indecisive. Feeling she should not proceed any further until she made a decision, yet not willing to linger in the restaurant, she returned to her car and drove to Artist's Point, the most famous and spectacular viewpoint of the Grand Canyon of the Yellowstone. The overcast sky which had threatened rain earlier had cleared magically, leaving a light cloud cover that allowed the sun to shine through.

Artist's Point was a natural outcropping of rock, to which the Parks Service had added a railing and a bench. For the first few minutes Deanna thrust her worries aside as she drank in the beauty of the scene before her. The sun's slanting rays reflected off the yellow sedimentary stone that made up the canyon, turning the steep jagged walls to raw ocher. Far in the distance, the Yellowstone River cascaded from the canyon's rim to its floor, hundreds of feet below, a splash of molten silver in the surrounding gold.

Gradually, however much as she might resist them, her problems nudged back into the forefront of her mind. Though her eyes might be staring at the Grand Canyon of the Yellowstone, her mind had returned to the Double S and the backcountry beyond.

Some of the remarks Jonas had made now took on greater meaning to Deanna. He evidently was in Rick's— no Roderick's—confidence. She could also understand Rick's initial hostility and his belief that she was at the Double S for ulterior motives. It was more difficult to understand why he refused to trust her once they were safely away from the ranch and access to the press. What had he said to her yesterday morning? She had been so wrought up from lingering fear, mixed with hot surging desire, that she couldn't be sure. That he wanted her, that he needed her, that he had fallen for her. *That he was testing her.*

She sighed and moved away from the railing, sinking with unconscious grace onto the cold stone bench. If Rick—no, Roderick... How would she ever get used to the name? It simply did not suit her Rick! If Rick had been testing her, she had surely failed. She thought of what she knew about Roderick Latimer. Not all that much, considering their fathers had once been the best of friends. One trait that stood out was his desire for privacy. Through most of his adult life, he had avoided the limelight.

Privacy, she thought, watching shadows shift, darkening the stone from gold to bronze as thicker clouds passed across the path of the sun. Roderick Latimer would not want to conduct a love affair in the full glare of the press. And that was what he would have to do if he wanted to see her. The tale of the children of two famous friends, later bitter enemies, coming together and symbolically healing the wounds between the two families was too much of a storybook romance for the world not to be excited by it. How could anything worthwhile grow between them while they played out their life in the glaring public eye.

I Need You. She sighed. When Rick had needed her most, to stand beside him and brace the mob of reporters and photographers, she had run, like a scared rabbit from a pack of hungry wolves. God, he must be furious with her. In her heart she could not blame him. She had behaved stupidly and deserved the numbing anguish she was feeling now.

If she went back to Mammoth Hot Springs now, to tell him she would face the press with him, he would only push her away. The moment for that had passed when she ran blindly from the barn to her car and drove thoughtlessly away.

The shadows were lengthening as the sun sank lower on the canyon walls. She stood reluctantly, her decision made. She could not go back. Her relationship with Rick might have grown into something quite wonderful, or it might not, but she would never know. Unconsciously, she straightened her shoulders and raised her chin as she walked back to her car. There was no sense in wistfully looking back on what might have been.

In her car, she consulted the road map and discovered the closest town outside the park was Cody, some two hours' drive away. Checking the accommodation guide, she was reassured to note that there were dozen of motels listed. She started the car and put it in gear. Time to be on her way if she wanted to get there while it was still light.

It took her longer to get to Cody than she expected, mainly because the road twisted through the towering Absaroka mountains then, once past the park gates, through the Wapiti Valley, its red stone walls carved into haunting shapes made even more eerie by the gathering dusk. It was dark by the time she reached the town and, as in Jackson, she had difficulty finding a motel for the night.

The thought of sitting in the small room she had located, brooding over what might have been, didn't appeal to her; when she discovered that Cody was the home of Col. William B. Cody—Buffalo Bill—she spent several hours in the excellent museum dedicated to his memory. The fascinating collection of memorabilia dedicated to Cody and his Wild West Show, Plains Indians artifacts, and a gallery of paintings and sculpture inspired by the west, kept her wayward thoughts at bay.

It was not until she was back at her motel, lying in bed staring sleeplessly at the ceiling, that she let her misery wash over her. Her decision this afternoon at Artist's Point had been the correct one. She couldn't have returned to the Double S then, but how she wished she hadn't run in the first place!

Her stupid flight had been as pointless a reaction to Rick's identity as his suspicions of her had been. Two people working at cross-purposes because of who their parents were. Yet the chemical reaction between them was strong—it deserved a chance to develop into something deeper.

Rick had know who she was, who her parents were, from the moment he met her. When she considered it rationally it explained so much. His initial reluctance to her presence on the trip, his careful effort to hide their mutual attraction and protect her from prying eyes. His caution about revealing his identity.

If he knew who she was, he was sure to know of her parents' rocky marriage and the strong beliefs that were all that held it together. He would also know that his father's womanizing reputation didn't go over well in Nigel Monroe's house. He undoubtedly assumed Deanna would be prejudiced against him if she knew who he was.

Would she? The question was a tough one, double-edged and painful. With cool honesty, Deanna admitted that what she knew of Roderick Latimer would have colored her reaction to him. Initially. Her responses to the hostile stranger, Rick, had melted from angry ice to passionate fire in a very short space of time. It wouldn't have taken much longer for Roderick Latimer, whatever his background, to heat her blood to a similar state.

She shifted uneasily on the bed. Had there ever been the possibility of a future with Roderick Latimer? He kept such a low profile, she had no idea where he lived, but she assumed it must be somewhere in L.A. She let herself fantasize a love with him that encompassed every possible phase of her life. They would have plenty of time to get to know each other without rushing into marriage, but the fiery spark between them would remain, sealing increasing affection with love. Her career would grow naturally, because with Rick beside her she knew she could surmount any obstacle, even the pressure that sometimes choked her imagination and reduced her designs to dreary mediocrity.

For a minute her thoughts lingered on the perfection her mind had created, then it dissolved, draining away, despite her frantic attempts to keep it close to her. She blinked back tears she wouldn't let fall. Her dream had collapsed because it could never happen. She had made sure of that by walking out on Rick today. What she must do now was forget him—and what might have been.

Chapter Nine

Deanna closed her eyes and let the hot pounding spray of the shower wash over her as she debated whether or not to attend the party she had been invited to this evening. Her shoulders felt tense, evidence of another in a succession of long, miserable days.

It was two weeks since she had left Yellowstone. Part of that time she had spent driving back to L.A. by an accidentally roundabout route. Despite the long hot hours cruising the well-traveled interstate highways, those few days seemed a heaven of peace compared to what was waiting for her in L.A.

The story of her week in the wilds with Roderick Latimer had already broken in the press, although no photographs appeared to back it up, and the exclusive garden-apartment complex she lived in was besieged by reporters when she reached it. Fortunately, there was a guard at the entrance and she was able to retain some privacy. Those times that she did venture beyond the sturdy iron gates she refused to comment on the impertinent questions, but that didn't stop the press from hanging around in front, waiting for something to happen.

Deanna knew they were expecting Rick to come to her, but she also knew they were wasting their time. She wasn't likely to see him again.

One of her few excursions from her apartment was to join her parents and sister for dinner at their Bel Air home. Deanna ate what was put in front of her in a somewhat absentminded way, and her sharp-eyed sister, Sylvan, rather scornfully told her she would waste away to nothing if she didn't pay more attention to what she was eating. Deanna flushed, miserably aware that since her return from Yellowstone she had lacked the energy or desire to cook a decent meal for herself, and restaurant meals were out of the question. Her father then zeroed in with a comment about the dark smudges of exhaustion under her eyes, betraying sleepless nights, and Deanna suddenly felt persecuted and trapped.

Her nerves were already strung up from hours of agonizing over the loss of Rick and from the constant presence of the press contingent. Her temper flared and she lashed out at those closest to her. Sylvan was disgusted, Nigel furious, and only Felicia's timely soothing kept a major battle from erupting.

There was uncharacteristic compassion in Felicia's violet eyes, so like her older daughter's. She guessed that Deanna was more deeply affected by Roderick Latimer than she cared to admit. Since Felicia couldn't imagine any rational impediment to a love affair between Deanna and Roderick, she naturally assumed that Max Latimer's son was a copy of his father, whom she had never liked, and that he had callously used Deanna for a short time, then cast her aside. The relationship between Felicia and her daughter had never been close, but she did love Deanna and wanted to help her.

Since Deanna was steadfast in blaming all her physical problems on pressure from the media, Felicia suggested she issue a press release denying any romantic link between herself and Roderick Latimer. Eventually, Deanna agreed, the unhappy droop of her full lips exposing more clearly than words her emotional state.

The release, drafted by Felicia's agent, was carefully worded to reveal nothing while denying everything that had been written on the subject of Deanna Monroe and Roderick Latimer. When it appeared in the newspaper and Deanna read it, she cried. It looked so final, so real, in cold black-and-white print. She knew that if Rick saw it he would be scornful and contemptuous and would be glad he never had the chance to talk about the future with her.

She switched off the water, stepping out of the little cubicle into a gold-and-cream tiled bathroom. The big bath sheet she wrapped around her slender body was gold, too, a color that reminded her painfully of Yellowstone and that dreadful day two weeks ago. She wandered the short distance from the bathroom to her bedroom, still in the same despondent mood. If only things weren't so complicated, she thought with a sigh. If only I had never gone to Wyoming. If only I had never met Rick. If only!

Slumping on the wide brass bed, with its delicate rose spread, she debated whether or not she would go to the party tonight. Half of Hollywood would be there and if she didn't show up she would not be missed. On the other hand, if she did put in an appearance, everyone would want to know the scoop about her and Rick. But, as the forthright Sylvan said, she was going to have to face all these people sometime. Why not get it over with?

Reluctantly she stood up, dropped the towel on the plush cream carpeting, and reached in the cupboard to pull out a silk robe that she wrapped around her small body, tying it snugly at her narrow waist. The soft ruby material, emblazoned with a writhing chinese dragon on the back, clung to her shapely breasts and the slight flare of her hips below her waist, stopping midthigh. With a decided lack of interest, Deanna began to brush back her hair, shaping it to her head. The party tonight would be her first social engagement since her return from Yellowstone. Was she ready for it? Mechanically, she set to work applying makeup while her mind still hovered between going and staying home.

Perfume came next, a drop on each pulse point and in the shadowed hollow between her breasts. She bit her lip, feeling a sudden lonely longing because the action made her think of Rick. That made the decision for her. She could sit at home and wish, or go out and face reality. Reality won. Firmly, she donned her outfit for the evening—tight black leather pants that hugged her hips and slender legs almost indecently and a soft, white silk blouse with a demure ruffle at the neck and wide dolman sleeves. The contrast between the snug, sleek slacks and the delicate, loosely fitting blouse made the combination strikingly effective.

She had just finished dressing and was checking her appearance in the mirror when the doorbell rang. She frowned, wondering who on earth could have gotten past the guard at the front gate of the complex without his calling to check with her first. Deciding it must be someone he knew, one of her friends or family who visited regularly, she hastened to the door and flung it open without checking the identity of her visitor through the security peephole.

What little color was in her face drained away, leaving the makeup a sharp red smudge on her cheekbones. "Rick?" she faltered.

At some point since she had last seen him he had shaved off the heavy dark beard, exposing the strong, well-cut planes of his face and the square cleft chin that was all, along with his dark eyes, that could be traced to his father. His sun-streaked hair had been cut, too—it was shorter, styled by an expert. His lean, muscled body, which Deanna now realized was a combination of his stocky, rather short mother and his tall, rawboned father, was clothed in a cream shirt, well-cut tan blazer, and darker slacks. The clothes sat naturally on him, as naturally as the old worn jeans and the casual shirts had in Yellowstone. He looked stylish, but at the same time very cool and masculine, at ease in any situation. Though he bore only a limited facial resemblance to his father, there was the same confidence in his mannerisms. She knew that had she seen him clean-shaven and dressed as he was now she would have quickly identified him as Max Latimer's son. The similarity between them went beyond the physical.

"May I come in?" he asked huskily, as if unsure of her response.

His words surprised her out of her thoughts and she realized she had been staring. "Of course," she replied breathlessly, opening the door wide and stepping aside to allow him access. He lounged easily in the narrow hallway, filling it with his presence and making her feel self-conscious as she closed the door. Not really sure what to say, or why he was here, she retreated to the security of the social amenities. "Would you like a drink?"

There was a flicker of amusement in his eyes, but he said seriously, "Please. Bourbon, if you have it."

"Of course," she said again. "On the rocks?" When he nodded she murmured, "I'll just be a minute. Why don't you make yourself comfortable in the living room?" That was the first opening on the left. He didn't move.

He was studying her with the same thorough intensity that she had used on him a few minutes ago. She wondered what he thought of the city Deanna, whether he liked her or the rumpled, tousled girl of Yellowstone better.

She bit her lip and moved away from the door. As she passed him she said, "How did you get my address?" hoping to divert both their attentions as she brushed by him on her way to the kitchen. It didn't work. She could feel her body tense as she fought an urgent desire to stop and wrap her arms around his neck. But she didn't stop; she continued down the hall, feeling little joy in her victory over herself.

"Jonas," he replied, his voice nearby. She almost dropped the tray of ice cubes she was pulling from the freezer, she was so surprised to see him standing in the doorway of her bright modern kitchen. She told herself she should have expected him to follow her. He had come here for a reason and it was not to sit in her living room and stare at the wall.s

As she plopped the ice cubes into glasses she remarked idly, "I should have a talk with my doorman. He's not supposed to let anyone in without announcing them first."

Rick grinned. "Don't do that, bobcat. It's my fault. I told him I wanted to surprise you. He thinks we're lovers."

"That damned story!" she snapped, replacing the tray and taking out a bottle of tonic, which she poured into the taller of the glasses.

"Exactly. All I had to do was identify myself and I was in." He watched her pick up the glasses, then added flatly, "That vehement denial you made to the press doesn't seem to have done much good."

Her hand shook and she had to return the glasses to the counter. "I'm sorry, Rick. I didn't know what else to do. You saw what it's been like when you came in. You have to force your way through that circus at the front gate.'' She sighed and willed her hands steady as she picked up the glasses again to carry them through to the living room, where she kept her liquor stock. As she passed him, she glanced nervously up into his hard-boned face. What she saw didn't reassure her. His mouth was curled derisively and his eyes were cold. She bit her lip and said miserably, ''I thought it might discourage them, you see. At least, I hoped it would....'' Her voice drifted into nothing and she hurried into the living room, anxious to have something to do.

As she splashed bourbon in one glass he said curtly, ''It didn't work, did it? If anything, your denying the rumors only gave them more status.''

Her hand tightened on the bottle and a little of the liquor splashed on the cabinet. She made an impatient sound in her throat and hastily mopped it up. ''The press sees things the way it wants to see them.'' she said stiffly. ''It's meaningless.''

There was a slight pause during which she could feel his eyes boring into her back. ''Then why bother with that press release?''

She closed her eyes for a moment, willing herself to be calm, then pivoted around to hand him the drink. Their hands touched briefly and felt her body leap in response. Carefully keeping her eyes from meeting his, she said slowly, ''It seemed the right things to do at the time. I was virtually a prisoner here and I do have to work. I hoped it would discourage the press.''

''Not me?''

Quickly, she turned away so he couldn't see the flash of desolation in her eyes. Needing something to do with her hands, she reached for the bottle of gin. ''Why did you come?'' she asked thickly, staring at the label and not seeing it at all.

"We have to talk, Deanna," he said softly. She could feel his body behind her, disconcertingly close, but he was making no move to touch her.

Her hand moved jerkily as she poured gin into her glass of tonic. Lifting the drink, she took a long, steadying swallow. "About what?" she asked, not looking around.

"Us." She heard the ice in his glass clink as he sipped the bourbon.

The word made her stomach knot in sudden pain. There was no "us" between her and Roderick Latimer, only between her and the ranch hand, Rick. She sipped the gin and tonic slowly, then announced more curtly than she had intended, "Tonight's not good for me. I'm going to a party."

"Okay," he said briefly, "this won't take long." She turned slowly, glancing at his face, noting for the first time a controlled nervousness there.

He was staring at her intently, as if trying to draw her thoughts into the open. He placed the glass on the polished surface of the drinks cabinet, then said clearly, "I came to ask you to marry me."

"You—you can't just walk in here and say something like that!" she said, her voice trembling with shock.

"Why not?" he demanded, raising one arched brow.

"Because I might take you up on it," she replied huskily, without stopping to think.

The dark eyes warmed and became soft as his lips curled into a delighted grin. "You won't regret this, bobcat," he promised, taking the glass from her hand and slipping an engagement ring onto her finger.

She looked from the blazing diamond to his face, then down at the ring again. "I wasn't serious, you know," she said, almost conversationally.

"I was," he replied, gathering her pliant body against his in one fluid motion. She knew he was going to kiss her and didn't resist. To be held against his hard, muscular length, to feel his hands on her body, to know the pressure of his lips on hers was what she had been longing for these last two weeks, and she gave herself up to the raw pleasure of his touch.

But when he had raised his head, his eyes gleaming with triumph, she covered his lips with her fingers and said softly, "Why?"

"Why what?" he asked huskily, still holding her tightly.

"Why do you want to marry me?" she demanded flatly.

Surprise made him let her go and step back one pace. "What kind of question is that, Deanna? Because I love you! What other reason would I have?"

She shook her head sadly. "But you don't know me, Rick!"

Anger flashed in his eyes, but he controlled it, saying mildly enough, "Would you mind explaining that remark?"

She lifted her hands helplessly. "Look at me, Rick. Do I look like the same girl you knew in Yellowstone?" She put her hands on her waist and stood with her head flung proudly back.

His eyes probed her face, then scanned her body, lingering on her breasts, jutting out beneath the soft, clinging silk, then on her leather-clad hips. "The clothes, the makeup, the hair style are all different. The body and face seem even more delicate than they did, but the girl is the same. She has the proud, courageous expression on that lovely face I saw dozens of times in Yellowstone. Why are you afraid, bobcat? I won't hurt you." As he spoke, his voice changed. Lazy amusement was replaced with husky concern as he reached out to draw a gentle finger down her cheek with a tender gesture.

It was almost more than she could bear. She spoke his name with tormented longing, knowing that she wanted to be near him, but unable to take the step he demanded. "I can't marry you—or any man—after knowing him a week! It's not long enough." Her gaze fell to her hand, riveted by the sparkling gem, and she began to tug at it with fingers that didn't seem to function properly.

He reached out, catching her hands in his, stopping her nervous movement. "No, don't," he said heavily. "I bought it because the stone reminded me of you. Bright, sparkling, precious. Keep it."

She bit her lip unhappily as she stared into his searching eyes. "Rick, I can't! It isn't right! I..."

He sighed, releasing her hands to run shaking fingers through his thick, dark hair. "This is not going the way I planned," he said ruefully. "I thought I'd sweep you off your feet, then carry you off to bed and make love to you until we were both too exhausted to move." A faintly rueful smile twitched his lips. "I'm not very polished at proposing. This is the first time I've done it."

She looked up at his well-made face, marveling at how much a beard could change and hide features. She had thought Rick was a good-looking, sexy man, but without the disguising beard he was handsome in a hard, totally masculine way that made her blood pulse faster in her veins. Her eyes darkened to deep pools a man could drown in. "I said I wouldn't marry you. I didn't say I wouldn't go to bed with you."

There was a long, heavy silence as he frowned down at her, searching her face for answers. Finally, he said questioningly, "I don't completely understand, Deanna. Are you telling me you don't find me unattractive?"

She moved close to him and put her hand on his chest. Under her fingers she could feel his heart pounding. "I find you very attractive," she murmured huskily.

"Then why won't you marry me?" he demanded, with frustrated passion.

Under her palm the tempo of his heartbeat speeded up. In a moment his irritation would grow into anger and they would quarrel, or he would leave. She didn't like either alternative. She raised her other arm, curling it around his neck. "I don't know if I can explain it, Rick. Marriage is a long-term commitment to me...."

"Do you think it isn't for me as well?" he broke in angrily.

"Then you'll understand," she continued smoothly. "Rick, I've seen too many marriages not work out because the couples didn't know each other, didn't both to look beyond the sexual attraction." She moved closer, until her body was draped seductively against his. "I want you," she whispered intimately, the fingers of one hand twining themselves in his hair while the other moved to caress the strong line of his jaw. His hands moved, almost reluctantly, to clasp her waist as he bent to kiss her. She could feel his desire growing as his lips moved slowly over hers, teasing her with light, gentle pressure when she needed so much more. For a moment she wondered if he was punishing her for her refusal to marry him, then his tongue stroked softly against her lips as his hand traveled up her silk-clad torso to cup one perfectly rounded breast. The heat of his hand radiated through the cool, sensuous material, tantalizing her. A low groan built in her throat, and she opened her mouth in sweet submission. The kiss deepened, drawing her into a whirlpool of emotion where nothing mattered but their mutual desire.

Not content with feeling cloth between his seeking hands and her soft skin, he pulled the blouse roughly from the waistband of her pants only to be frustrated by the lacy bra beneath. He broke away, breathing heavily. "You wear too damn many clothes, you know that?"

Deanna smiled but didn't reply. Her features had softened with passion; her eyes were dark and the lids heavy with her arousal. Without hesitation she reached up to unfasten the blouse, then drew it over her head in one fluid motion before dropping it to the floor. The pants followed, then she stood before him in nothing but her lacy underwear.

"God, but you're beautiful," he said thickly, unable to take his eyes from her.

She moved toward him slowly, with the languorous, seductive smile of a woman who knew what she wanted. Putting her arms around his neck, she pulled his head down for a kiss as she molded her body against his. The flames that were licking inside her, heating her blood and making her pulses race, were only fed by the stroking and caressing of his questing hands; she needed an outlet or they would consume her entirely. Her fingers worked on the buttons of his shirt, then at the buckle of his belt, before he took over, ridding himself of his garments with feverish haste. She watched him hotly, drinking in the contours of his hard, male body with eyes that were heavy with desire.

When he was naked he paused to study her before he disposed of the last of her clothing. He made the simple task an erotic caress, his hands stroking and teasing while his mouth burned along her neck, her shoulders, her breasts, then lower to nibble playfully on her satiny thighs. She felt her muscles tremble, then suddenly her legs could no longer support her. He caught her as she sank down and laid her gently on the carpet. Bending over her, his mouth fastened on her breast, his tongue circling the rosy tip and sending shock waves of feeling coursing through her. The fire inside her grew until she was aware of nothing but his hands, his mouth, and her own frantic need to be joined with him.

In a moment of panic, the memory of that other time, when he had held back, intruded, then it was gone, put to flight by Rick as she felt his weight descend—his need as great as her own. Still, the fire grew as they became one until, in a burst of searing heat, it was quenched.

It was a moment before he could bring his ragged breathing under control. He shifted his weight from her, then slid one arm under her shoulders to cradle her head and draw her against him. She snuggled close, eyes closed, a satisfied smile curving her lips. "Mmmm. That was nice," she murmured languidly.

"It certainly was," he agreed in lazy amusement.

They lay peacefully for a few minutes until the carpet began to feel rough against bare skin and the return to normal body temperature made the air feel faintly cold.

"Are you hungry?" asked Rick suddenly.

Deanna opened her eyes to blink catlike at him. Hunger was something she hadn't noticed much lately, so she paused to think about it. There was surprise in her voice when she said, "Why, yes, I am."

He chuckled. "Good, because I'm starved."

"Would you like me to make you something?" she offered tentatively, wondering if there was anything edible in her fridge at the moment.

He drew her against him, kissing her slowly, seductively. "No. If we stay here I'll only make love to you again."

She grinned tauntingly at him. "Is that so bad?"

"Don't tempt me, lady!" he murmured gruffly. He stood up, putting distance between them as a safety barrier. She watched him hastily draw on his slacks before finally giving up hope that he might return to her. Stretching slowly with warm contentment, and quite unaware of the sensuous appeal of her movement, she rose to her feet and began to dress, only to feel Rick's eyes on her in an almost physical caress. She blushed slightly, very aware of his regard and unashamedly slowing all her movements, tormenting him as she covered her body in the clothes she had discarded not long before.

He drew a deep, shaking breath as she tucked the blouse into the waistband of her slacks. "Are you ready?"

She nodded reluctantly.

"Okay," he said, taking her hand and leading her firmly toward the door. "I'll take you out and feed you and we'll do what I came here for."

"What was that?" she asked, somewhat confused.

"Talk."

The restaurant was elegant, secluded, and known to be the favorite spot of famous people who wished to dine out without embarrassing or annoying interruptions. Though it was haunted by gossip columnists, there was an unwritten rule that patrons were not to be bothered while they were in the restaurant. How Rick got a reservation at so exclusive an establishment on such short notice, Deanna didn't know. Like the car he drove, a long, sleek Ferrari, it was another shock that seemed to put the Rick she knew far in the distance, leaving behind an unknown Roderick Latimer. She was even further disconcerted when the maître d' greeted him with the effusive charm usually reserved for regular patrons.

They were the cause of a minor sensation as they followed the maître d' to their table. Interested eyes watched them and conversations buzzed, stopped, and began again once they had passed. Rick took it all in his stride, which surprised her. She could feel her nerves tightening with every step.

"Champagne," he told the wine steward, who materialized as soon as they were comfortably seated. "We're celebrating." The man bent his back in a small bow, caught sight of the diamond ring Deanna had forgotten to take off, and allowed himself a thin smile. "Our very best, sir."

"Thank you." Wicked amusement danced in Rick's eyes as he waited for Deanna to puzzle out the reason for the man's reaction.

Her eyes widened in horror when she glanced at her left hand. "I forgot to take off your ring! He must think we're engaged! You didn't help, talking about celebrations, Ri— Rod...." She was saved by the wine steward, returning with the champagne. It gave her a few precious seconds to pull herself together, after stumbling over his name.

When the waiter left she stared at the bubbling wine in her glass and asked, "What do I call you?"

"Rick," he replied flatly. He paused, then continued conversationally. "I've always been called Rick by my family. My full name is Roderick Maximilian Latimer. Pretty awful, isn't it?"

She looked up, smiling faintly. "Mine's Deanna Felicia. It's not so great, either."

He stared at her, his dark eyes wandering over her face with hot intensity. "I think it's beautiful. Delicate but strong, like you."

She felt her stomach knot with sexual excitement. Laying her hands flat on the tabletop to still their trembling, she murmured softly, "Thank you. I'm afraid I can't say the same about yours."

He laughed. "Grandiose, isn't it? My father wanted Max, but he hated his own name, Maxwell, so he chose Maximilian. My mother demanded Roderick, which was her father's name. The combination is appalling. Neither of them seem to have thought of that."

He smiled lazily at her, coaxing a smile in return. She was finding it difficult to believe that this controlled, sophisticated man was the person she knew in Yellowstone or the virile male who had made love to her—was it only an hour before?

She began to frown, shaking her head. "Rick, I..."

He leaned forward, catching one fluttering hand and clasping it strongly. "Sweetheart, don't! You said earlier that you wouldn't marry me because you didn't know me. So that's what we're doing. Getting to know each other." The serious expression was chased from his features by an unrepentant grin. "Pretend you've just met me and this is our first date."

She eyed him askance. "This *is* our first date!"

"There, you see? You're already in the right mood."

Finding it difficult to hold back a smile, she hissed, "Rick, we just made love! How many people do you know who go to bed together *before* they go out on their first date?"

"Anything wrong with being different, bobcat?" he asked mildly.

"No, of course not!" she replied impatiently. "But I can't pretend that what happened between us didn't!"

He leaned forward, caressing her jaw with a light, seductive movement. "You'd better not, my love," he murmured with lazy amusement, "because I have plans for you that do not including leaving you primly on your front doorstep."

She felt her whole body flood with heat. Regretfully aware of their surroundings, her eyes scanned the room nervously, met several speculative glances, and skittered warily away. "Rick!" she gritted through clenched teeth. "Remember where we are!"

"And on our first date, too," he agreed, removing his hand. Deanna swallowed some champagne and he refilled her glass. "Now," he began calmly, as if the last exchange had never taken place. "What would you like to know about me? Let's see. I'm thirty-three years old. My father, as you know, is dead. My mother is married to a wealthy rancher who has a huge spread in the Big Horn Mountains of Wyoming, as well as oil interests in that state and in Colorado. I'm single, but only for the moment, and in good health. By profession I'm an architect, reasonably successful. I have a partner whose name is Martin Thorne and we do business across the country. I have no financial worries. Anything I missed?"

"You're crazy," she chuckled, unable to remain serious.

He said slowly, "No. Just happy to be with you."

She stared into his eyes, feeling her body melt with love. "Careful," she suggested lightly, "or I won't make it through dinner."

He grinned at her. "I'll be good. Have some more champagne."

She sipped at the wine, then took a deep breath and plunged into speech. "Rick, what happened at the Double S after I left?" She watched his face harden with remembered anger and her heart sank.

"Why do you want to know?" he replied obliquely. "It doesn't matter now, Deanna."

"Yes, it does," she protested softly, her eyes searching his face, wondering if he had forgiven her for running away when he needed her. "Rick, I'm sorry I ran out on you, really I am! But it was all such a shock! I didn't know what to think." Her voice rose, then fell to a raw sob. "I know I should have stayed but..."

"Stop it, Deanna," he commanded sharply. He took her hands and cradled them in his larger ones, his thumbs caressing her silky skin comfortingly. "I was glad you left when you did."

"It doesn't bother you that I abandoned you to face the press alone?" she demanded incredulously.

He shook his head. "God, no! The Double S was a madhouse for hours. You would have hated it."

"As you did," she stated morosely.

"As I did," he agreed with a faint smile.

After a moment of tense silence she asked, "What happened to the pictures that were taken of us?"

"Jonas exposed the film."

"And the photographer?"

He stared down at her hands, still cupped by his. "I broke his jaw, then smashed his camera," Rick said flatly.

Deanna gasped, remembering the angry violence she had felt in him that afternoon.

Taking her gasp to indicate disapproval, he looked up quickly. "The pictures he took could have been used with all kinds of sleezy innuendos, bobcat. I wasn't going to let anyone throw mud on you! The bastard deserved what he got." He paused for a moment, ruthlessly dragging his still raw anger under control. "I had it all worked out how I was going to break it to you who I was so that you wouldn't get mad. Then that idiot has to come along and spoil everything. I was furious."

She laughed shakily. "I know." Hesitating a little, she continued, "What have you been doing these last couple of weeks? I haven't heard a word and..."

"You're dying of curiosity," he concluded, stroking her soft cheek.

"Well, not quite dying," she amended cautiously.

"I had to go back east to make arrangements with Martin...."

"Back east?" she gasped. "Is that where you live?"

"Yes, New York mostly, though I have a house in Virginia."

Her eyes widened at his casual admission. Forgetting for the moment that she had refused to marry him, she cried, "But Rick, my work is here! I can't live in New York!"

"Don't worry about it, sweetheart. We'll work something out," he said soothingly, taking note of her slip even if she hadn't.

Deanna felt like a tornado had picked her up and dumped her on the opposite side of town. "Then you're only here for a visit."

"A little longer than that. We have a client out here who wants a design for a house. He's been adamant that he prefers me to do the work, not Martin. So," he grinned conspiratorally at her, "I'm keeping the customer happy. Also, there are a few things from my father's estate that still have to be cleared up. Between the two, I think I should be out here long enough for us to properly get to know each other."

His mention of the estate brought another question to mind. "Rick, what's the true story about the will? Why did you suddenly disappear like that?"

He fiddled for a moment with the long stem of the champagne glass before he began, "When my father died so unexpectedly in that car crash there was some confusion about his will. He'd only recently been divorced from his latest sugarplum and since he always claimed he made a new will every time he was married or divorced, everyone was looking for a recent will. The only one the lawyers had was several years old. Written, I might add, when I reached my twenty-fifth birthday. It turned out that he used the inheritance ploy to keep his ladies in line.

"That was the will that left everything to you and your mother," she said softly, watching his somber face as he paused to sip his wine.

"Right. It caused a sensation in the media, but even more of one amongst his ex-wives. They were all promising to contest its validity and they were taking their claims straight to the press. The lawyers advised me not to grant any interviews and not to react in any way to their accusations." He shrugged. "Maybe I shouldn't have disappeared to Wyoming. Maybe I should have gone back to New York, but I thought I'd be more successful at dodging the reporters in the Big Horn Mountains than I would in New York City."

"How did you end up at the Double S?" she asked softly.

He grinned ruefully. "I got bored. I was eighteen when my mother married Dale Sands, and though I get along well with him, I spent very little time at his ranch. I didn't have any part in the operation of it and the reporters who camped outside the gates—er—curbed my movements. So I contacted Jonas, grew a beard as a disguise and one day I, and a bunch of the men, got in a pickup truck, drove up to the front entrance, and headed off into the sunset right under those damned reporters' noses." He grinned wolfishly at the memory.

"You look pleased with yourself," she murmured over the top of her tall, fluted glass.

"I am," he replied promptly. "It gave me a tremendous kick to know I was outsmarting them. They—or others like them—had made my life miserable for weeks. It's bad enough when someone you're close to dies. Having the funeral mobbed by nosy reporters simply rubs salt in the wound."

"Were you very close to your father?" she asked curiously.

"Yes," he replied briefly, refusing to add anything more. She realized he was not going to explain any further when he asked her what she wanted to eat. Letting her attention be successfully diverted, she told herself he had already exposed more of himself this night than she had ever expected, and she would have to be content with that. There was no need to rush things.

Chapter Ten

When the last plate was cleared away, to be replaced by cups of steaming coffee, Deanna leaned back in her chair feeling deliciously content and not a little sleepy. This was the first complete meal she had eaten since she had braved the hordes of reporters and visited her parents. Right now she was feeling the effects. She looked over at Rick to find him watching her with warm, rather amused eyes.

Straightening a little self-consciously, she leaned forward to pour cream in her coffee. "No reflection on the company," she said lightly, "but I'm beat."

"I know," he said gently, scrutinizing her face. "You looked like a wraith when I arrived tonight."

"Is that why you insisted on taking me out to dinner?" she teased.

"Bobcat," he replied shaking his head, "someone has to look after you. I guess I've taken on the job."

"It seems to me you said that to me once before," she retorted with a low chuckle. "But that was in Yellowstone, where even I will admit I was out of my element. Now that I'm back home I can look out for myself."

Suddenly serious, he said intently, "I'm not trying to smother you, Deanna, believe me. I just want you to know that if you need someone, I'm there. It's not only your beautiful body and heart-stopping face I love, you know. Though I'm certainly not complaining," he added, letting his eyes linger possessively on her breasts. Deanna found herself smiling suggestively as his gaze rose to her soft, full lips and felt her body temperature shoot up at the desire that leaped into his eyes. A silent promise passed between them before he continued, "You wouldn't be half as beautiful to me, bobcat, without the fire in your eyes or that indomitable spirit that drives you to tackle anything. I guess what I'm trying to say is I'll let you fight your own battles, but I want to be there to back you up if you need me." He paused and looked down at his coffee cup. "Even if you won't admit it."

At that, Deanna laughed. "Like that day in Yellowstone."

His eyes mocked her as he calmly sipped coffee. "Exactly," he said, putting the cup down and signaling for the check. "What about this party you mentioned?"

Flinging one hand over her mouth in a gesture of horror she exclaimed, "I forgot all about it!"

He grinned lazily. "You do my ego a world of good. Do you want to put in an appearance for an hour or so, or forget it?"

Deanna finished her coffee then said reluctantly, "You'll cause a sensation."

"I know," he agreed flatly. "I'm prepared for that."

"It will be a terrible crush. Everyone who's anyone and loads of people who aren't. Reporters all over the place."

"There were reporters at your front gate," he said dryly. "I managed to survive them."

"Maybe we should go," she mused doubtfully.

"Okay." He paid the bill swiftly and stood up. Almost before she knew it, he was guiding her out of the restaurant to the sleek silver car.

"Once you make a decision you don't wait around, do you?" she remarked dryly when they were seated in the plush interior.

He shot her a laughing look. "You noticed!"

She giggled, but countered, "You're not exactly subtle about it!" The Ferrari purred into motion. "Rick, where did you get this super car? It makes my little model look like a family compact!"

"It was one of my father's cars," he answered easily. "I used to drive it when I was out here. And, as I had a gorgeous girl I wanted to impress tonight, I thought I'd make use of it."

"Well, you did. Impress me, I mean. It's great. I love it," she announced enthusiastically, looking around her.

"I'll give you the spare set of keys," he offered casually, "on the condition that the first time you drive it, I'm with you. It's a powerful beast and takes a bit of getting used to."

She stared at him, awed and somewhat aghast at his generosity. It made her a little nervous.

The party, which she had dreaded, proved to be a lot of fun. She was surprised by the number of people Rick knew, most of them merely names and faces to her. She supposed she ought to have realized he would know people through his father, but truthfully she hadn't given the matter any thought. Both her friends and Rick's were curious, but the party had been going on for hours when they got there and everyone was wound up and too intent on having a good time to bother them. Music blared, liquor flowed, voices shouted and laughed.

One hour stretched into two then three before Rick and Deanna left. Despite the late hour, there was an even larger cluster of newsmen waiting outside the gates to Deanna's apartment, pressing to get close to the car despite the security men, with their German shepherd guard dogs, who held them back. Once again they were blinded by the blaze of a flashgun, but none of the reporters were able to do more than shout questions that remained unanswered.

Rick guided the Ferrari to the open visitor's parking area in heavy silence, his firm lips a hard, grim line, his face cold and set. Deanna felt her nerves knot as she remembered his violent reaction at the Double S.

"Thank goodness for security men," she yawned, trying to break the tension as they left the car.

Rick frowned and slammed his door hard.

Her nerves tightened another notch. Once again she attempted to lighten the atmosphere. "You're going to have to get used to this if you want to stick around me." Beneath her mild teasing was the very real fear that after another taste of heavy publicity he would decide she was more trouble than she was worth.

Very much aware that they were out in the open, visible to prying eyes, he didn't reply until they were safely inside her apartment with the door closed securely behind them. By then Deann's nerves were tight, quivering wires that prompted her to misread his silence. As the door clicked shut she turned in the small hall to face him, a fixed, but unconsciously wistful smile on her lips.

For a moment he silently studied her expression then shook his head, a small, tender smile playing on his mouth.

"My sweet idiot," he chided softly. "Do you think I'm going to walk out on you because of a few reporters?"

Her eyes lit up with revivifying hope. "You're not?"

His expression was ironic. "You sure do have a high opinion of me."

"No, that's not it at all!" she muttered, running her fingers through her hair and completely demolishing the careful set. It curled wildly around her delicate features in a manner reminiscent of the week she had spent at Yellowstone. She closed her eyes as a wave of fatigue hit her. Then opened them quickly when she felt Rick's fingers touch her face.

"You look exhausted," he said curtly, observing the dark areas beneath her eyes.

"I am." She moistened dry lips. "Maybe that's why I'm not thinking straight. Rick, I know how determined the press can be, what to expect from them. I've been the focus of cameras and reporters since I was born."

"Do you think I haven't?" he demanded humorously.

The question threw her off stride, as he meant it to. "Were you?"

"To some extent," he admitted. Putting his hands on her shoulders he began to ease the tense muscles there. "Despite the incident at the Double S, I'm not camera shy, bobcat. I can handle the media if I want to and in this case I want to, very much."

Her eyes were huge as she stared up into his calm, determined face, wishing she could believe what he had said, but afraid she could not. "They'll hound us, never give us breathing space, never a moment to ourselves. You'll start to hate me after a while, I know it!"

His hands stopped their rhythmic motion as he gripped her shoulders hard. "I could never hate you, Deanna, whatever happens! I might hate this town and what it does to people, but not you, sweetheart, never you."

She closed her eyes and let her head fall against his chest. "I don't want to lose you," she said, almost inaudibly.

Wrapping his arms comfortingly around her, he cradled her against his muscled strength. "Not a chance, lady." He held her closely for a minute, giving her a much needed opportunity to renew her confidence, then he tipped her chin up with one lean finger and commanded firmly, "Don't worry about the media, bobcat. After a week or two they'll find someone else to chase. You and I are interesting because of our parents, not because of who we are. Once people get used to the idea of our being together we won't be exciting anymore."

Warning bells jangled in her brain. Would he, too, find her unexciting once the novelty wore off? Her eyes studied his face, searching for evidence of this, but there was no mockery in his eyes, no overheated lust demanding conquest. What she saw was a tender smile and a concerned question in his dark eyes. She reached up and pulled his head down for a kiss.

"Love me, Rick," she begged against his lips. "Now. Always."

His lips brushed lightly over hers. "You know I will," he replied huskily.

Deanna stretched and snuggled closer to his warm body. "Do you have to go?" Her voice was sleepy and she was guiltily aware that she had dozed off, spent after their slow, tumultuous lovemaking.

"Yes," he sighed, tightening his hold on her shoulders briefly, before climbing determinedly out of the bed. "Those reporters saw my car drive in. They'll see it leave. Tonight."

She sat up, the sheet around her waist, her naked breasts firm and uptilted, the nipples still hard and flushed from the touch of his hands and mouth. She was unconscious of the seductive picture she made, the sheet covering her slender legs and hips, showing only the outline of what was beneath, but her breasts proudly bare.

Rick paused in the act of buttoning his shirt. "Don't tempt me, lady," he said roughly. He picked up her crimson dressing gown and tossed it to her. "Here, put this on."

She looked at him for a moment, smiling winsomely, then slid from the bed to shrug on the garment. His reaction was just what she had hoped for.

"God!" he rasped, "That doesn't help at all!" Though his words were critical, his eyes were telling her warmly that he liked what he saw.

"Which hotel are you staying at?" she asked softly, perching on the edge of her bed with one leg folded beneath her.

He glanced over at her, his expression lightly mocking. "Can't you guess?"

She frowned, wondering why he would imagine... "Of course! Your father's house!"

"Right, only it's my mother's property now. She's thinking of selling it, but hasn't made up her mind yet. Anyway, until she does decide, it's better off tenanted than empty."

She chuckled. "I'm glad to know you're going to a good home."

Rick made a wry face at her and finished dressing, then ran his fingers through his ruffled hair to restore it to some order. Deanna padded over to him to straighten his collar and make sure the lapels of his jacket were flat, a wifely task that amused him. She smiled up at him and he smiled back, a precious, intimate moment snatched from time. Then he kissed her lightly and said, "I'll see you tomorrow."

Her hand flew to her mouth. "Oh! Rick, I forgot! Tomorrow I have a meeting with the producers of the picture I'm working on."

A devil of mischief leapt in his eyes. "No problem. I'll meet you for lunch. That gives me the chance to take care of some of my own business."

"Lunch?" she repeated doubtfully. "But then everybody..."

"I want everything out in the open," he said soberly.

Drawing a deep breath she agreed. "One o'clock okay?"

He nodded. One more quick, hard kiss and he was gone. Deanna wandered disconsolately around the apartment for a few minutes, then returned to the bedroom. Discarding the silk robe, she curled up on the bed in the spot still warm from Rick's body. Her fingers plucked moodily at the sheet and the light from the bedside lamp caught and flashed. The ring. The diamond Rick had placed on her finger just a few hours before. She had intended to take it off twice. First here in the apartment when she told him she couldn't marry him, then once again in the restaurant after the sly look from the wine steward. Both times something held her back. Well, the damage was done now. Had she worn it only in the restaurant, it might not have been noticed. But by wearing it to the party she had made a public statement.

She stretched out on her back and examined it. The stone was flawless, the setting tasteful and timeless. A beautiful ring, one any woman would be proud of. On the whole she rather liked the way it looked on her slim finger. What did it matter if people naturally assumed she and Rick were engaged? She knew what the ring meant and so did Rick. She flicked off the light. The ring would stay on the finger Rick had slipped it on. Let people think whatever they cared to.

She wasn't surprised when Felicia called, full of probing questions. Since it had been her suggestion to issue the denial to the press, Deanna knew her mother would be curious, but she wasn't sure how Felicia would take the news that Rick Latimer and her daughter were seeing each other romantically. Deanna's childhood had been spent in the care of nannies and maids while Felicia worked on a succession of major films. Though there were infrequent periods of intimacy with her mother when she was between pictures, Deanna's relationship with Felicia was a tenuous one. Consequently, though she wanted her mother to like Rick, she had already decided that if Felicia did object, it wouldn't change the way she felt about him.

The first meeting between Rick and her parents was full of rocky, unvoiced hostility. They met in a neutral area, a small, secluded restaurant where none of them could make any violent emotional scenes. Deanna had the distinct feeling that Felicia had strong reservations about Rick and was annoyed when Deanna left with him and not her parents, almost as if she had committed some sort of disloyal act. She was astonished when Rick remarked that he thought, for an initial meeting, it had gone off very well.

A couple of weeks later Felicia issued a maternal command, thinly veiled as an invitation, to bring Rick to a family dinner. Her father astounded her by greeting Rick at the door with a warm handshake and a friendly clap on the shoulder. At first she thought he was acting the jovial host, but as the evening wore on she realized he both liked Rick for himself and because Rick was his old friend's son. When it slipped out that the two had met privately a few times, Deanna was surprised, but not overly so. It was the sort of thoughtful, considerate action Rick would take, working out differences with her father in private, where they could be honest and open with each other.

He was equally successful with her younger sister, Sylvan. Sylvan was in the last year of a course in business administration and was planning to be an accountant, a choice of professions that had initially appalled her parents until they discovered how useful a commercially inclined family member could be. Sylvan had long ago despaired of any of her family understanding her obsession with numbers, so when she discovered that her sister's new boyfriend was an architect and worked with figures as well as designs, she was delighted. After a long involved conversation, to which Deanna listened in silent amazement and her parents in amusement, Sylvan cheerfully informed Deanna, still in Rick's hearing, that her choice in men had improved dramatically. Deanna took one look at Rick's self-satisfied, but amused expression and burst out laughing.

It had taken a few more meetings before Felicia cracked under the full weight of Rick's determined charm, but she had. Felicia decided that Rick took after Leah and that emotionally, as well as physically, he had few of his father's features. After that she was as warm as the rest of her family and equally insistent that Deanna do the right thing and marry Rick.

Though he made no secret of the fact that he wanted to marry her, Rick never pressured her to make a decision as everyone else seemed to be doing. Deanna, falling ever more deeply in love, was too emotionally involved to realize that he was pressing his case far more effectively by allowing her to find her own path to him, than he ever would by badgering her until she caved in to his wishes.

By the time he told Deanna that his mother had invited them to the Sands ranch in the Big Horn Mountains of Wyoming, Deanna was ready to admit that her world was revolving around him. The thought of losing him because she didn't measure up to his mother's standards was too awful to contemplate.

They flew to Wyoming for the weekend and when they finally reached the ranch, Deanna had worked herself into a tight knot of worry that not even Rick's affectionate teasing could soothe.

Dale Sands was a tall, husky man whose western drawl belied an astute mind and wide-ranging interests. He was something of a shock to Deanna, who had vague visions of a hard-bitten cowboy whenever Rick mentioned him. Leah was even more of a surprise. Small in comparison to her husband, she was a few inches taller than Deanna, but much stockier. She had a round face with a small, uptilted nose and lips Deanna instantly noted she had passed on to her son. Her slate-blue eyes were thoughtful and rather amused as Rick introduced them. Deanna felt a little as if Leah had suspended judgment until all the facts were in, and her stomach curled with more nervous tension until Leah observed that she looked very much like her mother and promptly kissed her on the cheek.

Deanna was somewhat reassured by the warm welcome, but as she watched Rick with his mother and Dale Sands, she realized she needn't have worried about Leah changing his attitude toward her. He obviously liked his mother and stepfather as people, but he wasn't afraid to disagree with them or to form his own opinions. He made no effort to hide the fact that he and Deanna were very close, although he did acquiesce gracefully when his mother had their suitcases put in widely separate rooms. Deanna caught his eyes on her as Leah was remarking that she hoped Deanna would be comfortable, and she blushed. Leah broke off, looked from her son's amused expression to Deanna's embarrassed one, and drew her own thoughtful conclusions.

The next day she cornered Deanna in the living room when Dale had taken Rick out to the barns to show him some improvements made since he was last at the ranch. They talked easily for a while about the ranch, Dale, and finally, Deanna's meeting with Rick. Eventually, Leah said lightly, "Rick tells me he wants to marry you. Will you accept?"

Deanna blinked, feeling her mouth go dry with nervousness. She swallowed hard and said, "Marriage is a big step."

Leah studied her troubled face. "I know that. You don't like to make commitments without thinking them through very thoroughly, do you, Deanna?"

Deanna looked down at her hands and the big diamond that flashed up at her. "I've thought about this a lot," she said gruffly, picking her words carefully. She liked Leah Sands and didn't want to wound her with a casually voiced reference to her first husband's infidelities. "When I marry it will be forever. I don't want to make a mistake."

"Do you love him?" inquired Leah gently.

"Oh, yes," breathed Deanna, touching the ring as if it were a tangible part of the man who had given it to her.

Leah frowned. "Then what's holding..." Understanding lit her eyes and her expression became wary. Abruptly, she changed the topic. "You're not very much like your mother, are you, despite the very close physical resemblance?"

Deanna relaxed a little. "No. My mother is fire and I'm water," she admitted, somewhat wistfully.

Leah shook her head. "I think you're doing yourself an injustice, my dear, but you're right. Felicia is fiery!" She hesitated, then added briskly, "We're none of us our parents. And it's a good thing, too. If you were like Felicia, I'd advise Rick to stay away from you." She laughed at Deanna's dropped jaw and widened eyes. "Not that it would do any good."

Deanna raised her hands in bafflement. "I don't understand."

Slowly, choosing her words carefully, Leah said, "Even though you may be the image of your mother, you're a very different person. Well, it's the same with Rick and his father. Max was a dear man, but he didn't have Rick's self-confidence, or the hard, decisive core that makes my son so strong. Think about the differences, Deanna, not the small similarities."

Deanna felt herself turning crimson and mumbled some reply. Leah sat irresolute for a minute, then quietly left Deanna alone to think about what she had said.

Though there were other opportunities for Leah to return to the conversation, she didn't, leaving Deanna to assume that having said her piece, she was content to let the relationship seek its own course and allow the two young people to work out their problems for themselves.

Chapter Eleven

Deanna walked in a straight, unbending line from her parking spot to her apartment door, looking neither to the left nor right. She felt very tired, a fatigue caused not by physical exertion or mental exhaustion, but an emotional shock.

Reaching the apartment door, she carefully searched her purse for her key, knowing that if she didn't find it the first time her artificial poise would shatter like glass as her emotions sought an outlet. Her fingers closed over the key and she withdrew it to insert it slowly into the lock. The door slid open and she stepped inside.

She closed the door with a soft click, not with a loud, angry bang as her mother would have done in similar circumstances. Automatically, her mind clamped down on the thought of her parents and shuffled it aside. She wasn't prepared to cope with that yet. She moved calmly into the apartment, wandering from room to room, looking at each without really seeing it. Finally she stopped in the living room, sank down on the yielding couch, and let her head droop onto her hands in an attitude of despair.

She remained that way for a long time, forcing her mind into blank emptiness, refusing to let the pain she couldn't cope with tear at her. The seconds turned into minutes, then an hour, until finally the stabbing thoughts could no longer be kept at bay.

Everything had been moving so smoothly, she reflected bitterly. Too smoothly. Her relationship with Rick, their parents' attitudes, her own much stronger confidence in herself as a woman, as a person, as a designer. All smashed now, because of one angry, malicious woman.

She sighed and leaned back against the padded cushions of the sofa, fighting against the agonizing, aching pain that threatened to consume her because it had no physical cause; it was all in her mind. She wished Rick were here. She'd give her right arm to be able to talk to him. Even more, to have him beside her, just to know he cared and was nearby. But he was in New York and had been all this past week. He had promised to make it back for the weekend if he could, but that didn't matter now. She wouldn't be available.

She swallowed a lump in her throat and closed her eyes on threatened tears. She told herself that she was being stupid, that she was overly sensitive, and that Colleen Carlisle was merely being venomous, that she was using Deanna to ease her own personal problems. It didn't do much good, but it did help enough to give Deanna the energy to go to the kitchen and make herself a cup of coffee. Anything more than that was beyond her at the moment. She ambled back to the cozy living room, clutching the mug as if she were afraid of spilling the hot liquid inside. After sinking gracefully back onto the sofa she sipped at the hot beverage.

She couldn't continue as she was now, that was certain. She needed something to grab on to and the only solid, dependable thing in her universe right now was Rick. Looking slowly around the room, she remembered the night they had made love on the carpet, when she had been as down as she was now.

No, not quite. She had been worse then, thinking she had lost Rick for good. The memory cheered her, and she hugged it to her. What she had learned today hurt, but it didn't affect the central, most precious part of her life. Somehow she would get through the next few days—no, weeks—then it would be over, forgotten, past.

Deliberately, she focused her thoughts on the good times she and Rick had shared this last month and a half. She had discovered that beneath his controlled exterior was a sensitive, thoughtful man who listened to what was said and took careful note of what was going on around him. He could be charming when he wanted, and never hesitated to let her know that she meant everything to him. There were times when he was intensely protective of her, but he simply let her work her problems out on her own, as he had promised he would. Deanna wondered what he would do if he knew about today. But what could he do? How could he protect her? This was her job; it had nothing to do with her private life.

Or did it? Her father had started dropping hints lately about grandchildren, settling down, and a career not being necessary for a woman. Today had been the worst, she thought ruefully, when he had come out and said that she ought to forget about a career because she wasn't suited to one.

The phone rang. She looked at her watch and was startled to see it was already eight o'clock. She reached over, picked up the receiver, then said wearily, "Hello?" She didn't feel much like talking tonight.

"Hi, lover," said a low, seductive voice. "Miss me?"

She felt her stomach lurch and a smile of tender pleasure curled her lips. "Rick! I'm so glad to hear your voice!"

There was a warm chuckle at the other end of the line. "If that's the kind of response I get, I think I'll go away more often!"

Sudden panic assailed her. "No, don't!" she cried. Bringing her voice back to normal, she added gruffly, "Please."

There was the faintest of pauses. "Deanna, something's wrong. What is it?"

"Nothing, really. Just a few problems with the costumes." She hesitated, wondering if she should tell him she would have to work the weekend.

"What kind of problems?" he asked casually, breaking into her thoughts.

"Big ones," she groaned. "It's a mess."

"Tell me about it," he ordered gently.

Deanna felt much of the gnawing hurt of the last hours drain away. She closed her eyes, imagining he was in the room with her, not three thousand miles away. "Everything was going great until this afternoon. Then I had Colleen Carlisle in for her first fitting." Colleen Carlisle was the female lead in the picture. She was talented, gorgeous, temperamental, and, at times, extremely nasty. Like today. This afternoon she had been at her worst.

Deanna didn't realize she had stopped until Rick coaxed gently, "What happened?"

"It was a disaster," she admitted grimly. "The clothes made her look like a dump truck when she's supposed to be sexy and seductive, and the colors! Well, let's just say her complexion went from peaches and cream to sickly green."

There was a choked-off laugh from Rick. "Sorry, bob-cat. I know this must be frustrating for you. I've met Miss Carlisle a couple of times. She was, and I guess she still is, a witch."

"She has such a lovely face," muttered Deanna sadly.

"It's what's inside that counts, sweetheart. Was she un-pleasant about the costumes?"

"Very," Deanna agreed dryly.

There was a bitten-off expletive from New York. "I could wring her scrawny neck," Rick gritted savagely. "Don't pay any attention to her, Deanna. She enjoys stepping on people."

Remembering the look of triumph in the woman's eyes, Deanna said, "I can believe that."

"Look, sweetheart, I'm flying in tomorrow. Meet me at the airport and bring an overnight bag for the weekend. Sounds like you need to get away for a while."

"Oh, Rick, I can't!" she wailed. "I've got to redo all of Colleen's costumes—by Monday! At least have the sketches ready by then. I'm going to have to work all weekend. The producers are really upset and they're threatening to get someone else if I don't come up with the goods by then."

She was about to tell him the further messy details of the story when there was a high-pitched woman's giggle from the other end of the line, clearly audible, which meant the woman had to be practically on top of Rick. He grunted and said, "Hang on a minute, Deanna," then there was a low, indistinguishable murmur of voices, as if he had put his hand over the phone to muffle the words. Deanna felt tear-ing jealousy crawl up her spine. He had a woman with him. He had been away from her four days and already he had another woman. On top of the blows her ego had already suffered today, this was just too much for her to take. Ir-rational fury swept her.

"Who was that? An old friend?" she demanded nastily when he was back on the line. Her voice rose as emotions bottled up for too long pressed against her throat, threatening to explode. "I hope she's pretty," Deanna all but screamed, then jammed the back of her hand against her mouth, appalled by her outburst. "Rick, I..."

"That was Katie, the somewhat inebriated wife of my partner. And yes, she is pretty," he replied curtly, adding furiously, "Right now, she and Martin and half a dozen other people, are in the living room celebrating Katie and Martin's first wedding anniversary. I know what you're thinking, Deanna, and I don't much like it. Drag your mind out of the gutter and have the decency to trust me."

Deanna didn't need his clipped, cutting tone to tell her she had responded shamefully. She knew about Katie and Martin. Rick had been the best man at their wedding the year before. He had talked about Martin, and about their architectural firm based in New York City, many times. She knew enough about his life there not to be jealous, but her confidence was low tonight and she was so afraid she didn't have what it took to keep him.

Choking back a sob, she mumbled, "I didn't mean..."

"Forget it," he said harshly. "I've got to go. Meet me at the airport tomorrow afternoon. And bring a change of clothes."

"I've got to work this weekend," she said stonily.

"Just meet me," he repeated coldly. "And come prepared."

The flight from New York touched down in L.A. twenty minutes late. Deanna waited at the arrival gate, miserably defiant, her head up, her jaw clenched, her dark violet eyes brooding. She had lain awake last night, fighting the lumpy pillow, cursing the hard bed, hating her own hasty tongue. After a sleepless night she hadn't needed another problem-filled day, but she had gotten one just the same. It culminated when she announced that she was leaving after lunch. Her father and the producers had indulged in a shouting competition to see who could destroy her character faster. Her father won. Not to be outdone, the producers leveled an ultimatum—results by Monday or she could forget working in the business again.

She sighed and apprehensively twisted the diamond ring on her left hand. The events of the last two days had stretched her nerves thin and she never worked well when she was this tense. What she needed was time, a chance to relax, and a few comforting words. None of which she was likely to get.

Passengers were beginning to filter into the arrival bay from the New York flight. The luggage carousels were moving, though nothing was on them yet. Any minute now Rick would appear and the confrontation she dreaded would occur. Her eyes scanned the thin trickle of people, looking for his dark head. Nothing. Taut muscles trembled and she forced herself to stand still. It had been her decision not to do as Rick had commanded. Now she had to face the resulting wrath. She blinked, fighting back tears, and bit her lip. Everything was such a mess. She didn't feel that she could cope with anything else.

Rick's dark head and lean, muscular body appeared at the back of the crowd and, as the surging mob fanned out into the arrival area, he skirted the edge to stride toward her. Wearing a dark blue suit, white shirt, and a diagonally striped tie and carrying an expensive leather briefcase, he looked every inch the New York businessman and very, very alien. She swallowed and couldn't control the trembling in her drooping lips.

As he had sufficient clothes at his New York apartment, he hadn't bothered with a suitcase, stowing what he needed in the briefcase. Now he ignored the people gathering at the carousels as the first pieces of luggage dropped down from the loading area to go straight to Deanna. "Did you bring the overnight bag?" he demanded without preamble, his eyes swiftly taking note of the jeans and casual cotton blouse she was wearing.

She shook her head mournfully, feeling absurdly close to tears. This was the end between them. He would never forgive her for this.

"I suppose I should be impressed you bothered to come at all," he jeered, taking her arm and hustling her toward the exit doors. "Where's the car?"

"In the parking lot, where else?" she snapped, resenting the callous way he was dragging her along behind him.

"So she speaks!" he mocked cruelly.

After a brief, unsuccessful struggle that only served to tighten his grip painfully, Deanna cried, "Let go of my arm!"

"Not a hope, sweetheart," he grated. "I'm not going to give you the chance to run off. I've got a few things to say to you that won't keep."

They were out in the parking lot now, the warm, late summer afternoon lost to both of them. Deanna stopped dead in her tracks, forcing him to halt and face her. "Do you think I would do that?" she demanded wrathfully. "Run off and hide, instead of facing up to whatever it is you've got to say? Do you? *Do you*?"

There was an odd combination of emotions in his dark eyes, a mixture of iron control and tender compassion. Along the hard line of his jaw a muscle twitched. Slowly, he released her arm. "Since you know exactly where you parked the car, why don't you lead me to it?"

They didn't talk on the way to Deanna's car. She felt she had scored a major victory by forcing him to let go of her arm, but she wasn't at all sure what to do to follow it up. Also, she was miserably aware that Rick's return was poles away from his departure. When she had dropped him here on Sunday night they had been warm from the aftermath of lovemaking and he had kissed her passionately before striding off to board the plane.

She caught sight of the familiar lines of her green car and pointed. "It's over there."

"Keys," he said abruptly, holding out his hand, palm upward.

"What?"

"The keys. I'm driving." They were beside the car now and he stopped, still holding out his hand.

"This is my car," she retorted indignantly. "I'll drive it."

He shook his head. "Not today. The keys."

"I don't understand you! I drove you here and you didn't complain! What's different about today?" she cried, confusion, hurt, and annoyance lacing her tones.

"Deanna," he said very softly, "Let's not make an issue of this, okay?"

Their eyes met and locked. Deanna knew from his implacable expression that he would not give an inch. Reluctantly, she placed the keys in his palm. She was not about to force a breakup over a stupid little thing like who was to drive home.

He unlocked the passenger door, then walked swiftly to the driver's side, tossing the briefcase behind the seat. Deanna opened her door, but hesitated, hating the thought of quarreling in the small, confined space.

Over the roof of the car their gazes met. Rick raised a questioning eyebrow and said coolly, "What are you waiting for, darling? Hop in."

"I asked you never..." she began as he disappeared, sliding into the vehicle. She muttered in frustration, then dove in herself. "I asked you never to call me that!" she fumed. The engine roared and the car eased into motion. "You know how I hate that so-called endearment! It's so false! Everyone calls each other 'darling' and no one means it!"

"Fasten your seat belt," he ordered, ignoring her furious outburst. She sent him a seething look that was completely useless because he was concentrating on guiding the car out of the lot and onto the highway.

It took her several minutes before she realized they were heading in the wrong direction. By the time she got her bearings back they were well past their exit. She spent another few minutes telling herself that Rick was lost, that his years in New York had made him a little fuzzy on the layout of L.A.

"You're going in the wrong direction," she pointed out carefully, as he took an off-ramp to a northwest-bound highway that led out of the city.

"No, I'm not," he replied calmly, keeping his eyes on the road, but doing nothing to hide the smile twitching at the edge of his mouth.

Deanna watched, fascinated. It was the first time he had smiled since leaving the plane. "You're planning something," she probed cautiously.

The smile widened into a grin. "You bet," he agreed, accelerating into the traffic.

"Whatever it is, forget it, Rick," she said harshly. "I've got to get back to L.A. If I don't produce acceptable designs, I'm out!"

"Your car's running a little rough, Deanna," he said absently. "You should have it tuned up."

"Didn't you hear me?" she cried furiously. "Look, I don't know what your game is, but I can't play!"

"You don't have to. You're being kidnapped," he replied cheerfully, easing the car into the outside lane and pressing the gas pedal so the vehicle jumped well above the speed limit.

Deanna sat in stunned silence while her car ate up the miles. "Where are you taking me?" she said finally.

"You'll see."

She almost choked as she spat out, "I hope you're having fun! I'm not!"

He grinned happily. "I am. I spent the whole flight planning this and it worked perfectly."

"You planned this?" she repeated slowly, glancing at his face. There was a smug amusement there that made her blood boil.

"I had to," he answered seriously. "I was positive you wouldn't be prepared to come away with me, so I had to take matters into my own hands."

"So that whole thing with the keys was faked? You were—acting a part?"

"Well, I was hoping you might bring the Ferrari, since I left you the spare set of keys. Then there wouldn't have been any problem. Not," he added thoughtfully, "that there is anything wrong with this car that a good tune-up wouldn't cure. When did you last take it in for service?"

Deanna looked at him helplessly. "I don't know. Six months ago, I think."

"Hmm. Too long. Especially with an extended trip included."

"I can't believe you were just acting a part! You said some hurtful things to me, Rick!" she snapped, getting back on track. "And I didn't like it!"

The smile faded from his face. She saw the muscles tighten in his jaw. "I had to do something to make you angry," he muttered. "When I saw you, you looked so lost, as if you were fighting off tears. I thought if I made you mad it would bring back my spitting wildcat." He glanced over at her sparkling eyes and flushed cheeks and smiled slightly. "I was right."

Astonishment kept her silent as she struggled for words. Finally she said gruffly, "What would you have done if I'd burst into tears right in the middle of the airport?"

"Held you until you were finished," he said quietly. "But I didn't think you would do that. It's not your style."

Once again she was at a loss for words.

After glancing at her confused face he said gently, "We've got about another hour before we get there. Why don't you try and get some sleep?" He guessed shrewdly, "Spent last night awake and worrying, didn't you?"

"Yes," she said flatly. Weariness washed over her as she remembered the deadline facing her at the end of the weekend.

"It will all work out, bobcat," he said caressingly, reaching over to touch her cheek with one lean finger. "I promise. Trust me."

She sighed and caught his hand, bringing it to her lips and kissing the knuckles. "I do trust you," she said on a sigh. "I do!"

Their destination was a low Spanish-style house in a sheltered valley deep in the arid coastal mountains far to the north of the city. Rick braked in front of the house and swung out of the car. "Coming?" he mocked as Deanna sat motionless, staring at the white stucco building roofed with red terra-cotta tiles.

"Who owns this place?" she asked softly, feeling absurdly as if she were trespassing. She stepped from the car.

"Me," he said calmly. "Now."

"Oh. Part of your inheritance," she guessed, following him inside the house. The interior was immaculate. No dust anywhere, the wood gleaming with polish. "Do you have a housekeeper? Whoever looks after the house does an excellent job."

"Harry Aitken and his wife, Joan. Do you remember the building at the edge of the property?" She nodded. "They live there year-round. Harry looks after the horses and runs a few livestock of his own, while Joan makes sure the house is kept up."

The house was built in a square. Rick told her that when his parents bought the place it had been a simple four-room cottage with a living room, kitchen, and two bedrooms. Almost as soon as the purchase had been made, the renovations had begun. Leah hadn't been satisfied with the kitchen, so an extension had been added to accommodate a huge new one, with every convenience. Then, as they began to entertain friends at the secluded ranch, more bedrooms were needed and a larger living room, so a new wing was built at the opposite end of the house. Eventually the original bedrooms, now in the noisiest part of the house, were remodeled into a study and entertainment center, and the two wings were linked by a new bedroom area, returning the house to its original rectangular shape, but leaving a small, flower-filled courtyard to separate the sleeping quarters from the front of the house. Finally, a pool was added at the rear, with direct access from all of the bedrooms.

As they wandered through the rooms Deanna realized the house was important to Rick and that in bringing her here he had brought her to what was, for him, a special place.

She felt her heart swell as she stood in the doorway of the rather formal study and watched him familiarize himself with the furniture and the room.

"Aitken?" she said softly, half to herself. "Where have I heard that name before?"

"Harry is Jonas's uncle," Rick replied absently, touching the gleaming mahogany surface of the big desk that dominated the room. He turned back to Deanna and smiled. "That's how Jonas and I met. He used to visit Harry off and on when we were kids. We ran wild together. When we were old enough to be on our own I'd go up to Yellowstone and we'd take off into the backwoods for weeks at a time."

Deanna had a sudden vision of a young Rick, his eyes glinting, his face alive with excitement, paired up with a gangly, tow-headed Jonas as the two of them plotted mischief. After his stunt today she wouldn't put any devilment past him. She flashed him an exasperated look. "You know, I don't even have a toothbrush."

He grinned and came to her, wrapping his arm around her waist and leading her down a long hall to the kitchen. "I wondered when you would begin to worry about the practicalities of the situation. Don't. When I called Joan last night to tell her to get some food in I also asked her to pick up the necessities you might be missing."

Deanna sighed. He was amazingly organized. "Food. I hadn't even thought of that."

Joan Aitken had done more than simply buy supplies. She had also made a stew that was sending mouth-watering smells from the oven and tossed a salad. A loaf of freshly baked bread reposed on the counter and a note, welcoming Rick and supplying instructions for the final touches to the stew, was stuck to the refrigerator door with a magnet shaped like a running horse.

Rick read the note, glanced at his watch and grinned wolfishly at Deanna. "It seems we have an hour before the stew is cooked. Got any idea how we can spent it?" He bent and kissed her, leaving her with no doubt as to what he would like to do. She felt her blood heat and her pulse race as he coaxed a willing response from her lips. Briefly, guilt that she was here with Rick, enjoying his company, when she should be slaving over a sketch pad, dredging her mind for new ideas, made her draw back, but Rick was having none of that. His arms tightened around her as he forcefully held her against his hard body until she melted, her arms creeping up to twine around his neck, her soft body warm and pliant. Only then did he raise his head to smile tenderly at her before dropping tiny, teasing kisses on her eyes, her nose, the corners of her mouth.

"I missed you so much," she whispered, as his lips found the sensitive spot at the base of her neck and drove her to a frenzy of need.

"I don't know how long I can stand this," he groaned.

"Then why wait?" she managed to say in a gravelly voice. "We have an hour, don't we?"

Deanna drained the last of her coffee and set the mug down on the low, polished table in front of the long sofa-and-love-seat combination. The entertainment center, where they were drinking their after-dinner beverage, was a casually elegant room, boasting the latest in video and stereo equipment, including an enormous five-foot television screen. The furniture was all squashy and well padded, chairs and couches to relax and recline on. She looked over at Rick, sprawled indolently in the corner of the love seat, and found that he was watching her, his expression thoughtful.

"Dinner was delicious. Joan is an excellent cook," she said softly, feeling absurdly shy under his penetrating gaze. She felt her cheeks color and cursed herself for being foolish. Considering they had made love with wild abandon not two hours before, there was really no reason for shyness. But he was staring at her as if he wished to discover her innermost thoughts, and it made her nervous.

"Yes, she is," Rick agreed. "Feeling any less—frazzled?"

So that was it, Deanna thought. He was worried that she was still upset about his hijacking this afternoon. Frazzled was the last word she would use to describe herself right now. Satisfied, well fed, or deeply contented might be closer to the mark. She grinned lazily at him. "Much less."

"Good," he said cheerfully, stretching his denim-clad legs. He had unearthed the old, faded jeans from a drawer in the bedroom. She was beginning to think he had clothes stashed around the country. "You can use the study."

She gaped at him. "For what?"

"You have a deadline to meet, remember?" he said dryly.

She swallowed, feeling like a complete fool. She hadn't forgotten, but she never thought he would let her work on her designs if they went away together for the weekend. And he knew it. There was no use denying that she had misjudged him badly.

"One of these days," he said softly, holding her chin and forcing her to face him, "you are going to admit that I know you and understand you."

She stared at him, sudden perception in her eyes. "This is one of those times you mentioned, isn't it? When you would help me, even if I wouldn't ask for it."

He smiled a little ruefully. "There are moments when you can be too stubborn, my love. You're not alone anymore, you know."

She caught her breath, fighting down a ridiculous urge to cry. "I know, Rick. But I'm not sure I'll be able to produce anything."

"Take your time," he said, dropping his hand. "You've got all weekend. This is a good place to work. It's quite and I promise—no interruptions!" He grinned encouragingly. "Before you know it you'll be flooded with ideas!"

She stood up, shooting him a wry glance. "We'll see. I'm not holding out for any miracles."

Three cups of coffee and as many hours later, she was regretting her flippant words. Her sketch pad and the file of notes she had amassed during the time she had been working on the project had fortunately—or perhaps unfortunately—been in the trunk of her car when she drove out to the airport to pick up Rick. Now both were on the big mahogany desk in the study, the notes spread chaotically over the surface of the desk, the sketch pad open to a blank, empty page.

After three hours of trying to drag ideas from somewhere deep within her and being totally unsuccessful Deanna's nerves were crawling with tension. In her mind she could hear the scornful voices listing her inadequacies, and each time she forced herself to put the tip of her pencil to paper her thoughts emptied, leaving only the echo of the hateful voices.

She closed the sketchbook with an angry slap. An hour ago she had been more than ready to call it quits, but when she wandered out of the study to find Rick she discovered he was not in the house. Assuming that he must have gone out to the stables or to visit with the Aitkens, she had returned to the study to give her work one last try before she quit for the night. She had a feeling that was what Rick would expect her to do.

Well, she had done her duty, wasting another hour in the process. Three hours of frustration were enough. She would wait for Rick in the entertainment center and maybe try out some of the fascinating gadgets there. Slowly she gathered up the papers and neatly returned them to the file folder. Putting it on top of the sketchbook, she pushed both wearly to one side of the desk, then closed her eyes and stretched slow, gracefully.

When she stood up and looked toward the door Rick was leaning against the frame wiping what appeared to be grease from his fingers with a dirty rag. The smoldering gleam in his eyes made it clear he had been watching her as she stretched and that he had enjoyed her unconsciously seductive movements.

"What have you been up to?" she asked lightly, eyeing the filthy rag. "I looked for you about an hour ago and couldn't find you anywhere."

He smiled slowly and sauntered across the room to drop the rag in the wastebasket. "Tuning up your car," he replied casually.

For a moment she thought he was joking and an expression of irritable disbelief crossed her features. Then she realized that he was serious and laughed softly. "Rick Latimer, you are full of surprises. Tell me, did it have any major problems" Wait." She held up her hand, palm outward. "I wouldn't understand if you told me and I'm not in the mood to struggle through complex explanations."

"No brilliant ideas?" he said sympathetically.

"You might say that," she agreed dryly, then quickly changed the subject. "How on earth did you do a tune up out here? Where did you get the tools and supplies and—whatever you need?"

He grinned at her feminine lack of knowledge about the mechanics of her car. Seating himself on the edge of the

desk, he explained. "This is where Dad used to bring me
when I was a kid. It was his escape from the pressures of his
life in L.A. After the divorce no one else ever came here but
us. I guess you know every boy goes through a stage when
he's car-mad." He shrugged. "Since I happened to have a
wealthy and indulgent father, when my turn came along he
had a machine shop installed in one of the barns and made
sure I had proper instructions on how to service an engine." He laughed at her awestruck expression. "It's not
all that difficult, bobcat. I'll teach you sometime."

"Well, maybe," she temporized doubtfully, making him
chuckle softly.

He pointed to her sketch pad. "Mind if I take a look at
what you were doing, now that I've confessed how I spent
my evening?"

She sighed and sat down abruptly, burying her face in her
hands. "Don't bother," she muttered despondently. "I
didn't get a damn thing done. Not one thing."

Gently, he pried her hands away and lifted her chin with
one finger. "And you're frustrated, tired, and pressured."

Slowly she nodded, the beginnings of a smile touching
her lips.

His eyes scanned her face. "I think I have the solution to
your problem, my love. Since I'm still on eastern time I'm
more than ready for bed. How about you?"

"To sleep?" she asked innocently, the sparkle returning
to her eyes.

"No, not to sleep, hussy!"

"Well, in that case..." she drawled, standing up and
pretending to sway past him to the door. He grabbed her
around the waist and pulled her into his arms, kissing her
with slow, tempting expertise that built up her smoldering
desires and left her aching for more. "A deposit," he said
huskily, releasing her. "Come on, I want to make love to

you in my bed, and sleep with you curled beside me for the rest of the night.''

''Sounds lovely,'' she sighed, as he picked her up to carry her to their own private heaven.

Unlike their earlier joining, which had been hurried and driven by need, they each sought to tease and tantalize the other into ever greater heights. Again and again he brought her almost to the peak of fulfillment and each time he held off until she was wet and panting, as if she had just run a four-minute mile. Her own hands and lips worked their magic on his body until she broke his rigid control and he took her fiercely to the heights of pleasure and beyond.

Exhausted, they slept, still tightly entwined in the aftermath of love.

Chapter Twelve

The room was pitch-black when Deanna opened eyelids still heavy with sleep. At first she couldn't identify where she was, but the sensation of a man's hand resting possessively on her breast while his thumb gently massaged the nipple evoked tender memories of the night before. She lay on her side, her head cushioned by his strong arm, her back arching wantonly into the hard wall of his chest. Against her sensitized skin, the rough mat of body hair tickled deliciously.

"Morning," he said brightly, leaning over to nuzzle the sensitive spot where her shoulder and neck met. The scrape of early-morning beard along her soft skin was an irritating stimulant, dragging her out of sleep.

"Morning?" she murmured groggily. "It can't be. It's still dark."

"It's morning in New York. Eight o'clock. I'm usually in the shower right now." He nibbled on her earlobe, his warm breath fanning her skin. "Want to come shower with me?"

Deanna groaned. While his lips teased, his hands stroked her breasts and the smooth, silky skin of her flat stomach. Her body felt alive and wide awake, but her mind was still fuzzed with sleep. "Eight o'clock in New York? But you're not in New York, you're here," she stated, trying to sort things out. "And it's not eight o'clock, it's—it's..."

"Five a.m.," he supplied easily, proving he was certainly much wider awake than she was.

She shifted to lie on her back so she could look at him. Smiling with sleepy tenderness, she asked with mock irritation, "Are you always this—buoyant—when you wake up?" Very lightly, she let her fingers stroke down his side, feeling the bone and sinew beneath the smooth skin.

"Always," he said huskily.

Her hand reached his hip and slid down toward his most sensitive area. "I guess I should warn you that I'm a terrible grump until I'm completely awake." As she spoke his flesh quivered under her touch and she felt him stiffen. She let her questing fingers slide up along the corded stomach muscles to tease and caress his nipple until it was taut.

"I love you when you're grumpy," he muttered thickly before he kissed her with an unyielding desire that made her arch against him, then slide her arms around his hard body to bring him closer to her.

Their union was electric, deep and satisfying to them both. Afterward Deanna lay in the shelter of his arms, her body spent and drained, her mind still drugged with his caresses. A tiny smile curled her lips as he whispered words of love, and once again she slept.

The next time she woke the sun was streaming in through open windows. She was sprawled in the middle of the wide bed, one arm outstretched and the other hugging the pillow Rick had used during the night. Her eyes still closed, she savored their lovemaking once more, feeling a deep contentment. A satisfied smile curled her lips as she rolled onto her back, wondering lazily where Rick was.

The question had hardly formed in her mind when the bedroom door opened to admit him. Dressed in the same jeans as yesterday, with a disreputable black T-shirt covering his torso, he looked tough, virile, and incredibly sexy. He smiled down at her, his gaze loaded with intimate meaning. Deanna smiled languidly back, thinking that it seemed the most natural thing in the world to share his bed at night and see him when she woke.

"Good afternoon, sleepyhead," he teased.

Today it seemed nothing could shatter her cozy, insulated contentment, not even the knowledge she had slept half the day away. "It is really that late?" she murmured, half closing her eyes and stretching, catlike.

Her movement shifted the bed covers so that one smooth, golden breast was revealed. It seemed only natural that Rick should bend and cover the rosy tip with his mouth, lapping gently with his tongue until it hardened. It seemed only natural too that she should utter a rough little growl of pleasure and link her hands behind his head to keep him from abandoning his stimulating caress.

Very gently, he reached up to unwrap her clinging hands, then he kissed her lightly on her surprised lips and said, "Don't think I'm not tempted, lover, because I am."

She giggled and observed with a twinkle, "Well, it was worth a try."

"Insatiable!" He grinned. "It's a perfect day. How does a picnic sound to you? I know a spot with a view for miles."

She laughed. "Would this be a lunch or dinner picnic?"

"Lunch! It's actually eleven a.m., if you're interested, so if you get a move on we can eat at about one."

"Okay," she promised, bounding from the bed with a sudden return of energy and heading for the bathroom. "Just let me shower and I'll be with you in fifteen minutes."

It wasn't until she was drying herself on a thick terry towel that she remembered she did not have a change of clothes. The idea of donning the blouse and underwear she had worn the previous day made her wrinkle her nose distastefully, but she had little choice. It had been her dumb idea not to bring an overnight bag.

When she padded into the bedroom she was surprised to see a thin blue T-shirt, obviously of the same vintage as the one Rick wore, lying casually on the bed. She picked it up, giggling slightly at the size, the noticed a scrap of black cloth beneath it. Her eyes widened as she picked up the panties and inspected them. Hardly more than two triangles of lace held together by a single band of elastic, they were the most exotic undergarments she had ever seen. Hastily she slipped them on, biting her lip in amused consternation as she viewed herself in a mirror. They certainly didn't cover much, but then she suspected they were not supposed to.

Rick had bought them for her, but when? It could only have been in New York, before their angry phone call. It made her feel good to know he had been thinking of her while he was away, and she didn't even mind that the blue T-shirt billowed around her slender body, completely covering the underwear. She pulled on her jeans, tucked the bottom of the shirt into them as best she could, then hurried from the room to find Rick.

They rode to the place he had selected for their picnic—a sunbaked hollow in the long ridge overlooking the house and the narrow valley it was situated in. Even now, in late September, the secluded spot was pleasantly warm, the perfect place for an outdoor meal. After tying the horses, they spread a blanket over the coarse grass and laid out the contents of the picnic basket.

While they ate, Rick pointed out places he had roamed as a boy, then steered the conversation to his week in New York and gradually to the difficulties she was having with her designs.

"It's more than just problems with how the costumes appear on the star, isn't it?" he demanded gently, watching her stiffen and the muscles in her jaw tense. He smiled faintly, "When something hurts that badly it's best to talk about it, or it will fester and poison your whole system."

Deanna swallowed and stared at the chicken leg she had been eating. Rick was right; Colleen's words were eating like acid through her soul. "I can't talk about it."

"Sweetheart, look at me," he commanded calmly. Slowly, she did so, her violet eyes enormous and vulnerable. The expression she saw on his strong features was neither pity nor compassion, both of which she'd expected, but understanding.

He smiled wryly at her surprise. "I know how frustrating it can be when you have a deadline to meet and not one idea to put down on paper. When my father died I was designing a house for a client on Long Island. I brought the work with me, thinking I could finish it once the funeral was over. I knew I wouldn't get back to New York until after the will was read and it seemed the wisest course. But every time I tried to work on the drawings nothing came, until finally I had to ask Martin to finish the project." He smiled ruefully. "I saw the shell of the building last week. Martin handled it brilliantly."

"I can understand how your father's death would affect you, but Rick, I don't have an excuse like that!" she cried woefully.

He put his hands on her shoulders and shook her gently. "It wasn't Dad's death that tore me apart, it was those damn women seeing his death as a way to milk more money out of him—or his estate!" He stopped. Deanna could see that he was making an enormous effort to retain control of his temper, and after a time he succeeded.

"I was so disgusted I had to get away. If I'd stayed in L.A. I would have torn into those harpies eventually, which was exactly what they were hoping for. I stayed away because I had no desire to design a building or even see a city again. So I spent my time snarling at everyone, including Dale and my mother, and punching out the odd reporter."

Deanna giggled and he grinned. "There are a few people I wouldn't mind hitting," she said wistfully.

"That's one way of easing frustration," he agreed, his lips twitching and his eyes bright with laughter. "But sometimes it's better to get away from whatever is troubling you. Make a complete break so you can look at the problem more clearly."

She laughed softly. "Which is why I'm here."

"Right the first time," he agreed with a chuckle.

There was silence between them as Deanna absently finished the chicken leg and delicately wiped her greasy fingers on a paper napkin, her memory replaying the scene in Colleen Carlisle's dressing room while she weighed Rick's words. If she viewed the incident dispassionately, she realized she hadn't felt hurt by Colleen's words, but angry. It wasn't until her father had agreed with the woman's accusations that her confidence in her own ability had been shattered.

She stretched out on the blanket, leaning on one elbow and facing Rick. "I found out on Thursday that I got my job—by default, you might say. It seems that the producers wanted Colleen for the female lead, but my father had someone else in mind.''

"Your mother?'' he asked curiously.

Deanna laughed. "Hardly. My parents are barely civil to each other at home, as it is. They could never work together. No, that's not the reason he was so firm against Colleen. I'm not sure what it was, but he was very much against her getting the role.''

"Probably because she was one of my father's women,'' he said casually, dropping a bombshell without seeming to be aware of it.

"What?'' she cried, sitting up and staring at him, aghast. "How can you be so nonchalant about a thing like that?''

He watched her with narrowed, assessing eyes. "Easily. My father went through four wives after he divorced my mother and who knows how many girl friends. Some of them were pleasant, some weren't. Colleen was one of the nastier ones.''

Still amazed at his calm, she demanded, "But didn't it bother you?''

"Why?'' he responded sharply. "I knew who was important in his life, and it wasn't his parade of nubile young lovelies. Those women knew the score. If Dad used them, they certainly got what they wanted in return. Occasionally one had a little more character than the rest and he married her. It would last a couple of years, until they were thoroughly bored with each other, then there would be a civilized divorce, the lady would come out much richer, and Dad would go back to his succession of starlets.'' He shrugged, then reached out to touch her face gently. "Don't look so shocked. No one was harmed by it.''

"Except you.''

"Not even me," he reassured her tenderly. "The only time I hated the four he married was when they showed how greedy they were after he died."

"I wish," she said bitterly, "I could be as relaxed about my father as you are about yours. When he agreed to let Colleen have the role, he demanded a concession. Since he has a financial stake in the picture, they agreed." She stopped. Her hands busily wiped at a dust mark on her pant leg. "The concession was me."

"What's your experience?" he asked after a tense moment. She was glad he hadn't bothered with the usual platitudes about it being normal for families to help each other, that it didn't matter how she had gotten the job, that what counted was how she did it.

"Several television shows," she said gloomily, "a couple of made-for-TV movies, and some theatrical releases, which were all flops. Most of them went straight to the drive-ins."

"So they took a chance on you," he stated calmly, "because your father pressured them into it."

She looked at him and said slowly, "When you put it like that it doesn't sound too bad."

"That wasn't how Colleen phrased it," he said flatly.

"God, no!" Deanna shuddered. "She screamed and ranted and threatened to walk out. Next thing I knew, I had the producers on my back for distressing the star and..." Her voice died. Come on, Deanna, she told herself savagely, spit it out. "... and my father lecturing me on how he's engineered chance after chance for me in the business and how none of them have ever worked out and how disappointed he is in me because he thought I might actually succeed this time."

Rick reached out and cuddled her against his solid, secure chest. She could hear him mutter exotic curses against her tactless father.

"Oh, Rick!" she wailed, her carefully constructed dam finally bursting. "There's more!"

"Then tell me," he advised softly. "Get it all out."

"He said that I should marry you and make babies because that's all I'm good for!"

Unexpectedly, Rick laughed. She could feel the amusement rumbling in his chest under her ear and spilling out around her. She sat up, blinking away threatened tears, and stared at him in amazement. "What's so funny?"

"Your father was obviously never much of a family man," he gasped after a moment.

She sighed. "Nor was my mother. She was busy most of the time doing one film or another, and when she and Dad were both home they always fought. They still do. I can remember one particular night when they were shouting at each other so loudly I woke up and got out of bed to see what was going on. I sat upstairs on the landing and watched them standing in the hall, squaring off at each other. Then my mother flounced into the living room. Dad followed and after a bit there was silence. I went to bed, but nine months later my sister Sylvan was born. I didn't connect the two at the time, but later I realized they must have been stimulated by the quarrel and made love."

She shook her head. "The only reason they're still married is because Dad doesn't believe in divorce." She didn't add that her parents' tempestuous relationship was one of the major factors in her fear marriage. She didn't have to. The expression on Rick's face told her clearly that he understood the implication.

She was grateful that when he spoke again he referred only to the difficulty with the costumes.

The problem, she explained, was mainly in Colleen herself. The woman's natural coloring was delicately fair skin and strawberry-blond hair. The shades Deanna had chosen were to highlight that coloring, avoiding hues that would clash with the woman's beautiful hair, but accentuate her creamy skin.

In a long-running battle with the producers, her father argued that the main character should be a brunette, that a redhead would be too exotic for the plot, and at long last he had won that battle. The problem was that as a brunette, with her brows and lashes darkened, colors that didn't clash with vibrant red-blond hair looked insipid, and rather than accenting Colleen's complexion, they made her look pale and unhealthy.

Apart from the colors, there was a major disagreement on the styles. The plot was the story of a woman in the 1930s who pulled herself out of destitution into a position of power in Washington just before the Second World War. Deanna had been told that she was to capture the look of the thirties, from the grinding, depression poverty to the opulent glamor of the rich. With this in mind, she had studied old photographs, fashion magazines of the period, and examples of clothing still in existence. She thought that she had succeeded in her task. Unfortunately, Colleen Carlisle didn't suit the thirties image.

By the time Deanna had finished her vivid, pungent description of Colleen's appearance, Rick was shaking with laugher and she herself was grinning lightheartedly.

Looking at the humorous points of the incident broke down her few remaining barriers, although she wasn't conscious of it. Ideas began to filter into her thoughts, pictures forming of dresses and gowns, some completely new, some mere alterations of already completed designs. Her fingers began to itch for her sketchbook, yet she was reluctant to leave the tranquillity of this open, peaceful spot.

She didn't realize how absorbed she had become in her thoughts until she heard Rick say softly, "You look far away."

She started, then admitted breathlessly, "I was. Rick, I've suddenly got dozens of ideas running through my head! I wish I had my sketch pad. I'm afraid if I wait until we get back to the house to put these on paper I'll lose them."

He yawned and stretched, them climbed lithely to his feet. Deanna watched him, a puzzled frown on her face, as he walked quickly to the tethered horses and opened the leather bag resting behind the saddle of his mount. The bulk of his body shielded his actual movements and she wondered if perhaps she should be gathering up the leftover picnic things, if he was preparing to leave.

When he returned, holding a large manila envelope, she was baffled. She couldn't image what it contained. He dropped it casually in her lap, then sprawled on his back, his hands cradling his head. She opened the brown envelope and her eyes widened as the contents slipped out.

"While you work," said Rick, watching her carefully despite his relaxed position, "I'll catch up on much needed sleep."

"You—you devil!" Deanna cried in delight, flinging herself on top of him.

He laughed and his arms snaked out to wrap tightly around her, pinning her against the hard length of him. She lowered her head to kiss him and felt his hands stroking lightly along her spine.

"How did you know I'd want to work?" she asked huskily, a few moments later.

"I didn't," he said, rolling on his side and laying her gently on the blanket. "I hoped, though. It was a simple matter to bring the necessary tools along—especially since you snored away half the morning,'' he teased.

She rose to the bait. "I don't snore!" she said indignantly and he laughed.

"No, you don't, I can attest to that. I spent a long time watching you sleep this morning." She blushed a little, thinking of his eyes on her while she lay vulnerable and exposed in sleep. He grinned and prodded her gently in the ribs. "No more stalling. Get to work!"

She made a face at him, but she sat up and began sorting through her file, looking at the old designs, now seeing clearly where she had gone wrong and feeling sure she knew how to achieve a look that would satisfy both the producers and the star. Nibbling at the back of her mind was the terrible fear that her work would be unacceptable a second time, but she resolutely ignored it, determined now to make the attempt, even if it was unsuccessful.

Rick watched her work, smiling faintly as her expression ran the gamut from pensive to burningly excited as ideas began to come together. When he was satisfied that she was absorbed in her designing, he lay back and closed his eyes. An hour later when Deanna surfaced from her frenzied sketching and began a laughing comment on the success of his therapy, she realized he was fast asleep.

When he had said he would sleep while she worked she thought he was teasing her. He had always been so strong and alive that it never occurred to her he might have been as affected by this last week as she was. When she thought about it she realized that there were marks of strain around his compelling dark eyes and the mouth she loved to kiss. A wave of tenderness washed over her as she watched him, drinking in the contours of the powerful body, now supine and at ease, the way his strong features relaxed in sleep, making him look younger and decidedly vulnerable.

I love him, she thought slowly, but not the way she had in Yellowstone. The emotion she harbored for the rugged, sexy guide was nothing compared to what she felt for the complex man beside her. Tender, caring, strong, but giving. Her lips curled in a caressing smile. Arrogant, demanding, stubborn. So many facets to his character. Would she ever know him completely? Did she have to? Already her love had grown immeasurably as she slowly explored his personality. Why couldn't she let go of those fears that kept her from agreeing to marry him?

Because she had to be sure. The answer threw a momentary pall over her emotions. Sighing softly, she pushed the thought to the back of her mind. She had some very immediate problems to surmount and she never would if she didn't get back to work. An unconscious smile lifted the corners of her mouth. Besides, if she didn't produce something this afternoon Rick would have her hide. He was one person she wouldn't disappoint.

She continued to work feverishly through Saturday afternoon and might have worked through the evening but for Rick, who had other, decided ideas on how they would spend the night. But Sunday found her up early, leaving him sleeping peacefully while she worked. By the time darkness had fallen she was finished and, as Rick drove them back to L.A., the creative energy that had sustained her throughout the previous two days began to dissipate. With its departure, fears and tensions crept in to fill the void. so that when Rick parked her car in front of her apartment she was as tightly strung as she had been before he had carried her off to his hideout.

He regarded her ruefully as they entered the apartment. She was jumping at any unexpected sound and talking in short, jerky sentences. Very carefully, she placed her sketches and file on the big desk in the living room, but after that she wandered around the apartment distractedly, picking up an ornament and putting it down, moving a cushion an inch or two to the left. It was in the kitchen, when she gathered together the makings of a pot of coffee then never completed the task, that Rick caught her hands, forcing her to be still, and demanded with wry amusement, "Are you going to get any sleep tonight, bobcat?"

She blinked at him in surprise. Sleep was definitely not on her mind.

He groaned hoarsely. "You sure know how to force my hand, lady. I know one way of making certain you don't spend the night pacing the floor."

His nearness, the familiar male scent of him, kindled the desire that was never very far from the surface and wiped away the fog of worry that had steadily taken hold of her. Her eyes cleared and she smiled serenely up at him. "You'll stay the night." It was a statement, not a question, and her soft voice held joy, not hope.

"If this gets out it will damage your reputation," he said grimly.

Deanna laughed. "Oh, pooh! Who cares? Besides, the press has forgotten about us now. We're not exciting enough, just as you predicted."

"This may be all it takes to make us interesting again," he cautioned.

She twisted her hands out of his grip to twine them around his neck as she cuddled against him. "Rick, I love you. I don't care who knows it. If it weren't for my crazy hang-ups we'd be married right now. As far as I'm concerned the media can tell the world that you stayed the night."

His smile was lopsided and rueful as he looked down into her enormous violet eyes, and there was a trace of sadness in his own. "I'm not going to make a habit of staying with you, Deanna," he said somberly. "I won't live with you unless we're married."

"Just stay with me tonight, Rick," she murmured huskily, her eyes pleading, her lips tempting. "I need you tonight."

It was an invitation impossible to resist. He lowered his head to kiss her, then swept her up into his arms and carried her into the bedroom, his lips still plundering hers with hard, demanding passion.

The next morning they rose together and Rick joined her in the shower, lathering her body from neck to feet with slow, erotic strokes that made them both wish she didn't have an appointment to keep. She dropped him at his house before continuing on to the office building that housed the production company. Rick's presence, and the flush of desire lingering from his caresses under the shower, kept her reasonably calm until she was parking her car in front of the building. Then her stomach knotted and her muscles tensed as she prepared for what was ahead.

Her designs were accepted, but not without change. After the problems with her first line the producers wanted to have input, but the alterations they demanded were minimal, and in most cases Deanna admitted that they did enhance the look. There was also considerable debate on the fabrics and colors to be used and by the time the discussion was complete it was late afternoon and she had to drive back to her apartment through thick, slow rush-hour traffic.

She hadn't been able to phone Rick with the good news during the day, so the first thing she did when she entered the apartment was to call him. To her disappointment, the line was busy. She put a lid on her bubbling excitement and changed from the tailored skirt and jacket she had worn into a comfortable pair of jeans. Then she tried Rick again, only to discover his phone was still busy. She swallowed her disappointment and made herself a drink.

Halfway through it, the phone beside her shrilled. She picked it up on the first ring, certain the caller was Rick. "Hi!" she greeted him effervescently.

"Hi, yourself," said his rich, masculine voice, "I gather today went well."

"Did it ever! Oh, Rick! I'm so happy! They made a few changes and my father was positively sulky about my fixing everything, but the designs were accepted! Thank you! Thank you so much! Without your help I couldn't have done it! Are you coming over? Or do you want me to meet you somewhere? Or should I come to your place?" When her breathless stream of words finally petered out there was a stiff silence.

"Deanna, I've got to return to New York," he said at last, regret in his voice. "I just got a call from Martin. There are problems with one of the jobs he can't handle alone. I'll be back as soon as I can manage it. On the weekend, for sure."

"Oh," she said, her bubble of elation bursting and depression swiftly replacing it. Suddenly, her victory didn't seem as important as it had a minute ago, not without Rick to share it. "When does your plane leave?"

"Tonight. I'm booked on the red-eye."

"Then I can see you before you go?" she asked hesitantly, wondering, for a heart-stopping moment, if he was using this as an excuse to drop her.

"I'm counting on it," he said huskily, relief in his voice, as if he had been afraid she would not accept his sudden departure easily. "Why don't you come over here, then you can drop me at the airport."

"Okay," she agreed softly. "See you in a few minutes." Replacing the receiver in its cradle, she bit her lip and pressed the heels of her hands against her eyes to hold back threatening tears. She wouldn't cry. She wasn't going to make this unexpected departure any more difficult for Rick than it must already be, and arriving at his apartment with tear-reddened eyes would certainly do that. She breathed slowly and deeply, gradually regaining her composure. Then she hurried into the bedroom, stripped, sprayed herself liberally with spicy perfume, and donned an oriental-style silk dress that she wore without a bra. It clung to her breasts and the curve of her hips and shimmered a deep, rich sapphire when she moved. Long slits exposed her rounded thighs enticingly.

She had bought the dress only a week before, sure Rick would enjoy the seductive qualities of the fabric and cut, but with the problems of Thursday and Friday, she had forgotten all about it. Carefully, she made up her eyes, emphasizing their near almond shape with liner, and dusting deep blue powder on the lids. Her hair she combed forward, to frame her face with gentle waves.

When she stepped back from the mirror she was satisfied with her appearance. If her man had to leave her tonight, he wouldn't go away grim and depressed. He would take with him the memory of an evening impossible to forget.

Chapter Thirteen

September drifted into October and then November. Rick was residing permanently in New York, doing his best to arrange business trips and weekends out to the west coast. Deanna found that she missed his presence terribly during the long lonely days of the week and seemed to come alive only on his too short weekend visits. She tried to share the burden of cross-continent travel with him, flying out to New York whenever he couldn't make it to L.A. His stamina constantly amazed her. She found the long, tedious trip and the disorienting time change exhausting, but somehow Rick always seemed full of boundless energy when she saw him.

Her visits to New York were always fun. Rick made sure of that. He wanted her to like the city and to feel comfortable there. They went sightseeing, shopping, to a Broadway opening. One weekend he threw a party to introduce her to Martin and Katie and other friends he had spoken about. The party was a great success and Deanna had a

wonderful time, despite the excitement her ring caused.
Jokes were made about Rick's wild bachelor days being finally over and what a hard time Deanna would have trying
to tame him. Deanna had laughed lightheartedly with the
rest, but later, when she was back in L.A., missing Rick and
wishing she were with him, she began to wonder what his
friends knew that she didn't.

In a few short months she had surrendered completely to
him and it frightened her to think he might not love her as
passionately as she loved him. She knew that his father had
once loved Leah Dewart, but it hadn't lasted. Rick wanted
to marry her now, but how would he feel in four or five
years? Would he tire of her as his father had tired of his
mother?

When she was with him the questions never arose. He always made her feel needed and loved. He wrapped her in a
cocoon of warmth and tenderness that drove out all the
fears that haunted her when she was alone. She put worries
about the future aside to bask in the joy of the present.

As the days slowly progressed toward Thanksgiving,
Deanna told herself she had to make a choice—to marry
Rick or not. The hectic cross-continent travel couldn't
continue indefinitely. In the back of her mind Deanna had
known this for a long time, yet she couldn't bring herself to
make that decision because she felt torn by conflicting
emotions. Her mind said be cautious, hold back, don't get
involved. Her emotions said you love him, you're lonely
when he's not around, your greatest joy is his happiness.
Take a chance!

By mid-November her work on the picture had come to
a successful conclusion. Though she knew her talent had
finally found that elusive outlet and her future in the business was secure, she discovered she no longer cared. Proving herself didn't seem to matter when she knew she had

Rick's unquestioning belief supporting her. Ironically, now that her career was on the rise, she very seriously considered abandoning it. All her life her world had been centered on Hollywood and its productions. Now her interests were expanding dramatically and she felt a restless desire for change.

With no deadlines to speed the long weekdays past, she had plenty of time to brood. She began to forget about meals again and to lie awake worrying. Her eyes were shadowed and she had difficulty smiling naturally—until she saw Rick. Then the haunted look would disappear as her eyes lit joyfully, but not even the blaze of happiness could disguise the physical side effects of her nearly constant fretting.

The hints that her father had been dropping since his first meetings with Rick became outright suggestions, then exasperated commands. *Marry Rick. He loves you. He'll make you happy.* Nigel Monroe was a man used to giving advice and used to having it followed, but he had passed some of his stubborn determination on to his daughter, and Deanna was not about to be bulldozed into her future by someone else.

When her mother took her aside one evening for an unusual mother-to-daughter, heart-to-heart talk Deanna was startled and wary. She naturally assumed that this was all part of her father's campaign to wear her down.

They sat beside each other on a long sofa in the elegant living room, recently redone in a cold, but artistic way by a young decorator who was the current rage. Felicia began the conversation by observing critically that Deanna looked terrible and that she was wasting away to nothing.

It was not the opening Deanna expected. "I forget to eat sometimes," she admitted reluctantly.

Felicia raised beautifully arched eyebrows. "Do you mean Rick has to remind you to eat?"

"No, of course not!" Deanna replied, laughing. "But when he isn't around I don't seem to have the energy to make a meal, and I hate eating alone in restaurants."

"Aside from the fact that you are always welcome here, Deanna," Felicia stated dryly, "doesn't that tell you anything?"

Deanna looked at her and blushed.

"You never were much of an actress." remarked Felicia with amusement. "Thank God."

Deanna's brows rose and her eyes widened in astonishment.

Felicia's face twisted in self-condemnation. "Deanna, know I haven't been much of a mother to you. I'm just not the type to lavish care on anyone, not even on my own children, but I do love you and I do want the best for you. know I was against your seeing Rick at first." She hesitated. "I was afraid, you see, that he would be like his father, needing a succession of beautiful women, never staying long with any of them. I know you, darling. You wouldn't be able to stand being treated like that, and in the end you would be hurt." She paused as if she intended to say something more, but changed her mind. "I was wrong about him, Deanna. Very wrong. I judged him by his father, not himself. If Rick planned on being unfaithful to you, he would have shown it by now. It would be so much easier for him to find a beautiful woman in New York to satisfy his needs if that was all he cared about."

Her daughter blushed. "How did you know we were..."

Felicia laughed, a bright rippling sound of pleasure that delighted millions. "You're my daughter, aren't you? I can't imagine you being content with tepid handholding and chaste kisses."

Deanna took a deep breath then expelled it in a silent whistle. She wasn't sure she was ready for this frank, open discussion with her mother.

"Marry him, Deanna," Felicia urged gently. "If you love him, don't wait for him to prove himself. He already has."

"Marriage is such a big commitment," Deanna mumbled, unable to look at her mother. "I don't want to make a mistake."

Felicia drew in a quick hissing breath. "Absurb child! Your father and I only knew one another a week before we were certain we wanted each other. A month later we were married."

"Exactly," said Deanna with heavy emphasis.

Felicia stared at her daughter in amazement. "And you think we made a mistake?"

"Yes," replied Deanna flatly, deciding she might as well be honest about her feelings. The conversation was already extraordinary; a few more revelations couldn't make it any worse.

The charming, gay laugh rang out again. "Darling, your father is the most exciting man I know! I have to fight to wring even the most minor concession from him, he never lets me get away with tantrums or the awful things I sometimes say as other men do. He's always critical and I can depend on his opinion to be truthful—he spares no one, not even me! In short, he stimulates me constantly." She stopped and Deanna watched with awe as her sophisticated, controlled mother blushed. "And he's a wonderful lover. I couldn't live without him," she concluded simply.

That conversation gave Deanna a great deal to think about. She had always looked at her parents' marriage through the eyes of a child, desperate for security in a frightening world. Her mother's confession forced her to see it as an adult. For the first time it occurred to her that a

woman with Felicia's fiery temperament would never be
satisfied with the bland relationship Deanna's childish desire for harmony had envisioned. Felicia needed someone
to spar with; it was as important to her as Rick's quiet support was to her daughter.

Deanna found herself hovering, half of her willing to take
the risk, the other, more cautious part still undecided.

The impasse could not continue for long. Thanksgiving weekend was only a few days away and Rick had promised he would come out and spend the long weekend with
her, letting her cook a traditional turkey dinner at her
apartment Thursday night before they drove up to the
ranch. It was Wednesday and Deanna was humming softly
to herself as she juggled bags of groceries while she unlocked the door of her apartment, looking forward to the
idea of four long days alone with Rick.

The door flew open and he was standing there, dressed
in jeans and a sweater. She almost dropped the groceries in
her joy as she unconsciously started to fling her arms around
his neck.

"Whoa, bobcat!" he laughed, catching the bags and
bending to kiss her. Deanna wrapped her arms around his
neck and kissed him back, ignoring everything but the delicious sensation of his lips on hers.

"What on earth have you got in here?" he demanded
eventually. "These bags weigh a ton. How did you ever
carry them?" He headed for the kitchen.

Deanna grinned, content to follow behind. "A fifteen
pound turkey, to start with. And a couple of bottles of wine.
A turnip, a bunch of potatoes, lettuce, tomatoes..."

He groaned. "A fifteen-pound turkey! Are you inviting
your whole family to dinner?"

"No," she replied sunnily. "It was the smallest one I could find." She watched him put the bags on the counter. Her forehead puckered in a frown. "What are you doing here? Not," she added, sidling against him and running a familiar hand up his chest, feeling his steady heartbeat speed up as she touched him, "that I'm complaining. But I was supposed to pick you up at the airport tomorrow. What happened?"

"I caught an earlier flight," he said flatly.

Something in his voice told her all was not as it should be. She stepped back a pace and searched his face. What she saw didn't reassure her. His eyes were hooded beneath long lashes, but his mouth was grim, his jaw hard and inflexible.

Her voice was as flat as his when she said, "Why?"

"I couldn't wait to see you, lover. Isn't that enough?" he replied mockingly, smiling with his lips, but not his eyes.

Deanna felt her body go cold. "I guess I'd better put the food away," she said shakily, not daring to look at him for fear he would see the tears in her eyes. She took a platter out of the cupboard, carefully put the turkey on it, then picked it up. All her movements were mechanical; her mind worked furiously in a completely different direction.

Holding the platter with the turkey in both hands, she turned to face him. He was standing with his arms crossed over his chest, his expression still closed, but grim. She swallowed and lifted her chin proudly. A smile flickered on his lips, but before he could say anything she was speaking. "Is this it? The end? Have you found someone in New York?" Her voice shook and she sucked in a deep breath to steady it. "You know, you didn't have to fly all the way out here to tell me in person. You could have written, or maybe phoned. I'd have understood."

At her first words, Rick's jaw had dropped in amazement. He quickly clamped it shut, his expression changing to one of growing anger. As Deanna finished, he reached out and wrenched the platter from her and almost threw it on the counter, then he grasped her shoulders and shook her, hard. "You know damn well that I'm not interested in anyone but you!"

"How do I know?" she shouted, as furious as he. "I hardly ever see you anymore! What do you expect me to think when you stand there like a figure of doom, looking all solemn and serious!"

"For God's sake, Deanna, you know why I have to be in New York!" he roared.

"Yes, I do!" she shouted back, twisting out of his somewhat loosened grasp and flinging herself against his chest. "But I miss you!" She placed her palms flat against his body and rested her cheek on his shoulder. "I miss you so much," she repeated in a broken whisper.

Slowly, almost reluctantly, his arms closed around her. "Damn," he swore softly. "I know, sweetheart, I know."

"It's not working, is it?" she asked, her voice muffled as she spoke into his chest. "My being here and your being in New York."

"No," he replied gently, stroking her hair.

"What are we going to do?" she demanded in a small voice.

"Talk about it," he said calmly. "That's why I caught an earlier flight." He lifted her head with an insistent finger under her chin, smiling wryly at her watery eyes. "First put that damned bird in the fridge and I'll fix us a drink. I think we both need one. Then we'll talk."

Fifteen minutes later Deanna was curled on one corner of the sofa while Rick sat stiffly in a chair facing her. She thought wryly that he looked like a man ready to issue an ultimatum he knew wouldn't go over well.

"Do you remember the day Martin called and I had to return to New York suddenly? After we'd been up to the ranch?" he began, after taking a long gulp of his bourbon.

"Yes." She blushed delicately, remembering how they had spent the evening before his flight.

He smiled faintly, his eyes amused, but his expression quickly sobered. "Martin had been approached by the chairman of a large multinational firm that has decided to relocate its corporate headquarters to a small town in up-state New York. They bought the property and now they want an office complex built on it that will be suitable to their planned rate of expansion for the next twenty-five years. It's an enormous project, and it will take at least a year and a half to see to completion." He stopped.

Deanna understood the implications of his words im-mediately. "Your firm got the commission," she said with a calm she didn't feel.

"No. Me. Martin will handle the other jobs while I work on this project exclusively." His eyes searched her face and saw there only flat despair. "Deanna..."

She shook herself and smiled mechanically. "You'll be busy."

"Yes."

"No more visits to L.A. What will you do with the ranch?" She was finding it increasingly difficult to breath. She felt as if she were choking.

"Keep it, of course! Deanna, this does not mean I'm never returning to L.A.! But..." He put his drink on the table and grasped her free hand. "Bobcat, I'm asking you again to marry me. I need you with me. I love you."

"I don't know!" she cried. "Rick, what if I hate New York? And what will I do when you're up in rural New York working on the complex?" She bit her lip and lowered her lids to hide her anguished expression. "What if I don't measure up?"

"Measure up to what?" he demanded brusquely.

"Other women," she choked. He dropped her hand and when she raised her lashes he was staring at her with hard, angry eyes. "Rick?" she said tentatively.

"What?"

"Can't we give this a test? Let me come out to New York and live with you for six months. If it works out we can get married, but until then, we'd be together."

"No," he said baldly.

"Why? Why are you so stubborn about this?" she cried, hurt by his curt refusal.

"I've told you, Deanna. I will not live with you without marriage."

She tried again. "But lots of people do it! There's nothing wrong with it...."

"No," he repeated.

They glared at each other.

Finally he drew a deep breath. "We'll talk about this again on Friday, at the ranch. I think we'd best give it a rest now, before we both take stands we can't retreat from."

Mutely, Deanna nodded. She didn't want to lose Rick but she was terribly afraid she would.

By Friday Deanna was beginning to wonder if there was any point in their going to Rick's hideaway in the Coast Mountains. They had been acting like polite strangers with each other since the argument Wednesday afternoon. Rick left soon after his command that they forget the discussion until Friday, telling her he would be back about seven to take her out to dinner. She had been deliberately cool that evening, waiting for him to make a sign of reconciliation. She was determined that he must be the one to reestablish their relationship on its normal intimate level. When he matched her polite coolness she was hurt, then angry. She thought up several choice phrases, rejecting his presence in her bed, but he dropped her at her door and didn't even kiss her goodnight. After that she didn't attempt to go to bed, but sat in her dark living room and fumed.

By the time the rising sun chased away the last of the night, she had persuaded herself that she was being a fool and that she should simply tell Rick so when she saw him later in the day. She had a shower, made herself breakfast, then sat down in the living room to sip her morning coffee. The apartment was silent in the early morning quiet and without realizing it, she fell asleep curled in one corner of the comfortable sofa.

She woke with a crick in her neck and a cramp in one thigh from lying in an awkward position. Yawning, she stretched her legs as she rolled onto her back, still feeling tired despite her sleep. She told herself that she should get up, make the stuffing and clean the turkey so it would be ready to pop into the oven about noon. She estimated it must be about nine-thirty or ten o'clock and Rick would be calling soon to suggest how they spend the day. Yawning again, she swung her legs from the couch and stretched her arms out before her. Her gaze fell to the digital watch on one slender wrist and widened in horror. Twelve-fifteen. The turkey was already supposed to be in the oven!

She bounded out to the kitchen and began working at a frantic pace, finally slipping the roasting pan in the oven just forty-five minutes behind schedule. Only then did she allow herself to wonder if there was any point to her work because she wasn't sure whether Rick would even bother to show up for the meal.

He did arrive as promised, but his expression was wary and Deanna was so annoyed at not hearing from him all day that she forgot her pledge to apologize and was even frostier than she had been the previous evening. After spending another lonely, sleepless night she felt so physically and emotionally drained that all she wanted was for this prolonged parting to be over. She debated phoning Rick to tell him not to bother coming for her, but making the move that would cause an irrevocable break with him was more than she could manage. By the time she dragged herself through a shower, dressing, and pretending to eat breakfast, he was at the door and the chance was gone.

Standing face to face and telling him she wasn't going with him was more difficult than doing so on the phone, but she had to do it. She didn't think she could handle a whole weekend of their silent hostility.

He was wearing jeans and a checked shirt, over which he had tossed a lined leather jacket. She stared hungrily at him for a moment, then said to his black-booted feet, "I can't go with you."

"Yes, you can," he replied implacably.

"I'm tired. I didn't sleep well," she muttered sullenly, wishing she could slam the door and make him go away. There wouldn't be much point, though. He would just unlock the door with the key she had given him.

"You can sleep in the car," he said calmly.

Desperate now, she cried, "I'm not packed!" and lifted her head to glare at him.

He shrugged. "So?" He ran a practiced gaze down her slim form, noting the casual jeans and the dark green sweater. "You're dressed okay. Grab your leather jacket and let's go."

"No!"

He stared at her mutinous face for a moment then brushed past her, collected her jacket from the hall closet, grabbed her wrist, and pulled her firmly out of her apartment. After slamming the door her dragged he to his car and deposited her inside. She tensed, preparing to jump out as soon as he was on the opposite side of the vehicle. He gave her a hard look and said evenly, "Don't do it." She subsided into the seat, clutching her jacket in front of her like a shield.

"Put on your seat belt," he ordered as he settled into the driver's seat and switched on the engine.

"You're kidnapping me again," she said balefully.

He twisted in his seat to face her as the powerful car purred into a smooth idle. "Do I have to?" he demanded quietly.

She glared at him, wanting a fight and not understanding his restraint. He met her gaze calmly and forced her to look down. "No," she muttered at last, wishing she didn't love him so much.

He eased the car into motion and suggested gently that she try and get some sleep. She replied huffily that that would be impossible and promptly nodded off.

The cessation of movement woke her when they arrived at the ranch. A feather-light touch on her cheek, quickly retracted, made her turn her head. "We're here, sleepyhead," Rick told her in a gruff voice. She nodded, suppressing a shiver of apprehension, and climbed out of the car. She waited until he joined her, then followed him into the house.

As before, Joan Aitken had supplied food and seen to it the house was ready for Rick's arrival. A fire had been laid in the stone hearth in the entertainment room. Rick lit it, made sure the flames caught, then turned to Deanna, who was hovering on the edge of the room, feeling uncomfortable.

After a strained moment he said politely, "Would you like some coffee?"

"That would be nice," she agreed softly, feeling tension coil in the pit of her stomach as he came toward her. He passed without touching her, making her think bitterly that despite what he said it was over between them. Now even the physical charge that always flared when they were together was gone.

She was curled in front of the hearth, watching the orange tongues of fire licking at the logs, when he returned carrying a tray with a percolator, mugs, cream and sugar, and spoons. He set the tray near an outlet in the wall, plugged in the percolator, then crouched down beside her.

"I thought we might need more than one cup," he explained with a faint smile as she stared with surprise at the pot.

They sat in silence while the coffeepot burbled and groaned and the fire crackled and spat. Deanna refused to look at Rick, staring instead at the red and gold flames, but she knew he was watching her. She could feel the caress of his eyes.

"Why won't you marry me?" he asked at last, his voice calm, faintly curious. "Does the idea of living in New York frighten you that much? Or is it loneliness? That you'll miss the people you love? Or are you worried you'll be bored?"

She bit her lip, not sure how to answer. The log snapped and sparks shot up the chimney.

He tried again. "If it's your career, you can try Broadway. I know it would be tough to begin again, but surely with our combined family backgrounds, we could manage to get a door or two opened."

She shook her head mutely.

He held his breath for a minute, then expelled it in a puzzled sigh. "Then is it your family? I didn't think you were a particularly close-knit one but... hell, that's no problem. We can afford the plane fare so you can visit regularly. And it won't be as if I'm cutting myself off from California permanently. My roots are here, too."

"No," she said in a small voice. "Those are little things. We can work them out."

He stared at her averted face thoughtfully. "Then it must be New York. I'm sorry, sweetheart, it's not feasible for me to make my base anywhere else...."

She shook her head, halting him in midstream. "No, it's not that either. I wouldn't mind living in New York. It might be kind of fun."

"Then what?" he demanded in an anguished voice, turning her head to face him with insistent fingers. "I've got to know, bobcat. You've told me you love me, but you won't marry me. I have to know why!"

"I've already told you why," she said shakily.

"You told me you didn't know me well enough. That we didn't know each other well enough. That was nearly four months ago. Four intense months. Do you still feel we don't know each other?"

She swallowed. "I suppose you can never truly know everything about another person," she said lamely.

There was a pause. "Then you will never marry me." His voice grated harshly in the stillness.

"No! That's not true! You're twisting my words and changing my meaning!"

"Then explain it to me!" he ordered, exasperation edging his tone.

Pinned in a corner of her own making, she said hesitantly, "I—I don't think it's necessary to know *everything* about a person before marriage." She slid a quick glance at him out of the corner of her eye and wished she hadn't. He was watching her with unnerving intensity. Her tongue stumbled a little as she spoke. "Just the—the important things."

"Such as?"

Her eyes dropped to her hands, which were clenched on her lap. "Whether or not you love the person and he loves you," she said softly.

His hands closed over hers and held them strongly. "Then what's holding you back, Deanna?" he demanded. "You know I love you."

"I know you feel that way right now," she said softly. "But what about the future?"

He looked at her thoughtfully, then let go of her hands so he could pour out the freshly brewed coffee. He offered her a mug and watched her stir in cream and sugar. He drank his black. "You said something on Wednesday about other women. Now you're implying that in a few years I'll desert you for someone else. You think I'm a carbon copy of my father, don't you?"

"Not exactly," she whispered. "But..." She stopped, biting her lip. Said flatly it was an awful accusation. "It's just—you see—if we were married, I couldn't bear to let you go. If you wanted to leave me, I wouldn't give you an easy divorce and if we stayed together we would end up hating each other. I couldn't live like that."

He laughed shortly and stroked a soft tendril of hair away from her face. "Deanna, Deanna. What crazy ideas you get in that beautiful head."

"I wouldn't tolerate you running around with younger women," she warned fiercely, her eyes amethyst-hard.

"I promise I won't!" he replied, holding up his right hand as if taking an oath.

She sighed, the fight going out of her as quickly as it had come. "It's no good. I couldn't stand the suspense, the fear that one day it would happen."

The heavy silence that followed grated in her mind like a spoken admission. It was the nightmare she had forced to

the back of her mind all along. Rick did love her. Now.
Eventually he would want to move on. It wasn't in his blood
to remain constant.

She was startled when he began to speak, his voice heavy,
then smoothing to quiet reflection. "I guess there's only one
way to persuade you you've got it all wrong and that is to
tell you the truth about my parents. I haven't told you before because it's not really my story. But in this case, I don't
think my mother would mind.

"I was seven years old when my parents divorced. My
father was around forty and feeling his mortality when he
met Roxanne, the starlet he divorced my mother to marry.
She wasn't the first beautiful young creature to make up to
Dad, but she was the first he slept with. Up until then it had
been nothing more than harmless flirtations that fed his ego.
The divorce was very amicable. My mother didn't contest
it. Their property was split and she got me and a fat ali-
mony check every month, and my father got visitation
rights to his child and a bride half his age who made him feel
young again."

He paused to take a sip of his coffee before he continued. "As I said, it was all very amicable. Dad would show
up on the weekend to take me on some excursion and he'd
sit down and have a chat with Mom before we went out."
He grinned. "Then, when he brought me home, Mom
would have dinner waiting and insist he stay. I think at first
she was doing it for me, so the separation of my parents
would seem less strange. Then it got to be a habit, and one
weekend Dad asked me up here, to the ranch, and for some
reason he couldn't pick me up, so Mom drove me. Instead
of dropping me off and heading home, he persuaded her to
stay the night and then the whole weekend. They went on
like that for ten years, meeting here for weekends, weeks,
sometimes whole months. Dad would talk to her about

what roles he should take and advise her about investments."

"To a seven-year-old kid it seemed perfectly natural that they would share the same bedroom, just as they did when we all lived together, but as I got older I began to notice they never stayed together anywhere but here. But by that time it had become a habit none of us really questioned too deeply."

"Why didn't they get married again?" Deanna asked quietly, wondering how Leah could stand the uncertainty of the relationship.

"Dad needed beautiful young women like some people need drugs or booze. He used them to prove to himself that he wasn't aging. That he was still young enough, and good-looking enough, to capture any woman—and any role—he wanted. They stroked his ego, told him how sexy he was, and made him feel good about himself. They were essentially trophies. But Mom was his anchor. When he had problems he needed to discuss with someone or when something was getting him down he needed her, not the pretty young things the press agents wrote glowing stories about."

"It couldn't last, though. Not forever. I was at a university back east when I got a call from my mother saying she had met Dale Sands and was going to marry him. I wasn't really surprised, but Dad was. He was shattered. He hid up here for months putting himself back together. Afterward he wasn't the same. In his own mind they were still married and he felt she had walked out on him. He loved her all his life. He loved her until he died."

He stopped. The blaze had died down and he leaned forward to shift the logs.

Deanna watched the play of expressions on Rick's face. She knew that he had been torn by the conflicting emotions of both parents. Loving both of them, he could understand his mother's need for a more conventional relationship, but Leah's happiness meant his father's despair. "That's why you don't want to live together, isn't it?"

"Yes," he said flatly as he sat back. "I won't take the chance of losing you to some other guy because I don't have you bound securely to me."

"I don't want anyone else," she told him softly.

"Maybe not. But I won't take the chance," he repeated stubbornly. "I love you too damn much to risk your walking out of my life. You mean everything to me, Deanna."

Fleetingly, she remembered Leah's advice so many months ago. Leah was right. Rick was not like his father. Not in the ways that mattered. Her eyes kindled with mischief. "Then you're not going to disappear from my life if I say no?"

He closed his eyes, then opened them again and smiled ruefully at her. "I was hoping you wouldn't pick up on that."

Deanna felt as if an almost unbearable weight had been lifted from her shoulders. She was lighthearted, every emotion free and airy. Laughter bubbled in her throat and emerged as a husky chuckle. Her eyes dancing she said, "Okay."

"Okay? Okay what?" he demanded, confused.

"I'll marry you." She giggled at his amazed expression.

"That's it?" he said indignantly. "Just okay? No passionate declarations?"

"I love you, Roderick Latimer, because you are all I have ever wanted in a man and more," she said huskily, smiling into his serious eyes.

"Kiss me," he ordered softly.

She laughed throatily. "You know what will happen if I do."

"Exactly what I had in mind, Mrs. Latimer," he replied thickly, drawing her into his arms.

Genuine Silhouette
sterling silver bookmark
for only $15.95!

What a beautiful way to hold your place in your current romance! This genuine sterling silver bookmark, with the distinctive Silhouette symbol in elegant black, measures 1½" long and 1" wide. It makes a beautiful gift for yourself, and for every romantic you know! And, at only $15.95 each, including all postage and handling charges, you'll want to order several now, while supplies last.

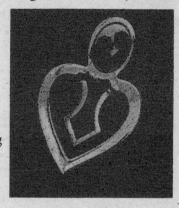

Send your name and address with check or money order for $15.95 per bookmark ordered to
Simon & Schuster Enterprises
120 Brighton Rd., P.O. Box 5020
Clifton, N.J. 07012
Attn: Bookmark

Bookmarks can be ordered pre-paid only. No charges will be accepted. Please allow 4-6 weeks for delivery.

N.Y. State Residents
Please Add Sales Tax

SBM-A

READERS' COMMENTS ON SILHOUETTE INTIMATE MOMENTS:

"About a month ago a friend loaned me my first Silhouette. I was thoroughly surprised as well as totally addicted. Last week I read a Silhouette Intimate Moments and I was even more pleased. They are the best romance series novels I have ever read. They give much more depth to the plot, characters, and the story is fundamentally realistic. They incorporate tasteful sex scenes, which is a must, especially in the 1980's. I only hope you can publish them fast enough."

S.B.*, Lees Summit, MO

"After noticing the attractive covers on the new line of Silhouette Intimate Moments, I decided to read the inside and discovered that this new line was more in the line of books that I like to read. I do want to say I enjoyed the books because they are so realistic and a lot more truthful than so many romance books today."

J.C., Onekama, MI

"I would like to compliment you on your books. I will continue to purchase all of the Silhouette Intimate Moments. They are your best line of books that I have had the pleasure of reading."

S.M., Billings, MT

*names available on request

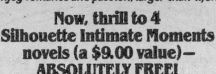

Silhouette Special Edition

COMING NEXT MONTH

THE HEART'S YEARNING—Ginna Gray
When Laura's search for the son she'd had to give up finally ended, she was content to watch him from afar…until Adam Kincaid, her son's adoptive father, unwittingly drew her into a triangle of love.

STAR-CROSSED—Ruth Langan
Fiercely protective Adam London was determined to stop B.J. Conover from writing his mother's biography, but B.J. had a job to do and she couldn't let her growing feelings for Adam stand in her way.

A PERFECT VISION—Monica Barrie
Architect Lea Graham envisioned a community nestled in the New Mexican landscape that Darren Laird was determined to preserve. Could the love that they shared survive a fight to the finish to save their separate dreams?

MEMORIES OF THE HEART—Jean Kent
Was it really possible that foundling Suzy Yoder was the long-lost Hepburn baby, heiress to a vast fortune? Attorney Rich Link had to find the answer, for reasons both legal and personal.

AUTUMN RECKONING—Maggi Charles
Deep in the Berkshire mountains, Marc Bouchard fell in love. Children's-book author Jennifer Bently was more than she'd led him to believe, and her deception threatened the love that they had dared to share.

ODDS AGAINST TOMORROW—Patti Beckman
Every jockey dreams of winning the Kentucky Derby, but for jockey Nikki Cameron the stakes were almost too high. If she triumphed on the bluegrass track, she risked losing the only man she'd ever loved.

AVAILABLE NOW:

ONE MAN'S ART
Nora Roberts

THE CUTTING EDGE
Linda Howard

SECOND GENERATION
Roslyn MacDonald

EARTH AND FIRE
Jennifer West

JUST ANOTHER PRETTY FACE
Elaine Camp

MIDNIGHT SUN
Lisa Jackson